$1.75

S0-AVS-260

SMILE OF DEATH

As Charles started down the brick sidewalk he was bumped hard by a man who was short but wide and carried a big pistol in a holster on his right side.

"Get the hell out of my way, you rich eastern bastard," the man said. "I seen you before. You're one of that bunch who think you own the Maxwell."

A hard work-gnarled fist suddenly came up and hit Charles in the nose and he fell back on the seat of his pants. When he looked up he was staring into the bore of a gun.

Charles couldn't believe it. He couldn't meet his death now, on a sidewalk in what was supposed to be a civilized town. And what on earth was the Maxwell?

"Please, sir . . ."

"Shut up," the man said with a smile, a crazy gleam making his eyes shine like bull's-eye lanterns. "Shut up and say your prayers!"

THE BOOK RACK
Thousands of used paperbacks
trade 2 for 1
for same price and type

2710 So. Academy #139
Colorado Springs
390-7657

ZEBRA'S HEADING WEST!

with GILES, LEGG, PARKINSON, LAKE, KAMMEN, and MANNING

KANSAS TRAIL (3517, $3.50/$4.50)
by Hascal Giles

After the Civil War ruined his life, Bennett Kell threw in his lot with a gang of thievin' guntoughs who rode the Texas-Kansas border. But there was one thing he couldn't steal — fact was, Ada McKittridge had stolen his heart.

GUNFIGHT IN MESCALITO (3601, $3.50/$4.50)
by John Legg

Jubal Crockett was a young man with a bright future — until that Mescalito jury found him guilty of murder and sentenced him to hang. Jubal'd been railroaded good and the only writ of habeus corpus was a stolen key to the jailhouse door and a fast horse!

DRIFTER'S LUCK (3396, $3.95/$4.95)
by Dan Parkinson

Byron Stillwell was a drifter who never went lookin' for trouble, but trouble always had a way of findin' him. Like the time he set that little fire up near Kansas to head off a rogue herd owned by a cattle baron named Dawes. Now Dawes figures Stillwell owes him something . . . at the least, his life.

MOUNTAIN MAN'S VENGEANCE (3619, $3.50/$4.50)
by Robert Lake

The high, rugged mountain made John Henry Trapp happy. But then a pack of gunsels thundered across his land, burned his hut, and murdered his squaw woman. Trapp hit the vengeance trail and ended up in jail. Now he's back and how that mountain has changed!

BIG HORN HELLRIDERS (3449, $3.50/$4.50)
by Robert Kammen

Wyoming was a tough land and toughness was required to tame it. Reporter Jim Haskins knew the Wyoming tinderbox was about to explode but he didn't know he was about to be thrown smack-dab in the middle of one of the bloodiest range wars ever.

TEXAS BLOOD KILL (3577, $3.50/$4.50)
by Jason Manning

Ol' Ma Foley and her band of outlaw sons were cold killers and most folks in Shelby County, Texas knew it. But Federal Marshal Jim Gantry was no local lawman and he had his guns cocked and ready when he rode into town with one of the Foley boys as his prisoner.

Available wherever paperbacks are sold, or order direct from the Publisher. Send cover price plus 50¢ per copy for mailing and handling to Zebra Books, Dept. 3850, 475 Park Avenue South, New York, N.Y. 10016. Residents of New York and Tennessee must include sales tax. DO NOT SEND CASH. For a free Zebra/ Pinnacle catalog please write to the above address.

DOYLE TRENT

TEXAS TRACKERS

ZEBRA BOOKS
KENSINGTON PUBLISHING CORP.

ZEBRA BOOKS

are published by

Kensington Publishing Corp.
475 Park Avenue South
New York, NY 10016

Copyright © 1992 by Doyle Trent

All rights reserved. No part of this book may be reproduced
in any form or by any means without the prior written con-
sent of the Publisher, excepting brief quotes used in reviews.

If you purchased this book without a cover you should be
aware that this book is stolen property. It was reported as
"unsold and destroyed" to the Publisher and neither the Au-
thor nor the Publisher has received any payment for this
"stripped book."

First printing: August, 1992

Printed in the United States of America

One

It was a foolish thing to do. He didn't need his degree from Columbia to know that. What chance did he have of finding a scheming, thieving scoundrel away Out West where there wasn't a railroad or even a telegraph?

He'd already spent three days of cramped, bone-rattling torture in a Concord stagecoach. Three days is what it took to travel from Trinidad in the State of Colorado, where the railroad ended, to the town of Lariat in the Territory of New Mexico. Now, because of a foolish promise, he had to go right back.

Just thinking about it made him groan.

At least he'd get a second night's rest. The stage didn't leave until early in the morning.

He'd arrived in Lariat only the day before. After climbing sorely out of the coach and trying to stretch the cramps and aches out of his body, he'd walked weakly across the hard-packed dirt street to the Lariat General Store. A sign over the door said Isaac Enderlee, prop. There he'd inquired about renting a horse and asked directions to the Double M Ranch.

Isaac Enderlee was a middle-aged paunchy man with a round pleasant face. He squinted with pale blue eyes. "You a kin of Joe Manderfield?"

"Yes sir, I am Charles J. Manderfield. Joseph Manderfield is my uncle."

"Oh. Well, you don't need to hire a horse. I was thinkin' about goin' out to the Double M anyway, and you can ride along."

"Why, that would be very kind of you."

"I'll take some groceries 'case Bertha's runnin' short. She don't want to leave Joe long enough to come to town."

"Aunt Bertha wrote that Uncle Joseph wasn't well."

"He's been sick in bed for some time now."

The buckboard wagon had a spring seat, but that didn't absorb the bumps across six miles of the St. Augustine plains. Charles had to constantly shift positions to ease the aches in his hips and back.

To their north was a high ridge covered with juniper thickets. Farther west, the steep, jagged Mangas Mountains stood blue in the late-afternoon sun.

"Bertha told me about you, son. Said you was about to graduate from some New York college." Enderlee let the driving lines hang slack while the two-horse team trotted along steadily.

"Yes sir." Charles gritted his teeth to stifle a groan.

"You don't talk much, do you?"

"Well sir, I am rather weary."

" 'Spect you are. Ever'body that rides the stage from Trinidad is mighty glad to get off. They tell me Trinidad is growin' like a hogweed now that the railroad's got there."

"Yes sir."

They traveled in silence for a time. The team of bay horses seemed tireless. An early-summer sun sent streaks of sweat down the young man's face.

Now and then Enderlee sneaked a glance at him. What he saw was a slender young man, average height, with brown hair combed across his forehead, topped by

6

a black derby hat. Charles Manderfield had gray eyes under thin, almost feminine brows. But in spite of the thin brows and smooth face, his straight mouth and firm chin hinted of an inner strength. He wore a string tie, hanging loose now, a soiled white shirt, badly wrinkled dark wool pants and a black finger-length coat. His shoes were the high-topped lace-up kind, made of soft leather.

"Reckon you heard 'bout your uncle's partner runnin' out on him."

The remark jolted Charles worse than the wagon did. "What? No."

"Rounded up all their cattle and trailed 'em up north and sold 'em and quit the country."

For a moment Charles forgot how tired and sore he was. "How could he do that?"

"Ol' Joe was too sick to do anything. But I'd best let your Aunt Bertha tell you about it."

The Double M ranch house was built of thick timbers hauled and dragged down from the Mangases, chinked with clay dredged from Bear Creek. With five rooms, it was the biggest house in Conejos County. Joseph Manderfield had intended to make his wife comfortable. There was also a barn, an open-sided shed a one-room log bunkhouse and three pole corrals.

On Bear Ridge to the north, the juniper brush was so thick that trails had to be cut through it with an axe. But under the ridge was Bear Springs. Cool clear water seeped out of a half-acre of ground and gathered to run downhill and organize Bear Creek. The creek had never been completely dry.

Uncle Joseph had bought patent to ninety-five square miles of grazing land, and the Double M holdings extended over a good portion of the St. Augustine plains and up into the Mangases where cattle grazed in the summer. All of which was meaningless to Charles. He

7

knew nothing about grazing land or the beasts that grazed. In New York he had driven and ridden horses as a means of transportation, but they were kept in barns and pens and ate hay and grain, which was grown somewhere else.

Aunt Bertha saw them coming and was out of the house and hurrying toward them by the time Enderlee whoaed the team.

"Evenin', Mizzes Manderfield," Enderlee said. "Brought you some chuck and this here young man."

"Thank you kindly, Mr. Enderlee." She stood with her hands on her plump hips, a wide smile on her face. "My, how you've grown. Charles. Why, you look just like your mother. Get out, both of you, and come in this house."

Charles climbed down, using a front wheel hub as a step. He had to straighten his back and stretch his legs before he could walk. His aunt wrapped her arms around him and kissed him on the cheek. "It must have been a horribly long trip, Charles. But I'm so glad you're here. Your uncle has been wanting very much to see you."

Inside, Mrs. Manderfield led them to a sitting room which was furnished much like his mother's house in New York. There was a cushioned, camelbacked sofa, two cushioned chairs covered with a flower pattern to match the sofa, a hand-carved oak chiffonnier and even a leather ottoman rocker with a matching footstool. A huge stone fireplace was part of the far wall.

Mrs. Manderfield invited Enderlee to sit, then excused herself and led her nephew into a bedroom. Charles wouldn't have recognized the man lying on a big brass bed, covered to his chin with a white sheet. This couldn't be Uncle Joseph. No, not at all. Uncle Joseph was a wiry, vital, masculine man over six feet tall, a man full of enthusiasm and always looking for a new adventure.

No. This man looked to be a hundred years old. His hair was white. His face was white. The only resemblance to Joseph J. Manderfield was the walrus mustache.

Mrs. Manderfield spoke softly. "Dear. Joseph, dear, are you awake?"

The eyes in the white wrinkled face opened, blinked, opened again. A hand moved from under the sheet. "Charles?"

"Yes, Uncle Joseph. It's me." Seeing his uncle like this made him feel like crying. Blinking back tears, he glanced at his aunt. "Is he . . . ?"

"He's very ill, Charles. We don't know for sure, but the doctor thinks it's some kind of cancer in his bones."

The old man spoke again in a gravelly voice. "Charles, you've grown up. You've got an education now."

Stepping closer to the bed, Charles said, "Yes, Uncle Joseph. Thanks to your contributions, I was able to graduate from Columbia with a degree in civil engineering."

"That's good, Charles, that's good. Your daddy would be proud of you."

Charles pleaded, "Uncle Joseph, can I do anything for you?"

A slow grin widened the white mouth. "Matter of fact, Charles, you can."

"Anything."

"Take care of your aunt."

"Of course."

"Either run this outfit or sell it. You're a smart boy. What you don't know you can learn. Just take care of your aunt and your mother."

"I'll certainly do the best I can."

"Sure you will. Now"—the voice was weakening—"talking is hard work for me. I'm powerful glad you're here, Charles." The watery eyes closed.

After Enderlee left, Aunt Bertha baked some biscuits in the best brass-trimmed cookstove that Montgomery Ward had to offer. She warmed a stew and set out a jar of plum preserves. "I apologize, Charles. I haven't felt much like cooking since your uncle took sick. He won't eat much. I'll do better in the morning, I promise." They sat at a table of hand-carved oak, and while they ate, Charles asked again about a doctor.

"Mr. Enderlee sent a man to Las Vegas to fetch him. I expect he'll be back here in a day or two. He has so many patients he can't attend to them all."

"What about the cattle? Mr. Enderlee said something about them being rounded up and driven away."

"Yes. Every animal we had. Two thousand and four hundred head. Except for the buckboard team and one saddle horse, there isn't a domestic animal on the ranch."

"Who did it?"

"Matthew Wyker. Joseph bought a lot of land, and he told Mr. Wyker he had more grazing land than he had cattle for. He and Mr. Wyker went into a partnership, whereby Mr. Wyker brought one thousand four hundred cattle from Texas to graze with our one thousand head."

"And then," Charles finished the tale for her, "while Uncle Joseph was in his sickbed, this Matthew Wyker rounded up all the cattle and sold them."

"Yes."

"And disappeared."

"I'm afraid so. I don't understand it. Joseph doesn't understand it. They were partners before, you know, and though Mr. Wyker was a mite reckless, Joseph thought he could be trusted."

10

"I know nothing about the value of cattle, but they must have been worth quite a lot of money."

"A lot of money. Joseph was planning to sell some beeves this fall. Now we're almost penniless."

The supper was tasty, and Charles was hungry, but he was too deep in thought to eat much. A worry frown wrinkled his forehead as he picked at his food. Then he reached a decision.

"I'll find him." he told his Aunt Bertha. "I'll find this Matthew Wyker."

That was how it started.

Two

Billy Johnson was also looking for Matthew Wyker. It was his third stop at the Conejos County sheriff's office, but he got no more information than he'd got before. "No," the deputy said, "I still ain't heard nothin' about that Wyker feller. I sent notices out in the mail, but I ain't heard nothin'. And like I already said, I couldn't get a warrant out for 'im. The judge says a partner's got the right to sell what he called 'the assets.'"

Deputy Arnold Phister sat in a straight-backed chair with his boots on top of a rickety wooden desk in the one-room sheriff's office. "Say, a young feller was in here while ago, said he was from Back East and said he was lookin' for Matt Wyker too. Said he's a nephew of Joe Manderfield."

"You don't say." Billy poured tobacco out of a small cloth sack onto a cigarette paper, licked an edge of the paper and rolled a smoke. "Didn't know ol' Manderfield had a nephew."

"Said he was, and he was ridin' a horse branded with two *M*s joined together. I told 'im about you boys trailin' them cattle up to Colfax County, and about Matt Wyker sellin' 'em and takin' off with the money."

"What kind of feller is this nephew?"

" 'Bout your age and size. Wore clothes that look like they come out of a Monkey Ward book."

"What's his name?"

"Manderfield. Didn't catch his first name. Said he's gonna stay at the hotel tonight so he can catch the stage north first thing in the mornin'."

"*Mañana*, eh? How long's he been in town?"

"Got here yesterday. Ol' Enderlee took 'im out to the rancho yesterday and he came back by hisself today."

"Wal, reckon I'll hunt 'im up and see what kind of gent he is." Spurs ringing, Billy Johnson left the sheriff's cubbyhole and headed up the boardwalk.

The town of Lariat, in the south-center of New Mexico Territory, had one main street two blocks long and two parallel streets. Houses and shacks, most with horse corrals in back, were scattered around the three streets and halfway up a rocky hill south of town. Most of the houses were built with adobe brick, but a few were of rocks and lumber. There was one mercantile which sold everything from sugar to saddles, a blacksmith shop, a laundry, a one-story hotel and a restaurant next door to the hotel.

Charles Manderfield was sitting alone at a table for four in the Corrales Steak House when he saw the young cowboy come in the door, glance around and then head right for him. The cowboy was about his age, smooth shaven, with a dusty, sweat-stained, curl-brim black hat on his head. He wore a gray muslin shirt with a black silk muffler hanging loosely around his throat. Big roweled spurs dragged across the wooden floor when he walked. He also wore a pistol in a holster on his right hip.

"Howdy," he said pleasantly. "Might you be Chas Manderfield, a kin of Joe Manderfield?"

13

"Yes sir, I am Charles Manderfield." Charles stood, ready to shake hands, but the young cowboy didn't offer a hand.

"I know Joe Manderfield. I usta work for 'im. A good man to work for. My name is Billy Johnson. My folks're holdin' down a claim a dozen miles south of the Double M headquarters."

"Won't you sit down, Mr. Johnson. May I order you a cup of coffee? Or some supper?"

The young cowboy pulled out a chair and sat. He took off his hat and dropped it onto a vacant chair. A sheaf of straw-colored hair fell across his forehead. "That's right nice of you, but I got to get back. I hear you're gonna go lookin' for Matt Wyker."

"Yes sir, I am."

"You got an idee where to look?"

"Only what Deputy Phister told me. Do you happen to know anything about the theft of my uncle's cattle?"

"Yup. I helped 'im do it. Only we didn't know he was gonna take the money and light out."

Charles forgot about his supper. "You . . . you helped him do it?"

"I was one of eleven men he hired to gather ever' cowbrute on the Double M and trail 'em up north to just under them Raton Mountains. Sold 'em to a feller that said he was gonna summer 'em on some good grass, and this fall he's gonna cut out the dry stuff and drive 'em up to the railroad."

"What is the buyer's name?"

"Jake Ingalls. He's got about a hunnerd sections up there around that big holler mountain."

"Then he still has the cattle?"

"I reckon. But he paid for 'em and he's got a bill of sale to prove it."

"Hmmm." Charles gave that some thought, then

said, "I don't suppose this Mr. Ingalls has a clue as to where Mr. Wyker went?"

"Not a one. Says he ain't. We ask 'im."

After pondering that a moment, Charles said, "Well, it's a place to start."

"You're leavin' *mañana?*"

"*Mañana?* Oh, tomorrow? Yes. I'll take the stage." Thinking about the stage ride made him wince.

"If you was to go horseback I'd go with you."

"Horseback? That far? And what's your interest in this?"

"Like I told you, ol' Wyker sold them cattle then quit the country. He owes us our wages."

"Oh, I see. You said you tried to find him?"

"Didn't try much. Couldn't. We didn't have more'n five bucks amongst us. All we had was the horses we was ridin'. Some of the boys stayed up there and tried to find work to keep from goin' hungry. I came on back by myself. Like to of starved before I got home."

"Do you really want to find him?"

"You betcha. I been ridin' for the Oxbow, 'tween here and the Double M, and I got a month's wages comin'. I swore as soon as I got some spendin' money I'd go back and try to find that *chingao* sonofabuck." The young cowboy's face had suddenly turned hard. "I hate thieves and I cain't stand bein' stole from."

"I don't blame you." Charles pushed his plate aside and took a sip of coffee. The coffee was cool. Could he trust this fellow? Billy Johnson seemed sincere. Could they work together? Lord knows he could use some help. Finally, he said, "Mr. Johnson, I'm going to take the stage to the Clifton House and start my search from there."

"Wal, you better take your saddle. You'll need a horse, and you can buy a horse almost anywheres, but

15

a good saddle for sale ain't so easy to find."

"Yes, you are probably right. I'll follow your advice."

Billy Johnson stood and put his hat on. Blue eyes with squint wrinkles radiating from them studied Charles a moment. "Wal, I'm goin' horseback. I cain't afford to buy a horse when I get there. Maybe I'll see you up there."

Standing too, Charles held out his hand to shake. The young cowboy shook it with a callused hand. "Yes, Mr. Johnson, I hope we do meet again."

Charles told the stableman at the Franklin Livery to keep the Double M horse until his Aunt Bertha Manderfield came to town. "Shore," the stableman said. "I'll keep an eye out for her. She can tie 'im to the hames on one of the wagon horses and lead 'im back. Say, I hear you're goin' up north to look for Matt Wyker."

"As a matter of fact, I am. I don't suppose you know anything about him or his whereabouts."

"No, I knowed 'im when I seen 'im is all. All's I know is he had a likin' for women."

"What do you mean?"

"He wasn't married, you know, and he was always lookin' for a woman to bed down with. Damn near got his *culo* blowed off once by a Mexican here in town 'cause he offered a woman some money to climb in bed with 'im. Deputy Phister talked the Mexican into puttin' his scattergun down."

"He was that kind of man, huh?"

"Yup. And I'll bet that wherever he went he spent a good chunk of that money on *pinche.*"

"Excuse me. On what?"

16

"*Pinche.* You know, what makes dogs run around."

Charles didn't know for certain, but he guessed. "Thank you. I'll keep that in mind."

He folded the stirrups under the saddle and tied them in place with a saddle string. He put that and a saddle blanket and bridle with his gladstone bag to be loaded in the boot at the rear of the stagecoach.

The ride north was no easier than the ride south. He sat between two men on one of two padded bench seats in the coach, riding backwards. A women and her two children, ages about five and seven, occupied the forward-facing seat. The country wasn't too steep, and the four-horse team kept up a steady trot, breaking into a gallop where the road went downhill. The stage stopped every fifteen to twenty miles so a fresh team could be hitched up. Those relay stops were all that kept Charles from dying. They gave him a chance to get out and stretch some of the aches from his body.

At Las Vegas, Territory of New Mexico, he switched to the Barlow and Sanderson's stage line and a bigger coach. This one had three bench seats, one on each end and one in the middle. But again he was crowded into the backwards seat, his feet tucked under the seat and his knees knocking against a man in the middle. They were traveling almost straight north now on the Santa Fe Trail.

It was at one of the relay stations that he was almost shot and killed.

He had to wait his turn to get into the men's outhouse behind a long, low adobe building. What a relief. When he came out he saw the three stage-line employees and the eight passengers, all men now, lined up beside one of the corrals. Their hands were held high. Four men with bandanas over their faces

17

and pistols in their hands were standing in front of them.

Charles stopped, blinked. He couldn't believe what he was seeing. Then one of the masked men spotted him. "Hey. You. Git over here. Git your goddamn ass over here before I blow another hole in it."

It took a moment for what was happening to penetrate his mind. Then Charles was scared. This was robbery. He was being threatened with a gun.

"Git over here, goddamnit, before I shoot the shit out of you. Move them feet, mister."

Great Scott. He was about to be robbed. The money he was carrying was about to be stolen from him. It was all he had. Without it he wouldn't be able to search for Matthew Wyker. He'd have to go back to Aunt Bertha and ask for more money to resume the search. And she'd said they were almost penniless.

"Move them feet, mister. Do it right now or, by God, you'll die right where you stand."

He started shaking with fear. He tried to say something, but all that came out was a squawk.

"Move, you dandy son of a bitch."

Charles moved. Without thinking, he turned and ran in the opposite direction. A gun boomed behind him, and a bullet sang an angry song past his left ear. Another boom, and he felt the heat of the bullet. He ran behind the outhouse, got it between him and the gunmen, then headed as fast as his feet could carry him to the cedar hills. More shots were fired. A bullet tugged at his shirt. He didn't look back, just ran.

There were shouts, men yelling, guns booming. Bullets spanged off the rocks and chipped bark off the cedars. Charles tripped and fell heavily onto his hands and knees. He scrambled up and tripped again. This time he fell into a shallow fold in the side of a cedar-covered hill. He stayed down, breathing heavily.

More gunfire. More shouting. Panting for breath, his heart beating a mile a minute, Charles thought he was done for. He knew the robbers were somewhere close, and if he jumped up and ran farther he'd be a target they couldn't miss. He stayed down.

Then he noticed that the bullets were not coming his way. And then the shooting ceased. Cautiously, he raised his head and looked. The victims were no longer lined up beside a corral. Three of them had guns in their hands. Two of the masked men were down. Another was standing nearby with his hands up. The fourth was walking down the hill back toward the stage. The stage driver had a lever-action rifle aimed at him, and that robber's hands were raised too.

"Hey mister," a man yelled. "Where are you? Are you hit?"

Three

Knees shaking, Charles Manderfield got slowly to his feet.

Someone yelled again, "Are you hurt?"

"N-no," he said weakly. Then louder, "No, I don't think so."

"You can come back now."

With unsteady steps he walked back downhill, a hill covered with chips of shale and flint. He stepped wide around the masked man who was face down with a bloody hole in his back. When he was closer, the stage driver asked again, "Are you hurt, mister?"

"Uh, n-no. I, uh, no, I am not injured."

"Wal, you sure saved our bacon."

"Uh, how . . . what?"

"You runnin' like that. Two of 'em took out after you and the other two watched and ol' Tobe here grabbed one from behind and swung 'im around and his partner tried to shoot Tobe but hit his own man and I grabbed a gun from the coach boot and shot that un and them two up there saw what was happenin' and threw their hands up like they was jerked up on ropes and that's all there was to it."

The two surviving robbers were ordered to stand up against the coach while one of the passengers pulled the bandanas off their faces. One had a knife scar on his chin. Both needed a shave and haircut.

"Listen," the passenger said, "there's no law officer for a long ways and no jail, so what're we gonna do with 'em?"

"We oughta hang 'em," another passenger said.

"Nope," the driver said, "we're gonna do things accordin' to the law. Jackson," he said to the station master, "you're gonna havta keep 'em here 'til the southbound comes along and send 'em down to Wagon Mound."

Jackson pulled a stem-winder watch from his shirt pocket and allowed, "She won't be along for nigh onto two hours, but don't you worry, I ain't lettin' these gents get away."

Soon they were traveling again, the four horses trotting, the coach bouncing and swaying on its leather thoroughbraces. Another passenger, a chubby man in a checkered suit and a homburg hat, chuckled, then said, "I never heard of anybody being a hero by running away, but mister, you sure saved our wallets." He stuck out his hand. "Name's Winderman. James T. Winderman."

"Manderfield, Charles J. Manderfield." Charles shook with him.

"Where you headed, Mr. Manderfield? Not that it's any of my business."

"Oh, to the Clifton House."

"Got business up there? Not that it's any of my business."

"Yes. Yes I have." His tone made it understood that he was not in a talking mood. The chubby man said no more.

* * *

The Clifton House was going to pieces. It was once a proud building that stood not far below where the toll road came out of the Raton Mountains. The first section was built of adobe, then added to with logs and later with rough-sawed lumber. A covered porch ran the length of it. Now there were loose boards at one end of the porch, and a broken window. The adobe section was deteriorating from the weather, and the chinks between the log walls were also weathering away. But two pole corrals just east of the house were in good repair. They held ten horses. At least eight of the horses had collar marks on their shoulders and were about two hundred pounds heavier than the saddle horses.

"Whoa-a-a," the teamster yelled, hauling back on the driving lines. The coach came to a rocking stop near the corrals. A man in baggy wool pants came out of the house and held one of the lead horses by the bridle while the teamster climbed down. "This here is as fur as we go tonight," the teamster said to the passengers. "You can feed your faces here and bed down. We ain't a-goin' over that there mountain 'til daylight."

Climbing out on both sides of the coach, the passengers stretched, lifted their suitcases out of the boot in back and walked on unsteady legs to the house. Charles leaned against a coach wheel a moment and let the others go ahead. The country was a little greener here than it was farther south. High, flattop buttes stuck up like sentinels, with rolling grassy hills between them. The yucca was in full bloom, with bell-shaped pods on stalks growing out of the jagged leaves. Some of the cane cactus sported small red flowers. The purple Raton Mountains

22

loomed to the north, and over east, away over east, was the towering cinder cone called Mount Capulin.

Jacob Ingalls's ranch was supposed to be somewhere near that cone-shaped mountain. Charles wondered how far. Oh well, he wasn't going to get on a horse and ride over there until morning. He hoped he could rent a horse.

He'd stopped at the Clifton House before, and while the food was simply beans, beef and biscuits, it was edible. He hadn't spent the night here, though, and the accommodations couldn't possibly be suitable. Oh well. Idly, he watched the coach driver and his helper unhitch the horses and lead them to the corrals. Moving stiffly, he picked up his gladstone bag, walked to the house, stepped onto the porch, opened a squeaking screen door and went inside.

"That's him," said the man in the checkered suit. "He ran like a rabbit, and whilst the hoodlums was watching him the driver and his helper overpowered them."

"Say, young feller," said a skinny man, bareheaded, wearing a dirty white apron around his middle, "where'd you learn to outrun bullets?" He also wore a wide grin.

"They're only joshing, mister," said a middle-aged woman in a long gray dress. "They're thankin' their lucky stars that you done like you done. It took more sand to run like that than to do what they tol' you to do." Her gray hair was pulled tight behind her head and tied in a knot. "Say, didn't you come through here just a few days ago?"

"Yes. I was on my way south. Can I rent a room for the night?"

The woman answered, "We only got one room and it's got ten bunks in it." She nodded toward the far end of the building. "Go ahead and pick out one. Rest your bones."

The building was divided into three sections. One end was a general store, the middle was a kitchen and dining room with a big wood-burning stove and a long table, and the other end was a hotel, or what passed for a hotel. "You got plenty of time to rest," the woman said. "Supper won't be ready for an hour and a half. You can warsh up out back." Wearily, Charles carried his gladstone bag back to the bunk room.

Supper was surprisingly good. A big bowl of soup was placed in the center of the table, and the woman ladled each customer's plate full. The soup was a mixture of beans, corn and bits of beef. Most of the customers dunked thick slices of bread in the soup, but Charles spread his bread with apple butter. He sipped the soup out of the side of his spoon.

"Where you from, young feller?" the skinny man asked as he picked up Charles's plate. "Want some more?"

"No thank you. It was delicious. I'm from New York."

"You don't say. We ain't ever had a traveler here from New York, have we, Maggie?"

The woman wiped her hands on a towel made from a flour sack. "Yeah, there was a gentleman came through here 'bout a year ago that said he was from New York."

Charles asked, "Did you ever meet a gentleman named Matthew Wyker?"

"Matt Wyker? Yeah. He's the cowman that drove

a big herd of cattle by here about a month ago." The skinny man chuckled. "I know some cowboys that'd sure like to see him again."

"You wouldn't happen to know anything of his whereabouts, would you?"

"Naw. If I did I'd sure tell you. What I heard is he vamoosed without payin' his crew."

"Do you know a rancher named Jacob Ingalls?"

"Sure. He's got a lot of country around that old volcano, and his house is over there just this side of it. You know him?"

"No sir, but I do want to meet him."

Checkered Suit changed the subject. "Expect you'll be goin' out of business pretty soon. The Santa Fe railroad's getting closer every day."

"Yes," the woman said, "Won't be long now. They say the railroad's got kitchen cars and bed cars and everything. People won't have to get off to eat and sleep."

"We're hopin' to sell this place to some rancher," the skinny man said. "We'll be lucky if we get anything for it."

"Well," Checkered Suit said, "I'll tell you folks, I've been over that pass with a wagon train before the railroad ever thought of coming here, before Uncle Dick built his toll road, and I'll tell you folks it took five days just to get about thirty miles, and we lost two wagons on the way."

"Yes, the railroad's a good thing, I reckon, but we don't know what we're gonna do for a livin' after it gets here."

There was no place in the bunk room to hang clothes, so Charles stripped to his underwear, folded his clothes neatly and placed them on top of his gladstone bag before crawling between the blankets. There were no linens on the bunks either, only rough, scratchy blankets. As a precaution, Charles put his wallet under the pillow. He spent the night listening to men snore, sputter and pass gas.

In the morning, after a breakfast of pancakes and sausage, a fresh team was hitched to the coach, the passengers were loaded, and the coach was gone. Charles stayed behind.

The skinny man, his wife, a short man hired to take care of the stage line's horses, and Charles had the Clifton House to themselves. "You say you're lookin' for Jake Ingalls?" the skinny man asked.

"Yes sir. Can I rent a horse? And can you tell me how to get to his ranch?"

"Yeah, but you'll be lucky if you find 'im at the house. He owns a lot of country, and he could be anywhere on it."

"I have to try. I do want very much to talk to him."

The brown horse was gentle but slow, and Charles had to be constantly slapping it on the rump with the ends of the bridle reins to keep it moving in a shuffling trot. The road east was an easy one to travel. Charles had been told it went all the way to the "Nation."

"The Nation?" he'd asked.

"Yeah, the Indian Nation."

"Oh." He remembered reading that the U.S. government had set aside a hugh area between Texas and Kansas for the Indians. Texas, Kansas and Colorado were official states now, with full representation in the U.S. Congress. New Mexico had only territorial status with one nonvoting representative in the Congress. These were things Charles had learned while studying the situation Out West.

The closer he got to the old volcano, the rockier the terrain was. Before he came to the ranch buildings, the horse was walking at times on solid sheets of brown lava. There was a long log house, two three-sided sheds, four corrals, a freight wagon and a buggy. Charles rode up to the front of the house, tied the horse to a hitchrail, walked up a dirt path to the plank door and knocked.

No answer. He knocked again. Still no answer. He went back to his horse and took a long look around. He saw no cattle, and only one horse in a corral. "Darn it," he muttered to himself, "there ought to be someone here." He went back to the door and knocked again.

"Hey." It was a man's voice coming from the barn. Charles backed away from the door and looked in that direction. "I'm comin'," the man said. He was old with a wrinkled, sun-dried face and a black, slouchy hat. His left foot and ankle were wrapped in a thick, dirty bandage. He was walking on crutches.

"Excuse me," Charles said, "but I'm looking for Mr. Jacob Ingalls."

"Well," the old man stopped and leaned on his crutches, "him and the boys rode out of here early this mornin'. I don't expect 'em back 'til late, maybe not 'til after dark."

"Oh." Disappointment showed in Charles's face.

"You come from the Clifton House?" The pale eyes went over Charles from the derby hat to the soft leather shoes.

"Yes sir."

"Well, it's too bad he ain't here. You can wait for

'im if you want to. Put your horse in one of them pens there and come on in the house."

"I appreciate your offer, but I'd like to get back before dark. Would he be here tomorrow perhaps?"

"Come to think of it, I b'lieve he said somethin' about goin' to the Cliftons tomorrow. We're gittin' low on chuck." The old man took his hat off, scratched his nearly bald head and reset the hat.

"Can you tell me, sir, whether he bought a herd of cattle from a Matthew Wyker recently?"

"That he did. We just got through putting his wagon wheel brand on 'em. Fact is, that's what him and the boys are doin' now, pushin' 'em up in the high hills for the summer."

"That's what I would like to talk to him about. Do you suppose you could give him a message for me?"

"Shore."

"Just tell him I want to talk to him. I'll be at the Clifton House for a day or two."

"I'll tell 'im that. Care to leave your name?"

"I am Charles Manderfield, nephew of Joseph Manderfield, who had a half interest in those cattle."

"Oh, is that so? I heard about Matt Wyker takin' the money and haulin' out without payin' his crew. Jake didn't have nothin' to do with that, but I'd better let him tell you about it. I just work here. That is, I did 'til I busted my ankle. Horse turned over on me. Now all I can do is stand around on these damned sticks. But I'll sure tell Jake you're lookin' for 'im."

"I would appreciate it." Charles turned to go back to his horse.

"Have you et?"

"Yes," Charles lied. "I brought a sandwich."

28

He waited until he was out of sight of the ranch house to stop and unwrap the sandwich the woman had given him. He sat on the ground and ate while the horse grazed on the buffalo grass. He had finished and started to get up when he heard a strange buzzing behind him. Turning half around, he saw something that made him gasp with fear and turned his blood to ice.

Four

The snake was about four feet long and as thick as his wrist. It was coiled with its head rising on one side, its tail sticking straight up on the other. The forked tongue was flicking in and out of its mouth. The buttons on the end of its tail were quivering, rattling.

Charles was petrified. Rattlesnakes, he'd read, were deadly. They could strike as quick as a wink, and their bites were fatal.

"Ohhhh," he groaned. "Ohhhh."

He dared not try to move. The slightest movement could cause it to strike. "Ohhhh." What to do?

Man and snake stared at each other. Neither blinked. Finally, the tail ceased its rattling, and the snake straightened slowly and started to crawl. Afraid to breath, Charles watched. Slowly, it crawled. Closer to him.

Death did not come quickly to rattlesnake victims. Charles had read about it in the *Police Gazette*. The victims became very ill, vomiting blood and sometimes going into convulsions. There was no one to help. He would die here by the side of the road all by himself. "Ohhhh."

Horror brought on an involuntary action. Charles

tried to jump up but only fell back on the seat of his pants. Immediately, the snake coiled again. Its mouth was open so wide Charles could see the two curved fangs. It struck.

The fangs buried themselves in Charles's right pants leg against the top of his shoe. With a scream, Charles jumped up. The fangs were stuck in his pants leg, and when he tried to move, the snake moved with him. He screamed again, kicked and cried, trying to shake the snake loose.

Finally, it fell free and instantly coiled, ready to strike again, tail rattling madly. But Charles was too horrified to stand still. He jumped back, fell onto the seat of his pants, jumped up and ran like crazy to the road. There, he stopped and looked back, half expecting the snake to be coming after him. He could see it, still coiled, its head up and its wicked beady eyes looking for something to strike at.

"Ohhhh, my God." Did it bite him? Carefully, he pulled up his pants leg and looked. "Ohhhh, my God." There was a scratch, one thin scratch, above the top of his shoe. He'd been bitten by a rattlesnake. He had to get help. He had to get on that horse and ride back to the Clifton House. But to get to the horse he had to walk through the grass. Where there was one snake there might be another. Maybe a lot of them.

"Here, boy," he said in a shaky voice. The horse went right on grazing. It wasn't worried about snakes. "Come here, will you?" The horse took three steps to get at another clump of grass. Could horses smell rattlesnakes? They could often smell danger, he'd read. "Please come here." It was useless. He'd have to go to the horse. Slowly, watching where he

31

put every step, Charles walked. The horse raised its head and watched him come. Every yucca, every clump of grass, could hide a snake. Careful. Look carefully.

Then he was at the horse's left side. It stood patiently as he gathered the reins and stepped into the saddle. Charles let his breath out in a long sigh. He was safe now. An animal as big as a horse could survive a rattlesnake bite. "Let's go back," he said. "Hurry."

Knowing it was going home now, the horse moved into a fast trot. Charles hung onto the saddle horn and endured the beating he was taking. His teeth rattled. His bones rattled. But he was in a hurry and he didn't try to hold the horse down to a slower gait.

How long would it take the venom to reach his heart? Would he lose consciousness before he got back? How much farther was it? "Oh-h-h." Then he saw something that brought the fear back into his throat.

Indians.

There were four of them. Off to his right. All on horses. Coming at a gallop, carrying long rifles.

"Giddap," he yelled at the horse, kicking the animal's sides with the heels of his shoes. "Run, you fool."

Run, it did. Heading for home with a terrified man on its back, it flattened out and fairly flew down the road. Letting the reins hang slack, Charles grabbed the saddle horn and continued kicking with his spurless shoes. When he looked back he saw the Indians were chasing him. Bloodcurdling yells came from them. A shot was fired.

"Please hurry." The brown horse was doing its best, hooves pounding. Another shot. Charles screamed as a bullet buzzed like an angry hornet past his right ear. "Please," he screamed.

Down the road they went. Indians were crying bloody murder. Charles was hanging onto his derby hat with one hand and the saddle horn with the other. His coattail was flying behind him. Then the buildings were in sight. Looking back again, Charles saw the Indians were farther behind. He was safe.

It was a badly winded horse and a terrified man that galloped up to the corrals at the Clifton House. The short hostler was raking manure in one of the corrals when he saw them. He ran out and grabbed the horse by the reins near the bridle bit. "What in hell's your hurry? What's goin' on?"

Charles was as breathless as if he'd done the running instead of the horse. "In-Indians. Back there."

The short man ran around the corner of the corral to where he could see down the road. Then he hollered at the house. "Luke. Maggie. Injuns." He took another look down the road and counted, "One, two, three, four. Four of 'em. Luke. Maggie." Then he dragged Charles off the horse and half pulled him to the house. "Come on, kid, we're about to get attack-ted."

The skinny man and the woman came out on the porch, carrying rifles. The man threw his rifle to his shoulder and fired. Charles made it to the porch before he looked back. The Indians weren't moving, just sitting their horses out of rifle range and watching.

"They won't attack," the skinny man said, lowering his gun. "There's only four of 'em."

"But there might be some more around somewhere," the woman said.

"The stage oughta be comin' down off the pass purty soon. That'll give us some more guns."

"Where'd they jump you, kid?"

"Down the road. I don't know how far. They shot at me."

"You hit?"

"No, I'm not shot. But I've been bitten by a rattlesnake."

"Where?"

"On the leg."

The woman said, "Let's go in the house and take a look." She led Charles by the arm into the kitchen. He sat on a bench at the table and pulled his pants leg up. She kneeled to get a closer look. "It's only a scratch. Don't think it got any poison in you." Looking up at Charles, she asked, "How come he only scratched you?"

"It, uh, it got its fangs caught in my pants leg."

"Oh. That could happen. I've heard of that happening. You're lucky it didn't get its teeth in you. You'd have a swole leg. Swole and sore for a long time. If it'd got you in a vein you'd be dead."

"You . . . you don't think it's serious?"

"No. It's just a scratch. I doubt there's any poison in you."

"Thank God."

"I've got some tincture of iodine here. I'll fetch it." She took a small bottle of red medicine from a kitchen shelf and, with a tiny glass dipper, spread some over the scratch. "That'll keep infection away.

34

I've got to get back outside and see what's happening."

Charles pulled his pants leg down and followed her out. The Indians had disappeared. "Which way did they go?" he asked.

"Back whar they come from," the short hostler said. "At least they're headed in that direction."

"Where did they come from?"

"The Nation. Some a them young bucks forget whar the boundaries are and they come over in the territory lookin' for somethin' to steal and some white folks to kill."

"They wanted to kill me."

"Yup. I don't doubt that for a minute." The hostler chuckled, "That ol' Brownie horse can run when he wants to. He's grain fed and he c'n leave them Injun ponies wonderin' whar he went."

"He carried me to safety."

Still chuckling, the short man said, "Yup. If he's headed for home and he thinks thar's somethin' on his tail, all's you have to do is throw the reins away and hang on."

"Here comes the southbound," the skinny one said.

Talk at the supper table was about the Indians and how they were far from being defeated. Most were content to stay on the reservations and let the U.S. government feed them, the conversation went, but there were always some leaving the reservations and looking for trouble.

"There ain't as many of 'em out there as there used to be," the hostler said, "but they're still out there."

35

"We havta keep our guns loaded and handy."

Then Charles thought of something else that had his heart pounding again. "I was told that Jacob Ingalls might be coming over that road tomorrow. Do you think . . . ?"

All were quiet a moment. Then the woman said, "I wish there was some way to warn him."

The southbound stayed only long enough for the passengers to eat and fresh horses to be hitched to the stage. Then it was gone. The teamster figured they would be safe from an Indian attack at night. Indians almost never attacked at night, he said. Sneak around, sneak up behind you and cut your gizzard out, but attack in force? Naw.

After the stage left, there were only two men at the Clifton House. Two men, a woman and Charles. "You might as well get some shut-eye," the woman said to Charles. "Nothing's gonna happen tonight. If it does, you'll know about it."

In his bunk, Charles ignored the scratchy blankets and wished he were back in New York. Sure, there were thugs on the city streets, thugs with knives who'd kill you for a half-dollar. But all one had to do was stay away from the sections of the city inhabited by thugs. Mind one's own business and stay away from them.

But Out West?

My God, in just two days he'd been shot at by robbers, bitten by a rattlesnake and shot at by Indians. He could be attacked by Indians again, maybe before daylight. With that on his mind, he turned over on his side and groaned:

"Ohhhh."

Five

Daylight was a relief. All night long Charles imagined every sound was a savage sneaking through the house. But at daylight everything seemed to be normal. The woman made some biscuits, fried some bacon and made gravy out of the bacon fat. As far as Charles could tell, the Indians had been forgotten by everyone but himself.

"What," he asked, "could they do about Jacob Ingalls coming to town, not knowing about the danger?"

"Well, there's not much *we* can do," the skinny man said. "If anybody went to warn 'im, he'd be in danger of losing his own scalp. Maybe he'll bring some of his crew with 'im. Sometimes they all come over here to drink some beer and eat a woman-cooked meal."

"Sometimes," the woman said, "the cattlemen and their cowboys bring a quarter of beef or some ribs, and we have us a feast. The beer is warm, but they don't care."

And that's the way it happened. Jacob Ingalls arrived shortly before noon with five mounted men following a light spring wagon pulled by two horses. The skinny man hoisted a keg of beer onto a kitchen shelf and began drawing beer by the cupful. The men sat in the kitchen or stood on the porch or squatted on their heels in the yard. They all wore big hats, tight denim pants and boots with spurs on the heels. And they all had big pistols in holsters hanging from their belts.

"Didn't see one damn Injun," a cowboy said.

"Bet they saw us."

"If there was only four, they wasn't about to attack us."

"Aw, I bet they went on back to the Nation. They was prob'ly a few young bucks out lookin' for some excitement."

"Way I heard it, them chiefs try to keep the young uns a-behavin' theirselves. If they don't the tribe bosses kick the hound dog out of 'em."

"I don't think we have to worry much about the Injuns from the Nation. It's them 'Paches down south that're always lookin' for blood."

Charles took it all in, his eyes going from one speaker to another. The speakers' eyes included him when they spoke, and the men didn't seem to consider him an outsider. Nor did they ask him about himself. He tried some of the beer but could only sip it and try to keep a straight face. Jacob Ingalls turned out to be the big man with a smooth-shaven face and curly brown hair. No matter how far down he pulled his hat, some of the curly hair stuck out from under it. Everyone called him Jake. He seemed to be good-natured.

"Mr. Ingalls," Charles said, trying to keep his voice low so only Jake Ingalls could hear, "I would like to question you about a Mr. Matthew Wyker. I understand you bought some cattle from him."

"Why, yes. Yes, I did."

"I'd like very much to find him."

"Well, son, I'd like to help you, but there were other men, some of his crew, asking about him, and I couldn't help them. I've been thinking about it a lot since then and I still don't know where he went."

"Oh." Disappointment showed on Charles's face.

"You got business with him?"

"Yes sir, I have. My uncle, Mr. Joseph J. Manderfield, owned a half interest in those cattle, and Mr. Wyker disappeared with all the money."

"Is that so?" They were sitting on the porch railing, Charles holding a tin cup nearly full of warm beer. The rancher seemed genuinely surprised. "I heard he cheated his crew, but I didn't know he had a partner. I bought his chuck wagon, harness team and everything."

"Would you mind telling me, sir, how you paid Mr. Wyker?"

"With a draft on the First National Bank of Denver."

Charles brightened. "Then he went to Denver?"

"Maybe. But he could have cashed that draft in any bank. Denver, Santa Fe, Chicago. Even New York."

"Oh." Disappointment again.

"One thing about selling cattle for grazing, if the check bounces he could always take the cattle back. My drafts don't bounce."

"Do you—you wouldn't have received the canceled check, would you?"

"Not yet. Might take a while. Depending on where he cashed it."

"Oh."

"Did you happen to notice in which direction he went after you paid him?"

"He got on his horse and headed west, this way, but he didn't get here. He could have doubled back and headed east, or he could have gone cross country to Taos and then Santa Fe, or he could have gone over the Trinchera Pass to Trinidad."

"Hmm, I see. Tell me, Mr. Ingalls—"

"Call me Jake. Only my banker calls me Mister." Jake Ingalls grinned. "And, believe me, I call him sir."

"Of course. Tell me, could Mr. Wyker have been robbed on his way back here? Or could he have been attacked by Indians?"

Shaking his head sadly, Jake Ingalls said, "All that is possible. His bones could be lying in an arroyo somewhere. I hope someday we find out."

"Well, Mr. Ingalls—I mean Jake—eventually your canceled check will be returned to you and you'll know where it was cashed and who cashed it."

"Yup, yup, you're right about that. Unless the Indians got him. They wouldn't have any use for a bank draft."

"If that's what happened, then we all owe Mr. Wyker an apology."

"Yup."

"Would you mind answering one more question, uh, Jake? How much did you pay for those cattle?"

"Well, we had to do some dickering and figuring. There were all kinds of cattle in that herd—some prime beeves, some young bulls, some old bulls, some dry cows, some mother cows with sucking calves. All kinds. And we figured an average of twenty-one dollars per head."

"And that brought the total to . . ."

"Fifty thousand four hundred dollars."

"That," Charles said, "is a great deal of money."

"That's a lot of money. I had to hock my soul to borrow that much. If the cow-calf business isn't pretty good for the next bunch of years, the First National Bank of Denver is gonna foreclose on a damn good ranch."

Charles absorbed it all, then stood and held out his hand to shake. "Mr. Ingalls—Jake—I appreciate your time, and I hope, I sincerely hope, the cow-calf business is very good." Jacob Ingalls shook hands with him.

Charles walked by himself out to the corrals and around them, staying on bare ground where there was no grass, yucca or cane cactus for snakes to hide in. He didn't like what he was thinking. Jacob Ingalls seemed like a nice man. He wasn't the kind that would . . . was he?

Well, he thought silently, there was a way to find out.

Dinner was soup and the leftover breakfast biscuits warmed up. But the woman promised everyone a feast for supper. She had the ribs roasting slowly in the oven, she said, a pot of Mexican beans and eight potatoes simmering, and three dried apple pies baking.

It was almost suppertime when they saw a rider coming from the south. He was alone, following the Santa Fe Trail, riding at a jog-trot. They watched him come, wondering who he was. When he was closer, Jake Ingalls allowed, "Why, I believe that's one of the Double M riders."

Sure enough, when he was closer still, Charles recognized him too. It was Billy Johnson from Lariat. He was still wearing the black, curl-brim hat and the black silk bandana slung loosely around his neck. He was also wearing the walnut-handled six-gun.

The young cowboy rode up to the long porch and grinned. The skinny man said, "Git down. Put your horse in a pen."

The woman said, "We're fixin' to have some supper. There's enough for you too."

"Wasn't you here before, with the Double M herd?" the skinny one asked.

"Yep. That's why I'm back." To Jake Ingalls, Billy said, "You remember me, don't you, Jake?"

"Sure do."

To Charles, the young cowboy said, "See you're still here. Doin' any good?"

"I'm afraid not."

"There's some hay in the rack yonder. Put your horse in there."

Charles walked with him as he led his gray horse to the corrals. "I'm afraid I haven't learned anything useful. We have to talk."

"Soon's I off-saddle this horse." He pulled the saddle off and sat it carefully astraddle a corral pole. Then he squatted on his heels and pushed his hat back, allowing a sheaf of straw-colored hair to fall across his forehead. "Did you learn anything at all?" He began rolling a smoke.

"Only that Jacob Ingalls paid Matthew Wyker with a draft on the First National Bank of Denver. I think it's safe to surmise that he went to Denver to cash it, although that is not necessarily so."

42

"I never been paid with a bank draft in my life. Fact is, I never even seen one. I wouldn't know what to do with one if I had it."

"Well, the draft can be cashed at almost any bank, but if he cashed it at any place other than the bank it was drawn on, it would take a while for it to clear."

"And you're thinkin' he wouldn't care to wait?"

Charles let out a sigh. "You know him better than I. Did he seem to be the kind of man who would be willing to wait?"

"I'd guess not. I'd guess he'd be in a hurry to get to some big city where he could lose hisself."

"There is another possibility. I was attacked by Indians yesterday. Is it possible that—"

The cowboy interrupted, "The hell you was? Apaches, or one a them other breeds?"

"Everyone thinks they came from the Indian Nation. But if it happened to me it could have happened to Matthew Wyker, couldn't it? Is it possible he could have been murdered by Indians and his body hidden?"

"Shore. We thought about that. And we looked. We thought we should've found some sign of a horse race or somethin'. We looked on both sides of the road for his carcass. We didn't see a sign of anything."

"But it's still possible?"

Shrugging, Billy said, "Yup."

"But you don't really think that's what happened?"

"I don't think so, and neither did the rest of us."

"Then I suppose the thing for me to do is to go to Denver, find out whether he cashed that draft and try to find a clue as to where he went from there."

43

"Wal, if you can stand my company, I'll go with you."

"That's fine with me. We can catch a train at Trinidad, but how should we get to Trinidad?"

"When's the next stage north?"

"They said it won't be here until late tomorrow and won't leave until early the next morning."

"Wal, I don't know about you, but I don't wanta set around here all day *mañana*. Can you buy a horse?"

"I can try. If I can we'll leave first thing in the morning. How long will it take to ride over the Raton Pass?"

"We'd best go over the Trinchera Pass. They said it's not bad for horsebackers, and it don't cost anything. You havta pay to go over the Raton Pass."

"Whatever you think is best."

Supper was as good as the woman said it was going to be. Everyone sat on the benches at the long table. The cowboys ate quietly, and were polite. "Please pass the spuds." Or, "Dick, will you push the gravy down this way?"

When the meal was over, before cigarettes were rolled and pipes were filled, the men scraped their plates in a garbage pail and stacked them inside a washtub. The woman had a bucket of water heating on the stove to wash dishes in. "Nobody pays for this supper," she said. "Jake and his crew brought enough beef to pay for ever'body with some left over."

Jake Ingalls said, "It was our pleasure. We butchered last night, and we remembered how good you can cook ribs and mash spuds, and we wanted a woman-cooked meal." To his crew he said, "You boys have one more beer and we gotta be going back."

When he lay between the scratchy blankets that night, Charles had a load on his mind. Whether he'd learned anything of value here remained to be seen. He wondered what kind of traveling companion Billy Johnson would be, he wondered if he would encounter any more Indians or robbers, he wondered if he would ever see New York again, and he wondered if he would ever find Matthew Wyker.

Six

Billy Johnson, lying only ten feet away, had a question on his mind too. He'd been planning for the past month to come back here and try again to find Matthew Wyker. Partnering with this easterner might or might not be a smart thing to do. They might have to spend some time horseback, camping on the trail and maybe even fighting. Some of the cities were rough, mean places, and some city men were plenty tough too. But this dandy didn't even have a gun, and probably never fired one in his life. He was something of a hero for foiling some would-be stage robbers, but he didn't do it by fighting. He did it by running. There were times when a feller had to stand and fight. A man needed a partner he could depend on to do his share.

On the other hand, this nephew of Joe Manderfield knew his way around the cities, knew about bank drafts and things like that. He would be taken seriously when he asked questions, while some dumb semi-illiterate cowpuncher like Billy Johnson would be shrugged off. Aw well, he thought as he turned over onto his stomach, all he had to lose was a month's wages. As long as he had his nearly new Remington

Army-sized six-gun and plenty of the metallic .44 center-fire cartridges, he could take care of himself.

They hadn't even got started up the trail before he had to save the dandy from being skinned. "Sixty dollars for that brown horse?" Billy shook his head. "That gent saw you comin'. Don't do it. Offer 'im thirty-five and go as high as forty, but no more."

"What if he won't sell at that price? I have to have a mount."

"He will. I'll bet he bought that pony off some drifter for twenty bucks."

So Charles went back to the short hostler and said, "See here, I believe thirty-five dollars is a fair price, but if you insist I'll pay as much as forty dollars."

Billy, standing within earshot, had to grind his teeth to keep from yelling "Fool!" It hurt to keep quiet, but he kept quiet.

"Nope," the hostler said. "I got to get at least fifty for 'im."

Charles looked over at Billy. Billy shook his head. "No sir, forty dollars is my best offer."

The hostler saw the exchange of glances and knew he was dealing now with an experienced horse trader. "All right, make it forty-five and I'll write out a bill of sale."

"Forty." "Nope, forty-three." "Forty-one." "Well, all right, if its cash money. I ain't got no use for them bank notes."

Billy had to intervene again when Charles bought himself a blanket to take along. "Goddamn, them Injun blankets are purty, but they ain't worth a diddly for keepin' the cold air out. They ain't worth a diddly for saddle blankets either 'cuz them squaws weave sagebrush in 'em. I've seen men bucked off for puttin' them blankets on a horse."

47

For a second, Charles was close to asking Billy to mind his own business, but if they were going to be traveling partners . . . "Well, that's all she has."

"Better buy two or three of 'em, then. See if she's got a tarp."

They rode east to get on the Trinchera Trail. Billy had helped Charles rig the gladstone bag so it hung from Charles's saddle horn. Billy had a pair of saddlebags hanging across the fork of his saddle and a blanket roll covered with a canvas tarp tied behind the cantle. "You were right about bringing a saddle," Charles said.

At the bottom of the Raton Mountains the hills were covered with dwarf cedar, juniper and lava rock, but the higher they climbed, the taller the trees became. Soon they were in a forest of lodgepole pine and tall ponderosas. The trail was single file most of the way, and Billy took the lead. Charles told him about his close call with a rattlesnake, and Billy agreed that he was lucky. "If he'd a got you deeper you'd be mighty sick about now."

Billy told about Charlie Goodnight, who drove cattle up this trail on his way to Wyoming to keep from paying Uncle Dick's toll on the Raton Pass.

"Is Uncle Dick Wootton a huge man, about six feet four?"

"I've never seen 'im, but that's what they say he looks like."

"I saw him when I traveled by stagecoach over the Raton Mountains. We stopped to change horses. He seemed congenial."

"Nobody's got any quarrel with 'im." Billy chuckled. "As big as he is, nobody wants a quarrel with 'im."

In places the trail was so steep they had to stop every few minutes and let their horses blow. Riding through tall timber, Charles thought he saw the crest of the pass ahead. Just a little farther, he thought, and they would be over the top and going downhill. He was disappointed. At the top of that hill, he looked across a narrow valley at another, higher ridge.

"Hey Chas," Billy said, looking back, "down there's a good place to stop and rest these ponies and eat them biscuits."

"What did you call me?"

"Chas."

"Why Chas?"

Billy reined up, twisted in his saddle and rested his right hand on his horse's rump. "First time I ever saw you I looked at the book in the Lariat Hotel to see what room you was in, and there was your name: *Chas J. Manderfield.* It was spelled C-H-A-S sure as anything."

"Oh, well, that's just an abbreviation of *Charles.*"

"I can spell. It was spelled *Chas.*"

With a shrug of his shoulders, Charles said, "If you insist. How much farther do you think it is?"

"Damned if I know. I never been over this trail before. I never been any further north than the Clifton House. I've been plumb over to Albuquerque, though, and I've been to Las Vegas three times."

A wry grin flashed across Charles's face. "You're well traveled." Then he added, "I'm sorry. I have no reason to be sarcastic."

"To be what?"

"Sarcastic. I mean, I didn't mean to be . . . insulting or anything."

Billy said no more, just straightened in his saddle and sent his horse downhill.

It was late afternoon when they rode out of the mountains and picked up Trinchera Creek not far from the towering Fisher's Peak. Turning west on fairly level ground, they could see the town at the foot of a long flattop shale hill. The Purgatoire River ran through the town, then curved to the north. When they rode into town, Charles discovered that the Mexican influence was as strong here as it was farther south in the territory. He was amazed at the mixture of cultures. Adobe huts and hovels of mud and straw were mixed with fine two-story brick buildings. A new hotel had gone up on Commerce Street, and there was a bank. Bricks were plentiful here. They seemed to be the favorite material for new buildings.

He guessed that the Atchison, Topeka and Santa Fe Railroad was bringing rapid growth to Trinidad. Thank God for the railroads. Now he could get off this horse for good. Or at least for a few days. He thought his knees were going to collapse under him when they dismounted in front of a barn with a sign over the front reading LIVERY.

"Give our horses a good feed and a rubdown," he said to the old man in slouchy overalls who came out of the barn.

The man stopped and stared, mouth open, bill cap pushed back on his bald head. "A rubdown? Whatta you mean?"

Remembering what he'd read about Out West, Charles said, "Yes, a, uh, rubdown." That's what cowboys always said when they rode up to a livery barn.

"How in hell do you do that?"

Grinning, Billy said, "Naw. They don't need any rubbin'. What kind of hay you got?"

"Good grass from over along the Picketwire."

"That'll do. This old pony I'm ridin' ain't ever seen the inside of a barn. You got a feedlot?"

"Shore. I can put 'em in there if they don't fight. I

50

don't want no goddamn cannibals in there with them other horses."

"They won't fight."

"Four bits per day per horse. How long you plannin' on stayin'?"

Charles answered, "We don't know. Perhaps as long as a week."

Horses cared for, Charles lugged his gladstone bag toward the new hotel he'd seen on Commerce Street. Billy walked alongside, his saddlebags slung over his shoulder. The hotel had a big lobby with a polished wood floor. The long desk with pigeonholes behind it, the chairs, the staircase—all were of waxed and polished mahogany.

"We'd like two rooms, please," Charles said to the clerk behind the desk.

"Two dollars per night per room," said the clerk, peering from under a green eyeshade.

Hanging back now, Billy whispered, "Wait a minute, Chas. I, uh . . ."

"What?"

"Come over here, will you?"

He led Charles back to the doorway. "Listen, I ain't got so much money that I can stay here. I got to find a cheaper place."

"Well, for heaven's sake. I need a clean, comfortable bed and a bath."

"You stay here. I'll find some other place."

"What other place?"

"I don't know. I'll find somethin'."

Studying the floor, glancing at the clerk, studying Billy's face, Charles said, finally, "Oh well. I'll go with you." They walked out and down a brick sidewalk, passing all kinds of stores—from a gunsmith to a men's haberdashery. When they crossed an intersec-

51

tion, they saw another hotel sign a block away on the corner of a parallel street. WARD HOTEL, the sign read. ROOMS FIFTY CENTS.

It was a one-story adobe building. Inside was a scarred desk and a long corridor with doors on one side. Charles sighed, "I hope it's at least clean."

Grinning, Billy quipped, "Don't worry. They prob'ly change the bed sheets at least once a month."

"Ohhh," Charles said.

A short, bald man with a billy-goat beard came out of the nearest room. "You want somethin'?"

"Two rooms," Charles answered.

Their rooms were side by side. Charles suggested they meet in a few minutes and find a restaurant. His room had no window, and only a narrow spring cot, one clothes tree, and a tin pitcher and washbasin on a small table. Carefully, as if he expected something to jump out at him, Charles pulled back the one blanket on the cot. The sheets were of muslin, and so was the pillow slip. Because the sheets were naturally gray, he couldn't tell whether they were clean. After washing his face in cold water, he went out to the corridor and found Billy waiting for him.

"I wonder where the toilets are."

"Out back, I'd reckon."

It was wide open, a two-holer. Charles didn't like the idea of standing side by side with someone while he relieved himself. "You go first," he said.

Billy shrugged, said, "All right." When he came out, Charles went in. That taken care of, Charles said, "I have to go back to my room a second."

"How come?"

"Why, to wash my hands."

"Oh."

They went into the first restaurant they came to. It

52

had no tables, no booths, just a long counter. Ten men sat at the counter, leaning on their elbows, eating or sipping coffee. A middle-aged woman, plump, with a work-worn face, was moving as fast as she could to keep up with the demand. Billy and Charles took two of the remaining three seats.

The menu, scrawled on a big sheet of white card-board tacked to the opposite wall, listed two dinners: roast beef and pork chops. Below that was peach pie and chocolate cake. They didn't have to ask to see what was served with the main courses. The man next to Billy was digging into a small pile of fried potatoes and onions.

Surprisingly, it wasn't bad. Both young men finished a pair of pork chops apiece and all the potatoes and onions on their plates. They finished their meal with peach pie. The peaches, Charles guessed, were the dried kind that came in a sack. But the pie was right tasty. The coffee was good too.

Outside, Charles spotted a laundry across the street and wondered aloud whether he had time to get some shirts and underwear laundered.

"Dunno," Billy said.

"I need to brush my clothes and hang them up to get some of the wrinkles out. I guess I'll go back to that hole-in-the-wall they call a room and do that. Wonder if I can buy a newspaper somewhere."

Instead of answering, Billy said, "Some town. Brick sidewalks and ever'thing. How's about a beer?"

Remembering the warm beer at the Clifton House, Charles said, "A beer? No thank you. I think I'll go find a newspaper and go back to that so-called hotel."

"B'lieve I'll walk around a little. See the sights. Maybe have a beer."

"The sights? What sights?" Without waiting for an

answer, Charles added, "Oh well, if that's what you want to do." He turned and started walking in the opposite direction. He was bumped hard by another pedestrian. "Sorry, sir."

"Sorry, hell. Get the hell out of my way, you goddamn rich eastern sonofabitch. You think you own the goddamn sidewalk too?"

"Wha . . . Are you talking to me, sir?"

The man was short but wide, with a thick neck, a dirty collarless shirt and a floppy black hat. He needed a shave and his breath could have killed a buffalo. "Yeah, you. I seen you before. You're one a them rich bastards that thinks you own the Maxwell." He had on jackboots and baggy wool pants, and he carried a big pistol in a holster on his right side. "Well, I got somethin' to tell you, mister, I ain't movin', an' any of your hired goons that tries to run us off is gonna get the shit shot out of 'em."

Surprised and flustered, Charles sputtered, "Sir, I, uh, I don't know what . . . sir, you have mistaken me for someone else."

"I know you. You and your little round hat and that Prince Somethingorother coat, and that shit-eatin' look on your face."

"Sir, I, uh—"

A hard work-gnarled fist came up and hit Charles in the nose. He fell back onto the seat of his pants. When he was able to look up he was looking into the bore of a gun.

Seven

Stunned, Charles couldn't believe it. He couldn't meet his death now. Not here on a sidewalk in what was supposed to be a civilized town. He tried to talk but could only squawk. Blood was running from his nose into his mouth and down his chin.

"I oughta put a hole in you right here," the man muttered. A crazy gleam made his eyes shine like bulls-eye lanterns.

"Uh . . . uh . . ." Charles sputtered. He wanted to get up, but he was afraid to move. "Please, sir, I . . ."

"Shut up. Say your prayers."

"Oh no. Don't . . ."

Suddenly the short man stiffened. A hard voice came from behind him. "This is a forty-four center fire, mister. One move and your backbone is gonna git blowed plumb through your belly."

The man moved only his eyes, trying to see who was behind him, who had a gun in his back. Billy's left hand came around the man and took the pistol away from him. "Can you get up, Chas?"

"Why, uh, yes, I think I can." Slowly Charles stood. He tried to stop the flow of blood from his nose with a white handkerchief, but soon the handkerchief was red.

"All right, mister," Billy said, "I'm gonna let you live this time. I'll put this cannon of yours in that alley up yonder. Don't be in a hurry to go get it. Come on, Chas."

A small crowd had gathered, but the people stood back and gawked as the two young men moved away.

"What . . . who did he think I am?"

"I dunno. I heared him say somethin' about the Maxwell."

"The Maxwell?" Charles was still holding the handkerchief to his nose. "Oh, the Maxwell. Now I remember."

They walked down an alley where the young cowboy dropped the pistol in the dirt. "I don't know much about it. It's a big Mexican land grant."

"I've read about it. Yes, I remember now."

"Let's git back to that hotel before some marshal or sheriff or somebody comes lookin' for us."

Before they went to their separate rooms, Charles thanked Billy for saving his life. The young cowboy shrugged and allowed, "You'd a done the same for me. Sleep tight, don't let the bedbugs bite."

But in his room alone, the young cowboy wasn't so sure. Hell, the eastern dandy couldn't have done the same. He didn't have a gun.

In his room, Charles washed the blood off his face, went outside to a long-handled pump and refilled his washbasin. Back inside, he washed his shirt and shorts the best he could in cold water. Standing nude, he hung them on the clothes tree, then went to bed.

Now that he was thinking about it, he remembered most of what he'd read about the Maxwell Land Grant. It was more than one-and-a-half million acres from southern Colorado deep into New Mexico Territory. When the United States took over the southwest from Mexico, people thought the land belonged to the United States, and many settlers, looking for free land, settled on it. They believed their squatter's rights would eventually become homesteader's rights. But the U.S. Congress finally decided the land still belonged to a man named Maxwell, and Maxwell sold it, or most of it, to a conglomerate of entrepreneurs from the eastern states, London and Holland.

Then the settlers had to go. Some, perhaps most, refused. The Maxwell Land Co., as the conglomerate was named, hired so-called guards to force them off. Angry words flew. Shots were fired. Men were killed.

This man, the one who had confronted Charles on the street, had mistaken him for a member of the conglomerate. The man was, no doubt, one of the settlers who had worked his heart out to establish a farm or a ranch on the Maxwell grant, and now was ordered to leave. Go. Get.

Thinking about it, Charles wondered whether he should try to find the man, explain that he was not a member of the conglomerate and offer his sympathies. Would that be the right thing to do? Perhaps not. There was nothing he could do for the man. Perhaps the best thing to do was to just forget it. Yes, that was the best thing to do. Now that he had reached a decision on that subject, Charles turned over on his side and tried to sleep. Suddenly, he sat up.

Bedbugs? Did Billy Johnson say something about bedbugs?

"Ohhh, my God."

At breakfast in the same cafe, Billy Johnson

grinned. "Aw, they won't hurt you. Sure, they bite and they can keep you awake, but they don't stay with you. Not like seam squirrels."

Between sips of hot black coffee, Charles asked, "Seam squirrels? What are they?"

"Graybacks. You know, lice. When you pick up some a them, they ain't so easy to git rid of."

"Well, I'm not staying in that place another night."

"Me neither. That's the kind of livestock I don't need. What're we gonna do next, Chas?"

"Go to the bank as soon as it opens and try to learn whether Matthew Wyker cashed his draft there."

"What if he did?"

"Then we'd know he wasn't murdered, and was here. And perhaps we can ask enough questions to learn where he went from here. Perhaps the railroad officials will remember him."

"It was a month ago. It'll take some luck."

"I knew right from the beginning that it would take some luck."

"Wal, I'm gonna hike over to the livery and see to the horses. Then I'll wait outside the bank for you."

Luck wasn't with them. The bank teller looked Charles over carefully, from the derby hat to the soft leather shoes, and guessed that he was an eastern businessman. Charles didn't lie, only asked to see the cashier. "I must apologize for my appearance. I have been traveling." The clerk, a slender young man with a bow tie, a narrow face and thinning dark hair, believed him. He excused himself to go in search of the cashier.

While he waited, Charles took in the room. It was elegant. The floor was polished wood, and so were the

58

tables where customers could do their paperwork. Wrought iron surrounded the tellers' cages and separated customers from the executive offices. Lamps with etched glass shades hung from the ceiling.

The cashier came out of an office and also looked Charles over. "May I be of service, sir?"

Again Charles apologized for his wrinkled appearance. "Sir, I am looking for a gentleman by the name of Matthew Wyker. I have been advised that he was carrying a rather large draft on the First National Bank of Denver, and I believe he stopped here for a time. Could you tell me, please, whether he cashed that draft in your institution?"

The cashier's pudgy face screwed up in thought. He hooked his thumbs in his vest pockets, then asked, "How large was the draft?"

"Over fifty thousand dollars?"

The mouth formed an O and the eyebrows went up. Finally, he spoke, "Sir, we, uh . . . what did you say your name is?"

"Manderfield, Charles J. Manderfield. From New York City."

"Well, Mr. Manderfield, I would like very much to be of service to you, but we have a policy that I must adhere to. All private transactions are confidential. I'm sure you understand."

"But, sir . . ."

The cashier was shaking his head. "I'm very sorry sir. I'm sure you understand."

"Isn't there some way I—?"

"Only with a court order."

A disappointed Charles left the bank and joined Billy Johnson on the brick sidewalk. "As you would put it," he grumbled, "I didn't learn diddly."

"Wouldn't talk to you, huh."

"I should have known. Private transactions are confidential."

"Huh," Billy snorted. "Wal, I'm guessin' that if he was here he stayed at the best hotel in town. I can describe 'im purty good. Shall we go ask?"

With a shrug, Charles said, "I don't know what else to do."

They went to the hotel on Commerce Street, the two-story brick one they'd stopped in the day before. Charles asked the desk clerk about a cattleman named Matthew Wyker who might have stayed there a month ago. "It would have been, let's see, June eight or nine. Would you please check your registry?"

The clerk reached under the counter for another registration book, thumbed pages. "June eight, let's see." After running his forefinger down the list of names, he shook his head, flipped a page and studied it. "No sir, no Matthew Wyker."

"He could have used another name. My friend here can describe him."

Billy described him, but Charles knew it was useless.

"I'm sorry, sir, but many cattlemen stop here. The man you described just doesn't stick in my mind."

"Thanks just the same."

"What now, Chas?"

"I don't know. Have you any ideas?"

"It prob'ly won't work, but we might try at the train station. I always wanted to see one a them train engines anyway."

"You've never seen one?"

"Naw. As much as I've been around, I've never seen one."

"The depot ought to be easy to find."

They couldn't have missed it. Not with a train whistle splitting the high-altitude air. The two-room depot was new, made of the same brick, with a split-shingle roof. A huge water tank on high iron legs stood beside it. A railroad engine sat hissing and billowing smoke and steam in front of it. Billy stared, mouth open, at the engine. He walked the length of it, and when a spurt of steam blew out of it he jumped back.

"Gaw-ud damn. That thing could eat you up alive. That thing could eat up a herd of elephants. Hope they keep it well fed. Hope it don't get mad at nobody."

Charles had to chuckle. "It will pull a long string of railcars."

"Gaw-ud damn."

But they learned nothing. A ticket agent lifted his eyeshade, wiped his forehead with a shirtsleeve and shook his head. "I don't remember anything that far back. Damn near ever' body that buys a ticket's got a cowboy hat and boots. Except the women and kids. And the easterners, like you."

"Is that a telegraph over there?" Charles asked.

"Shore is."

"I'm glad to see you have telegraph service. It could come in handy."

"Oh, we've had that for ten years. It usta be the United States and Mexico Telegraph Company. We can send a message plumb down to Mexico. When the lines're up, that is."

Charles tried to think of a way to make use of the telegraph, but nothing came to mind. He asked, "When is the next train to Denver?"

"Soon's they get that engine filled with water and coal and turned around."

"An hour?"

"About that."

61

"We goin' to Denver?" Billy asked, outside.

"I don't know what else to do. Unless you're ready to give up and go back."

"Not yet, I ain't. That feller at the livery barn wants his money in advance."

"All right, we'll go pay him for, let's see, say five days."

That done, they went back to the hotel, picked up the gladstone bag and the saddlebags and then walked back to the cafe. They had just finished a roast beef sandwich when an "Excuse me, sir" came from Charles's right.

It was the bank teller. He had a conspiratorial look on his narrow face. "I overheard what you said to Mr. Underwood. I know about that cattleman and his draft."

"You do?"

"Yeah." The slender man looked around quickly and said, "Everybody in the bank heard about it."

"What do you know?"

Another glance around. "I'm breaking the bank's rules. I could get fired."

"Then why mention it?"

"I could use some extra money. They don't pay much at the bank. Not us peons, anyway. The bigshots pay themselves damned good, but not us."

"Oh, I see." Charles reached for his wallet. "Here's five dollars."

The money disappeared immediately. "Well, he came in and tried to cash that draft on the First National in Denver, but Mr. Underwood wouldn't cash it right away. He said he'd have to wire the Denver bank to check the draft's validity. What he was really afraid of was taking that much cash out of the safe. It would've left the bank short of cash on hand."

"I see," Charles said. "I take it, then, that Mr. Wyker didn't wait."

"No, he didn't come back."

"So where did he go?"

"That I don't know, but I can guess. So can you."

"Yes. There's little doubt about it."

A few minutes later, after the teller had left, Billy said, "Now it's for sure we're goin' to Denver, huh?"

"For sure," Charles said. "Let's go buy some tickets."

Eight

The seats were just as hard in the railroad's passenger coach as in the horse-drawn stagecoach, but at least the passengers could stand up and walk. That is, if they didn't mind being thrown from one side of the aisle to the other. The coach swayed and screeched. Charles tried to sleep, to make up for the sleep he'd missed the night before in a bug-infested bed. Billy didn't try. His face was pressed to the big glass window, and his eyes missed nothing. His only problem was trying to see out of both sides of the car at the same time.

"How fast you reckon we're goin', Chas? I'll bet we're doin' purt' near twenty-five mile an hour."

"Faster than that. When I crossed the Kansas plains by rail I was told we were traveling almost fifty miles an hour."

"You're joshin'."

"That's what I was told."

"Nothin' goes that fast. Not even a hawk can fly that fast."

Their first stop was at El Moro, a settlement owned by the railroad company. On their left were the dark mountains. On their right the land changed from rolling hills to flat prairie and back to rolling hills. At Pueblo they got out for a few minutes to stretch their legs.

It was dark when the train pulled into Colorado Springs, another town founded by the owners of the railroad. Only this one was growing fast and becoming a sophisticated city. How the town got its name, no one knew. There were no springs here. Some railroad officials thought the words sounded good, and they adopted them. On his way south, Charles had been told about the real soda springs over west, on the other side of the older town called Colorado City, just under the front range of mountains.

As they traveled north, they moved farther away from the mountains, and the scenery wasn't as spectacular, but Billy didn't care. He could see nothing in the dark anyway. The young cowboy settled back on the hard bench seat and went to sleep, using his hat for a pillow. Charles envied him. How could he sleep like that? His body swayed and bounced, but he slept on. Charles tried. His derby hat would be ruined if he used it for a pillow, so he tried leaning his head back against the seat. His head took a beating. Out of desperation he took off his finger-length coat, folded it and used that for a pillow. Eventually, he dozed.

Once, he woke up and found his head on Billy's shoulder. "Oh, excuse me," he said, straightening up immediately.

Billy mumbled, " 'Sall ri.' "

The next time it happened, he found Billy's eyes on him. "I'm sorry, I didn't mean to."

A half smile turned up the corners of the young

65

cowboy's mouth. "If you was fetched up with a bunch of brothers all sleepin' in one bed you'd be used to it."

"Yes, I suppose so. I'll try not to let it happen again."

Billy's eyes closed. " 'Sall right."

Charles was sleeping fitfully when the steam whistle screeched twice, then again. Awake immediately, he looked out the window to see pale daylight. The whistle sounded again. Then the conductor in his black bill cap staggered through the car, yelling, "Denver. Denver in ten minutes."

Billy awakened, sat up, punched the crown of his hat out with a fist and stuck it on his head. "We're burnin' daylight. Ten minutes, he said? If I don't put a *morral* on purty soon, my big guts're gonna eat up my little ones."

"Put what on?"

"A *morral*. You know, feed bag."

"Oh."

Finally the train hissed, screeched and hooted into Denver's Union Station, where it shuddered to a stop. Charles lugged his gladstone bag in his right hand and Billy hung his saddlebags over his left shoulder as they walked through the huge room. It was a busy place, with people rushing in all directions, carrying luggage.

Outside on a brick sidewalk, Charles said, "Larimer Street is only a few blocks ahead. The Great Northern Hotel and Restaurant is on that street. I've stopped there before, and it's fairly decent."

"Wal, if it's good 'nuff for you, Chas, I'll try to stand it."

Charles gave him a sidelong glance to see if he

66

was joking. Only a twitch of the mouth gave Billy away.

The sidewalk was crowded. Billy had to constantly step aside to keep from colliding with other pedestrians. Charles had fixed a look on his face that caused others to step aside for him. At the registration desk of the Great Northern Hotel, Charles asked for two rooms.

"Four-fifty each," the clerk said.

Billy took Charles by the arm and pulled him aside. "Do we havta have two rooms? I started this trip with only a month's wages."

"Well, I . . . I thought we would be more comfortable that way."

"Why? I can sleep on the floor if you want."

"Well, I . . ." He wanted a room to himself. He'd shared a room at the university, but now that he was a graduate he was entitled to more privacy. On the other hand, he might have to travel with this cowboy for some time, and he didn't have unlimited funds either. "Well, all right." He paid for the room, but as soon as they were in it Billy counted out three silver dollars.

"No, I'll pay."

"Huh-uh. I'm payin' my way."

"Well, if you insist, but you gave me too much money."

"How much is half of four dollars and fifty cents?"

"Two twenty-five. You gave me three dollars."

"How much is three dollars minus two dollars and twenty-five cents?"

"Seventy-five cents."

"That's six bits, ain't it? Wal, you can owe me if you want to."

The room overlooked Larimer Street. It had a rug on the floor, a washbasin, a slop jar, a pitcher of water, a dresser and a small closet with wire clothes hangers. Billy sat in the one chair while Charles took off his shirt and washed himself from the armpits up. He poured the water in the slop jar. "I'm going to take a bath before the day is over, but I don't want to waste any time. The bank should open in about an hour."

"We just got time to eat," Billy said.

"Look here, Billy, don't you think you should leave that gun here? No one else we've seen in Denver is carrying a gun."

"Maybe you're right." Billy unbuckled the gun belt and hung it — holster, six-gun and all — over the top of the chair. "I feel a little lopsided without it."

The hotel's dining room boasted linen tablecloths and a printed menu for each table. Sitting at a table for four, Charles ordered a soft-boiled egg, toast and marmalade. His cowboy companion ordered a stack of hot cakes, two eggs fried and ham. "You live like a coyote, you learn to eat all you can hold ever' chance you get," he said. "If I had a bunch of money I'd double that order."

Though Charles's meal was light, the cowboy had finished his meal and was draining his coffee cup before Charles ate the last bite of his toast. Billy grinned. "I'll chew it later."

Shaking his head in disbelief, Charles snapped his fingers and ordered the check. "I'll pay and we'll be even," he said.

The First National Bank of Denver was easy to find. A short walk down Seventeenth Street, and they saw the sign: FIRST NATIONAL BANK ESTAB-

LISHED 1865. Below that was the message: GOLD DUST EXCHANGED. ALSO COIN, BULLION, GOVERNMENT VOUCHERS AND SCRIPT. The interior was even more elegant than the bank in Trinidad. The floor here was white marble.

But the answer was the same. "I'm very sorry, sir."

"Well," Charles said when he met Billy outside, "that stumps me. I don't know where to turn next. If you're not a police officer or a bank examiner you just do not have access to bank records. And even if you're a policeman you have to have a warrant from a judge."

"A cold trail, huh?"

"A lost trail." Charles was silent a moment, staring at the sidewalk, then he swore, "Damnit, I should have known. We haven't a chance in the world of finding Matthew Wyker. I was a fool for thinking I might."

"Wal, I figured the odds were against us, but I had to give 'er a try. I'm a lost child in this city. That's why I partnered with you."

"I'm sorry. I just don't know where to turn next."

"Don't apologize. We done the best we could."

Walking back to their hotel, both young men were silent. Billy, who had been fascinated by the people and the displays in the store windows, was now looking at the sidewalk. Suddenly, he spoke through clenched teeth, "Know what frosts my ass? It's lettin' 'im get away with it. I'd go to hell to find that sumbitch."

"I almost would. I'd almost rather go to hell than to go back to Lariat and tell my Aunt Bertha I failed."

69

They walked past a stairway in the middle of a brick building, and a sign above it caught Charles's eye. He stopped and read it silently. Billy stopped too and tried to read it: "P-R-I-V-A-T-E. I-N-V-E—"

Charles finished it for him. " 'Private Investigator. Very confidential.' "

"Does he investigate stuff?"

"Apparently."

"Could he find out anything at the bank?"

Charles made a quick decision. "He might know a way. Let's go see."

Wooden stairs creaked. Billy's boots thudded with every step. At the top of the stairs was a long corridor lined with glass-paned doors. The third one repeated the message. Charles tried the door. It opened. There was a desk, a wooden filing cabinet, a window with no shade, a dead cigar in an ashtray, a straight-backed chair—and a man. The man was middle-aged and bald. He wore a dark vest over a blue chambray shirt and had a puzzled look on his face.

"Are you a private investigator?" Charles asked.

Wise eyes took in the derby hat and the well-cut but wrinkled businessman's clothes. "You bet I am. Hank Brown, a man of renown." The eyes shifted to the cowboy. "You name it, I tame it. I'm a lover, a fighter, and a, uh, gentle horse rider." He chuckled at his own joke. "What can I do you for?"

Taking off his hat, Charles dabbed at his forehead with a white handkerchief and sat in the one chair. "Can you get a peek at some bank records?"

"How long you been in town?"

"A few hours."

Hank Brown leaned forward on his elbows. "I can

not only take a peek, I can get you a copy."

"Then that is what you can do for us."

"It won't be cheap."

"How much?"

"I get five bucks a day and expenses, and I gotta pay the judge."

"Pay the judge?" Charles's eyebrows went up. "You mean a bribe?"

"Whatta you think? You think you can look at bank records without a warrant signed by a judge?"

"No. But . . . how much total?"

"The judge don't do nothin' for less than fifty bucks."

"That's a bit steep."

"Where'd you come from?"

"New York City."

"How about your friend?"

"Lariat, Territory of New Mexico."

"Whose records do you wanta see?"

"A gentleman named Matthew Wyker. We want to know whether he cashed a rather large draft drawn on the First National Bank, and anything else you can find out about him. But fifty dollars, that's more than we're prepared to pay."

"Maybe he'll do it for thirty-five. That'll make it forty bucks total."

"Agreed."

"In advance."

Shaking his head, Charles said, "No sir. Payment when services are rendered."

"Okay. Where you stayin'?"

"At the Great Northern."

"It's, uh . . ." — Hank Brown pulled a stem-winder from a vest pocket — "almost ten A.M.. If the judge is

71

in, I ought to have your information by the middle of the afternoon."

"See here," Charles said, "what we really want is to find this Matthew Wyker. Where he cashes that bank draft may be a clue as to his whereabouts."

"I'll see what I can find out."

When the deal was finalized and they were outside, Billy Johnson shook his head. "Damn. The way we're goin' through money, I might have to get a job before I can get home."

"Yes," Charles said, "but maybe, just maybe, we'll learn something useful."

Nine

On the way back to the hotel, Charles took a newspaper off a stack on the sidewalk and put a nickel in a cigar box. The cowboy rolled a cigarette, lit it with a wooden match and, out of habit, shook the match, pinched the head of it and broke it in two before tossing it aside. With nothing to do now but wait, Charles took a bath out of a tin tub on the hotel's first floor and put on the shirt and underclothes he'd washed by hand in Trinidad. That six-gun hanging from the back of a chair continually attracted his attention, but eventually he managed to ignore it. Billy also took a bath, and said, "At least I don't smell like a goat now. Wanta take a little *paseo* around town? I ain't ever been in a town this big before."

"No, I think I'll read the paper and take a nap."

"A nap? You mean sleep? In the daylight?"

"Yes. I didn't get much sleep last night or the night before, you know."

"Whatever suits you."

There was so much to see in the city a man could walk himself to death. Billy wished he had a horse. He could see more from the back of a horse. He missed the feel of the Army-sized Remington six-gun on his right hip, but as Chas had said, nobody else in the city was packing iron. Traffic on the streets was heavy. There were freight wagons pulled by four-horse teams, light delivery wagons pulled by two horses, and buggies pulled by prancing, well-groomed bays and sorrels. He'd been up Seventeenth Street, so now he turned his steps in the opposite direction and found himself on Holiday Street. Here, the street was lined with saloons and gambling houses. Most of the men on the street wore working-men's clothes, but there were a few dandies with homburg hats and wool pants creased down the front.

Out of curiosity he stepped inside a saloon named the Queen City's Best. It was cleaner than the saloons at Lariat, Las Vegas and Albuquerque, but not much cleaner. The floor had been covered with sawdust, but foot traffic had pushed most of it aside, exposing bare wood. The bar was nothing fancy, just pinewood. Behind it was a shelf filled with bottles of liquor. On the opposite side of the long room were card tables. At the rear was a roulette wheel and more card tables.

Billy stepped up to the bar and ordered a mug of beer. It was cold and good. He smacked his lips, licked the foam off his upper lip, turned his back to the bar and studied the room. The roulette wheel was spinning, and a man in a striped vest was standing behind it, telling all interested people to place their bets. Only three bets were placed. The players lost. He saw the girl approaching, her eyes fixed on him, but he couldn't believe she was interested in him, not until she spoke:

"Hello, cowboy. You're new in town, ain't you?"

Grinning, he said, "How'd you ever guess?"

74

She smiled, and she was pretty. Her red dress was cut low in front, revealing a deep V at her breasts, and high enough at the bottom to show thin ankles above patent leather slippers. "I'll bet you just came down from Wyoming with a herd of cattle."

"Nope. I come from the other direction. New Mexico."

"Really? I met a man from New Mexico once. He was a cattleman too."

"Who would that be?"

"Why don't you buy me a drink, cowboy, and we can have a nice visit. What's your name?"

"Billy."

"Mine's Wanda. We can sit at a table over there and visit."

Charles was disappointed with the *Daily Rocky Mountain News*. It was dull, with one-column headlines and more advertising than news. Sitting up on the bed with his shoes and coat off, Charles scanned it. Even page one was mostly ads. There was an ad announcing the "Greatest Medical Discovery of the Ages," another inviting customers to Sargent's Hotel and Restaurant, and another by L.N. Greenleaf & Co., which sold everything from cigars to musical instruments. A column inside was devoted to "Telegraphic News," and another to "Territorial News." Page three was mostly ads, but one headline caught Charles's attention. It said: "Murder Victim Discovered."

The story told about the body of a man being found in an alley. The man had been clubbed to death, and his pockets emptied. The police had no clue as to the killer or the identification of the dead man. The story was told in only four paragraphs. Apparently it wasn't anything new in Denver. Murder and robbery weren't news in New York either. They were too common. Charles felt his eyelids getting heavy. He refolded the paper and rested his head on a soft pillow.

Hunger gnawed at Billy Johnson's insides. He didn't want to leave Wanda, but he had things to do. She was disappointed when he left, and showed it with a pretty pout. He promised to be back later. Damn, she was pretty. Smelled good too. Her perfume smelled so good a man could get drunk on it. Just the touch of her hand sent a tingle through his body and made his head swim. Damn right, he'd be back.

A cafe sign was something he'd learned to recognize, and it attracted him like a magnet. For a moment he considered going to the hotel to see if Chas wanted to have dinner with him, but decided against it. Chas could take himself to dinner when he wanted to.

A meal of pork chops and fried potatoes had him feeling steadier. The smell of cooking wiped out the memory of Wanda's perfume. He'd wait until after dark to go back to the Queen City's Best. Wanda would still be there. Meanwhile he wanted to hear what that private investigator had to say.

Charles had sleep in his eyes when he opened the hotel-room door to let Billy in. "I thought it best to keep the door latched from the inside," Charles said. "Crime is not unusual in the city."

"You're prob'ly right."

It was too early for the private investigator to

show up, so Billy sat in the one chair and tried to read the newspaper. He could make out the words, but it was slow going. Charles allowed he'd go downstairs and "grab a sandwich." While he was gone, Billy forced himself to keep reading, trying to improve.

It was a long afternoon. Charles was content to read from a book he took out of his gladstone bag. Billy looked over his shoulder and made out some of the words. "What's it about?" he asked.

"It's Charles Dickens's *Great Expectations*."

"Oh."

Restless, Billy spent long moments looking out the window at Larimer Street. He wanted to go outside, but he didn't want to miss the private detective. Hank Brown, the Man of Renown, didn't show up until late afternoon. His knock on the door spun Billy away from the window. Charles closed his book carefully, stood and went to the door. He stepped back to let the investigator enter.

"I got it."

"What did you learn?"

"It's pay-up time."

"Oh, of course." Charles took the money out of his wallet, then slipped the wallet back in his hip pocket.

"A man named Matthew Wyker cashed a check on June eleven for fifty thousand and four hundred dollars. The check was written by a Jacob Ingalls of Wagon Mound, Territory of New Mexico."

"Any idea where he went from the bank? Did he say anything to anybody?"

"Nothing. He seemed a little nervous, but the cashier figured it was because he was carrying so much money."

"He took it all in cash, did he?"

"Yeah. Wouldn't settle for anything else."

"That would be very unusual in New York. Most transactions of that size are made on paper. I was hoping he would have most of the money transferred to another bank in another city."

Shaking his head, Hank Brown said, "He didn't. I double-checked on that. He took it in cash. All U.S. greenbacks, legal tender anywhere in the U.S. of A."

"I assume he had some sort of identification."

"He had papers with his name on 'em."

"You had a warrant signed by a judge?"

"I had a duly authorized warrant and a police detective's badge."

"Who is the judge, and are you authorized to carry a badge?"

"You know I can't tell you that."

"Is there nothing else you can tell us?"

"That's it. That's what you said you wanted, and that's what I delivered."

"Oh." Charles couldn't keep the disappointment from showing.

"Well, I gotta be goin'. If you need any more investigatin' done, look me up."

"Yes," Charles said. "Yes, I . . . we certainly will."

When Hank Brown was gone, Charles slumped in the chair and let out a long groan.

"Didn't help, did it, Chas?"

"No. All we've learned is that Matthew Wyker was not murdered by Indians or by Jacob Ingalls, and that he came to Denver and cashed the bank draft. Where he went from here, we have no clue. No clue at all."

"Could he still be here? This is a big town, big enough to get lost in."

78

Another sigh came from Charles. "Not likely. Yet it is possible, I suppose."

"Listen, Chas, I don't know nothin' about bank drafts or banks, but maybe it's like you said, or almost said. Matt Wyker wouldn't want to pack that much money around and maybe he . . . there's more than one bank in town. I've figured out how to read the word."

Charles jumped up and snapped his fingers. "By gosh, you're right. And it will be easy to find out. We did see another bank, the Colorado National Bank, and there are probably others." Hastily, he pulled on his finger-length coat and slapped his derby hat on his head. "Want to come along?"

"Will I get in the way?"

"Not at all."

Down the stairs they went, Billy's boots thumping, then up Seventeenth Street. Charles was in a hurry, and Billy had to half run to keep up with him. "Slow down, hoss. We ain't in no damned race."

Into the lobby of the Colorado National Bank they went, and Charles marched straight up to a teller's window. "I have a legitimate question," he said to the goggle-eyed clerk. "I have been promised a draft on this bank by a gentleman named Matthew Wyker. Would you be so kind as to tell me whether Mr. Wyker has an account here?"

"Y-yes, sir." The teller adjusted his glasses, went to a wooden filing cabinet, pulled out a drawer and ran his fingers over a row of cards. Next he went to a desk, opened a drawer, took out a thick ledger, opened it and ran his finger down a page. "No sir," he said when he came back. "There is no account listed for a Matthew Wyker."

"Thank you kindly, sir."

After they'd walked the length of Seventeenth Street, and asked questions in two more banks, Charles was dejected again. "Well, that does it."

"He left town for sure."

"As sure as we can be."

They were quiet on their way back to Larimer Street, and Charles walked slower. At supper Charles merely dabbled at his food and ate very little. Billy cleaned his platter. "I know how you feel, Chas. All I lost is a month's wages and what it cost me to come up here. You lost a hell of a lot more'n that. I reckon I'd feel purty low too."

"The money is very important to my Uncle Joseph and Aunt Bertha. The loss will probably force them to sell their ranch. And me? I have to admit defeat. That is painful."

Charles went straight to their room after supper. Billy allowed he'd see more of the city before they went back. He headed for the Queen City's Best, where he hoped to find Wanda.

A persistent knocking finally awakened Charles from a troubled sleep. He got out of bed and staggered weakly to the door. "Who is it?"

"It's Billy Johnson."

Charles slid the latch back and let Billy in, then crawled wearily back into bed. "Wait a minute," Billy said. "I got somethin' to tell you." Billy scratched a match and lit one of the coal-oil lamps. "What?" Charles asked, a little irritated. Billy said, "I got word that Matt Wyker might have gone to Albuquerque."

"What?" Charles was suddenly wide awake. "Whose word?"

"A woman's. Listen, she pilfers drinks out of men at a saloon called the Queen City's Best, and she knows another woman that left town with a man named Matthew Wyker. She said the other woman told her they was goin' to Albuquerque."

"Is she certain the man was Matthew Wyker?"

"That's the name he was usin', and he was the same size and ever'thing, wore the same kind of clothes."

"Did he fit Matthew Wyker's description?"

"Yup."

"But . . . but why would . . . ?" A puzzled frown pulled Charles's eyebrows together.

"It don't seem likely, does it. Matt Wyker wouldn't go to Albuquerque where he might be seen by somebody from Conejos County. Would he?"

Charles didn't answer. He was going over it all in his mind. Then he asked, "Is this woman absolutely certain they went to Albuquerque?"

"All she knows is what the other woman told her. She said they were good friends and told each other their secrets."

"Then . . . you know, Billy, I . . . I probably shouldn't say this. I probably shouldn't even think it, but . . ."

Billy rolled a cigarette and waited for his partner to think it over and say what he wanted to say.

"It's crazy, but . . . look here, Billy, it's possible that we can quit looking for Matthew Wyker, and . . ."

"And what?"

"And look for his murderer."

81

Ten

Billy Johnson had to give that some thought. Then he said, "I getcha. You're thinkin' Matt Wyker was killed and robbed and the killer took everything out of his pockets—his papers and that bank draft."

"It's farfetched, but don't you think it's possible?"

"It's possible, all right. The killer had his papers and ever'thing, and he could take that draft to the bank, say he was Matt Wyker and walk out with a hell of a lot of money. And maybe the killer wouldn't know where Matt Wyker came from."

"Correct. Of course, we're only speculating now."

"So how can we find out if there was a man murdered that looked like Matt Wyker?"

"Easy. The newspapers."

"And if we find out there was . . . ol' Matt, he prob'ly didn't have any kin here and he was travelin' alone and there wasn't anybody that could look at his carcass and put a name to it."

"It's not unusual for a murder victim to remain unidentified. They're usually buried in paupers' graves."

"It'd serve 'im right."

"Well"—Charles was pensive now—"I don't like to think of anyone being killed."

"But if it happened to anybody it ought to happen to a thief like him."

"Yes, well, we'll go to the newspaper office first

thing in the morning. Surely they'll let us look through the back issues."

"First thing. Right now I got to get some shut-eye. Which side of the bed do you want?"

"Which side of the bed? Do you mean you want to sleep two in a bed?"

"Hell, Chas, many's the night I slept three in a bed."

"Well, all right. But—"

"I'll sleep on the floor if you want. Many's the night I slept on the floor and the ground and even in a tree."

"In a tree? You're joshing."

"No sir. A big ol' grizzly run me up a tree and didn't leave 'til purt' near daylight. I found me a spot between two limbs and scrunched down and got some sleep."

"Where was this?"

"Up in the Mangases."

"All right, you can sleep on one side of the bed and I'll sleep on the other side."

"Fair 'nuff."

Billy sat on the bed and pulled off his boots and socks. He stood and unbuttoned his shirt and pants. Wearing only his shorts, he crawled between the sheets and let out a long contented sigh. Charles went around the bed and crawled into the other side. "Good night," he said.

Billy said, "Only one thing I ask."

"What's that?"

"Don't fart."

Charles sat up suddenly. "What?"

"I said don't—"

Charles interrupted, "I heard what you said." He sat up for a moment, then lay back down. "I wouldn't think of it."

The offices of the *Daily Rocky Mountain News* were open when they got there, but the morgue attendant hadn't arrived yet. "The morgue?" Charles asked.

"Yeah," said a cigar-chomping fat man in a wrinkled white shirt and a loose necktie. "That's where we keep the old newspapers."

The morgue attendant turned out to be an elderly lady wearing a plain dress that was high at the top and almost dragged the floor at the bottom. Charles asked to see the newspapers published around June ninth and tenth. She pointed to a shelf and said, "Be sure to put them back the way you find them. Don't leave them for me to put away like these reporters do." She picked up a newspaper, turned a page, then began cutting out something with a pair of scissors.

Charles scanned the June ninth and tenth issues and was on page three of the June eleventh issue when he found it. The one-column headline said: "Another Murder." Subheads under it read: "Man's Body Found in Alley. Unidentified Victim Stabbed To Death. Pockets Emptied." The story read:

The body of a man, obviously the victim of a murderer/robber, was discovered early Monday morning in an alley off Holiday Street. Police stated that the body had two stab wounds to the chest, either of which could have been fatal.

The pockets had been emptied, and the body was minus shoes and hat. There were no papers on the body. The only identification police found was an orange kerchief with the initials MW embroidered on one corner. Police stated the dead man was in his early fifties, average in height and weight.

It was the third murder/robbery in Denver this year. The body was discovered by . . .

Putting the paper down, Charles said, "This is it."

"What does it say?"

"It says an unidentified body was found in an alley off Holiday Street. Judging from the way Matthew

84

Wyker was described to me, the body was approximately the same height, weight and age as he. No identification papers, of course, but there was a kerchief with the initials *MW*. No boots nor hat. It was found on a Monday morning."

"Now we know."

"I would say we can be at least eighty percent certain."

"Dead certain. Almost. I remember that wildrag with his initials on it. Some woman gave it to him. It was orange colored. He wore it around his neck tied in a square knot."

"Then we're ninety-five percent certain." Charles read the story again, then said, "It was early on a Monday morning. The private detective said the check was cashed on a Monday morning. It had to have been cashed after the body was found."

"The killer cashed it."

"Yes. That's why he took all the papers from Mr. Wyker's body. He used the papers to fool the bank clerks into thinking he was Matthew Wyker."

"Wal, do you wanta go all the way to Albuquerque on the chance we can find his killer?"

"I don't know. That's a long trip, but it's not far from Lariat, and I have to go back to Lariat anyway. I'd like to know more. Can you introduce me to this woman you told me about? What's her name? Wanda?"

"Sure, but she prob'ly sleeps late."

"Darn. Well, I guess we'll just have to wait."

"You don't b'lieve in wastin' time, do you, Chas?"

"No. I'm not looking forward to the trip back, but since I have to go I would like to get started."

"You're right. Sometimes I don't hurry enough."

They both thanked the morgue attendant and went out onto Fourteenth Street. Walking back to the Great

Northern Hotel, Billy was again gawking at other pedestrians, wondering where they were going, what they did for a living, how they lived. He repeatedly looked up at the three-story buildings, and stopped now and then to study the displays in store windows. Charles was impatient, then realized they had no reason to hurry. He slowed his steps to keep pace with his cowboy partner.

On their way they passed two beggers, one blind and the other with no legs. "Lordy," Billy said, "ain't that awful?" He dropped coins in their cups.

"In New York," Charles said, "there are so many beggers one cannot possibly give money to all of them."

"Is that so? I never seen one before."

"In the big cities, one sees so much of that sort of thing one becomes immune to it."

"Huh," Billy snorted.

They walked to the railroad depot, where they learned that the southbound left every morning at seven-thirty. "Well, that leaves us with time on our hands," Charles grumbled. "I'm going to the room to read. Perhaps I can wash some clothes."

"I'll go on over to the Queen City's Best and wait for Wanda. When she comes in I'll come and get you."

Charles had washed his extra underclothes and socks and had almost finished reading *Great Expectations* when Billy knocked on the door. "She's there," Billy said.

Wanda surprised Charles. He had expected a barroom hag with stringy hair and bad teeth. Instead, Wanda was well coiffured, neat and clean. Her dress revealed too much, and she wore too much makeup and perfume but otherwise she was an attractive

86

young woman.

She warned Charles that he had to order drinks all around before she could sit at a table and talk with them.

"Of course." Charles ordered beer for himself and Billy, and a gin for Wanda. "Now then," he said when they were settled at a table with the drinks before them, "tell me about your friend and her gentleman friend."

"Well, Effie knew him for only a few days, but she was crazy about him. When he said he had to go back to Albuquerque and asked her to go with him, she said yes."

"What did the man look like? A cattleman?"

"Well, he wore a cattleman's clothes, but . . . well, he didn't look much like the other cattlemen that come in here."

"Would you please explain that."

"Well, he had on boots and a cattleman's hat, but somethin' was different. I guess it was the way he wore the clothes, like he wasn't use to 'em."

Billy said, "I know what you mean. I've seen phony cowboys and cattlemen, and you can tell 'em at a glance."

"I see," Charles said. "Did this man have a lot of money?"

"Yes, he did. He took Effie to the best store on Sixteenth Street and bought her a new dress and shoes and everything. He spent money like it grew on trees. Uh, I hate to say this, but the bartender is givin' me dirty looks, and I have to order another drink."

Charles had taken only one sip of his beer, but he ordered another round. "Did he say why he was going to Albuquerque?"

"He'd been there before, and said he had business there."

87

"And he called himself Matthew Wyker?"

"Matt Wyker. Yes. Said he was from Albuquerque."

"One more question. Make that two. What's Effie's last name, and would you describe her?"

"Her name is Effie Osgood. She's got blond hair, shoulder length, and she's about my size. She's real pretty." Wanda shrugged. "I don't know what else to tell you about her."

Looking over at Billy, Charles asked, "What do you think?"

"That cinches it." To Wanda, Billy said, "The man is a killer. He murdered the real Matthew Wyker and took ever'thing that was in his pockets."

Her breath caught in her throat. "Does the police know?"

"Naw."

"Oh, my God." Then she said, "I warned her. I told her somethin' about that man didn't seem real, but she wouldn't listen. Oh, I hope he doesn't hurt her. She was my best friend."

"We want very much to find him," Charles said. "We'll notify the police, but I doubt they'll be much help. Perhaps they can at least try to notify Matthew Wyker's next of kin."

The police department wasn't hard to find. They merely asked an officer who was walking on the nearest corner, swinging his billy club. In the police building they were seated at a desk by an overweight detective who wore a derby hat like Charles's and a vest and pearl-handled pistol in a holster under his left armpit. Charles did the talking. When he finished, he asked, "I don't suppose you have identified the body?"

No, they hadn't, and no, they didn't have a clue to the identity of the killer.

88

"My uncle, Joseph Manderfield, first formed a part-nership with Matthew Wyker in Kansas City. They drove a long wagon train of trade goods to Santa Fe. At Santa Fe they went separate directions, but formed another partnership later at Lariat, Territory of New Mexico. That is all I know about Mr. Wyker. But per-haps the police in Kansas City can learn the where-abouts of his next of kin."

"We'll send a telegraph."

"I can guess what happened," Charles said. "I've been advised that Mr. Wyker was a womanizer. He got into Denver on a Saturday or Sunday, and he couldn't go to the bank until Monday. Meanwhile he just had to enjoy the pleasures of the city. That's what he was doing on that street."

"Yup. There's plenty of whores in those saloons. If he went up to the rooms with one, some thug knew it and waylaid him when he came out."

With a sigh, Charles added, "So ended the life of Matthew Wyker. It's sad, really. My uncle trusted him. It's too bad."

"It happens." The detective stood, shook hands with first Charles and then Billy. "We'll do what we can."

They separated in front of the hotel. Charles said he would have a sandwich in the hotel restaurant, then go up to the room. Billy decided to eat somewhere, then walk around, see the city.

Charles finished reading *Great Expectations*. He'd read it before, but enjoyed the adventures of Pip as much the second time. He lay back on the bed, and somehow his mind went to his Uncle Joseph and Mat-thew Wyker. He didn't know all the details, but he'd been told that the two pooled their resources and bought thirty-two freight wagons and enough oxen to pull them. Then they loaded the wagons with trade goods — cloth, dry goods, hardware and jewelry, mostly hardware — and started down the long Santa Fe Trail.

It was not an uneventful trip. Once they were attacked by Indians. But the bullwhackers they'd hired were well armed and crack shots, and the Indians were driven off. The wagon train moved slowly, but eventually it arrived in Santa Fe. There, the partners sold everything, even the wagons and oxen, at a profit of more than a thousand percent. Uncle Joseph went south, looking for some good grazing land, and Matthew Wyker went back to Kansas City.

A few years later they met again. Charles wasn't sure how. Uncle Joseph had spent so much money acquiring land and building a house that he had too little left to stock the ranch. Matthew Wyker went to Texas, bought a mixed herd and drove them to the Double M. The herd did well. Next spring the Double M had a good calf crop. The cow-calf business was looking good. And then Uncle Joseph became ill.

Charles was depressed. Matthew Wyker was dead, Uncle Joseph was probably dying, and Aunt Bertha was depending on him to . . . do something. With a groan, he closed his eyes and hoped that he could recover at least some of the money.

It was late, dark outside. Charles's stomach was growling. He began to worry about Billy. Then Billy knocked on the door. When Charles unlatched it, Billy glanced up and down the hall and rushed in, a wild look on his face.

"I got to get out of here," he said, breathless. "I got to get out of town."

"Why? What in the world happened?"

"I just robbed a man."

Eleven

Billy had been disappointed when he'd gone back to the Queen City's Best and found Wanda visiting with another customer. He left without buying a drink and walked. In another saloon on Holiday Street he drank a mug of beer, then went on down the street to another. The saloons were pretty much the same. All had women ready to drink and visit with the men. In one — Billy didn't notice the name — the roulette wheel had attracted a small crowd. Men were placing chips on numbers and shouting, "Spin 'er. Spin 'er my way." "Don't stop yet. Not there. Goddamnit."

At the tables men were playing cards, serious, deadpan. Billy drank two mugs of beer, then went back to the Queen City's Best.

Wanda wasn't that kind of woman, Billy found out when he finally got up enough nerve to ask. "If you want a whore," she said, "there's Margaret over there, and Jeannie." Billy didn't like the looks of Margaret and Jeannie, and he apologized to Wanda. It was another disappointment. He thought he ought to go to bed with a woman at least once before he left Denver.

Walking the streets again, he stopped in a saloon on Lawrence Street — an emporium, rather. This one was elegant, with a long glass mirror behind the bar, a floor covered with sawdust, a brass rail under the bar, and hand towels hanging from the bar so gentlemen could wipe beer foam from their mustaches. The customers wore long coats like Charles's, with fancy vests and creased trousers. Billy didn't belong here, but he didn't want to turn right around and leave either, so he ordered one. It cost a nickel more and was no better than the beer on Holiday Street.

When he left, it was dark outside. Street lamps had been lighted. He found a cafe on Holiday Street where he sat at the counter and ate a tough steak and more fried potatoes. He felt more at home here with customers in workingmen's clothes—overalls, brogan shoes and headgear that ranged from ragged bill caps to floppy hats.

Back in the Queen City's Best, Billy was standing at the bar when the woman named Jeannie swaggered over. "Buy me a drink, cowboy?"

"Yeah, all right."

"Are you lookin' for a woman?"

Jeanne's brown hair was stringy, her clothes were wrinkled, and her breath was bad. Billy would have bet that when she removed the props, her breasts flopped to her navel.

"Not right now," Billy answered.

"Wanta hear a toast?" She smacked her lips over her drink.

"Yeah, all right."

Holding up her glass, Jeannie said, "Here's to the girls of the golden West. Their tits hang down like a hornet's nest. The skin on their belly's as tight as a drum, and a wiggle of their ass would make a dead man come."

If a man had proposed that toast, Billy would have laughed, but he didn't appreciate that kind of language from a woman. In fact, she was disgusting.

"Let's go up to my room?"

"Naw. I reckon not."

"Why not? Ain't I good enough for you?"

"It's not that. It's just that, uh . . ."

"I'm not good enough for you, huh?" Jeannie's voice was rising, and Billy was embarrassed. "Well, I'll tell you somethin', cowpoke, I'm better than your hand, and I'm better than a stump-broke mare, and—"

"I gotta go."

The high-altitude night air smelled good compared to the air in the Queen City's Best. Hell, Billy said under his breath, even if she'd been good-looking her language would have ruined her. Wanda didn't talk like that. He went next door and drank two more mugs of beer while he listened to a monte dealer's spiel. He realized when he was outside again that he was feeling his liquor, even staggering a little. Maybe, he thought, he'd better walk it off. It wouldn't do to go back to the hotel and let Chas see him drunk. He walked.

Billy Johnson was passing the entrance to an alley when, out of the corner of his eye, he saw the man step up beside him. Then he felt something poke him in the ribs. Looking down, he saw the nickel-plated revolver. The man's voice was low and ominous. "Get in that alley, bub, and be quick about it." When Billy hesitated, the man said, "Do it right now, bub, or I'll kill you right here."

"Uh," Billy said, "What—?"

"Move, goddamnit, or I'll kill you. Now, goddamn it."

Mind spinning, trying to comprehend what was happening, Billy turned and walked into the alley.

"Keep goin'. Walk, goddamnit."

Halfway down the alley, in the dark, the man said, "Right here. Get them hands up. Reach for the sky, goddamnit."

Suddenly sober, Billy tried to figure out what to do.

The man wore a bill cap, but his face was indistinguishable in the dark. What little light there was gleamed on the nickel-plated revolver.

"Keep them mitts up." Rough hands went through Billy's shirt pockets and found his roll of bills. "Now, make one move and I'll kill you and leave your body for the rats to eat." The man backed away. "Stay here 'til I'm outa sight or you're a dead sonofabitch." He turned and walked rapidly away.

It took only three seconds for Billy to decide what to do. Running on his toes, making as little sound as possible, he came up behind the man. He was heard, and the man wheeled and fired. The shot sounded like cannon fire in the alley, and a bee stung Billy's left side. But he had the man around the neck now. Had him around the neck with his left arm while his right hand grabbed the gun.

Billy Johnson was an experienced fighter. Growing up the youngest of five boys, he was always "rasslin' " and fist-fighting with his brothers. Within two seconds he had the man on the ground, had his left knee on the gun hand and his right knee in the middle of his chest. He easily twisted the gun free.

Bucking and twisting, the thug tried to wriggle out from under Billy, but gave up when Billy shoved the bore of the gun under his nose. "No, don't. I . . . I didn't hurt you. Don't shoot me."

Billy hissed through clenched teeth, "You goddamn *pendejo* sumbitch, I oughta blow your head off. You ain't fit to live."

"No, don't. Please, I'm beggin' you."

Holding the gun in the prone man's face with one hand, Billy went through his pockets with the other. The first wad of bills he found was not his, but he shoved it in his pants pocket anyway. He found his roll in an overall pocket and put that away.

Standing, Billy growled, "I'm givin' you the same orders you gave me. Stay put. Get up and I'll shoot you with your own gun."

A shout came from the mouth of the alley. A man stood there, yelling, "Hey, what's goin' on? What're you doin'?" He was joined by two more men. "Hey, it's a robbery. He's a robber."

Billy turned and walked with quick steps down the alley. There were more shouts, and running footsteps. Looking back, Billy saw three men running after him. He fired a shot in the air. The men stopped. Billy ran.

Now—without taking time to tell the whole story—Billy said to Charles, "I gotta get out of here. They might have seen me come in here." Hastily, he buckled on his gun belt, slung his saddlebags over his left shoulder.

Charles couldn't believe what he was hearing. "You . . . you robbed someone?"

"Yeah. He robbed me first. I got my money back and his too. I don't wanta get you in trouble, Chas, so I'm gettin' outa here."

"What . . . what are you going to do? Where will you go?"

"I don't know. The train pulls out at seven-thirty in the mornin'. Buy two tickets. I'll meet you there. Give me one of the tickets and then pretend you don't know me."

"Yes, I . . . I will. Is that spot on your shirt blood? Are you injured?"

Billy was at the door. "It's *nada*. If anything happens to me, Chas, pretend you don't know me." Then he was gone.

Charles lay awake most of the night, worrying and waiting for a heavy-handed knock on the hotel-room door. Were the police really after his cowboy partner? What would he say if they came here looking for him? Wherever he was, would they find him? Where was he? Was he all right? How could he let himself get into trouble? It was those saloons. If he had only stayed out of those saloons, he wouldn't be hiding from the police. Perhaps he, Charles Manderfield, was asking for trouble himself by traveling with the young cowboy. Perhaps he should go to Albuquerque alone. Let Billy Johnson solve his own problems.

No, he couldn't do that. He'd do what Billy said.

By daylight he was bleary-eyed from the lack of sleep. Wearily he washed his face and got dressed. Breakfast was toast, marmalade and coffee. At seven by his watch he checked out of the hotel and carried his gladstone bag to the depot. Keeping an eye out for Billy, he bought two tickets to Trinidad. Then all he could do was wait.

What if Billy didn't show up? Should he get on the train without him? No, if Billy didn't appear before the train left, Charles would stay in Denver and try to find him. If he was in jail, Charles would bail him out. It would be foolish, but he decided that was what he'd do.

The train was on time, chugging, hissing and whistling up to the depot. People got off, carrying luggage. People got on. Come on, Billy, Charles pleaded under his breath. Please, Billy. As Charles watched, the big steam engine was unhooked and driven away. Soon another engine was backed up to the string of cars. A brakeman was giving arm signals to the engineer. The engine collided with the coal car, and the impact was heard all down the line of cars, but no damage was done.

The conductor, in his dark blue suit and dark blue cap, looked at his watch, put it back in a vest pocket and yelled, " 'Board!" Come on, Billy.

Then Billy was there, disheveled but able-bodied, his six-shooter on his right hip and the saddlebags over his left shoulder. "Got the tickets?"

"Yes. Here."

"Thanks, partner. You don't know me. See you later."

He watched Billy walk without looking around to the coach car, step onto the iron stool, then climb the steps and disappear inside. He followed and took a seat near the door. Out of the corner of his eyes, appearing to be looking out the window, he saw his partner take a seat at the far end next to a rough-looking bearded man in overalls. A well-dressed gentleman type took a seat next to Charles. "Fine morning," he said.

"Yes," Charles answered, and turned his head away.

With two screams from its whistle, the big steam engine spun its drive wheels and jerked the first car, which jerked the second car, and on down the line until the train was moving. Not until they were out of the city and rolling down a long low hill did Charles relax. The man next to him opened a newspaper and tried to read, but soon gave up. The way the coach was swaying and bouncing, no one could read.

A woman in a striped dress came through the coach car about noon with a basket of sandwiches. Billy bought one, and so did the bearded gent sitting next to him. As hungry as he was, Billy wished he'd bought two.

"Yup," the bearded one said, "I'm gettin' off at Colorada Springs, but I ain't stayin' there. I hear that town's got so uppity a workin'man ain't welcome. Little London they call it 'cause of all the foreigners that're buildin' big houses there. Over west is Colorada City. Now that's my kind of town."

"You been there before?" Billy asked, chewing a mouthful.

"Yup. It's got ever'thing a man could want. You can buy anything you want there. I was in Colorada City before Colorada Springs was born. Hell, in Little London you can't even buy a drink of whiskey — 'less you know the right people."

Billy finished his sandwich. The bearded one talked on. "I scratched for gold all over that big mountain, that Pikes Peak, and like ever'body else I had to give up. But you know what? I think there's gold over on the other side. That's what I think. I'm gonna get me a jackass, some grub and some giant powder and go have me a look-see."

"Some men've got rich diggin' for gold," Billy said, "but I wouldn't know it if I saw it."

"I do. Wanta go partners? If you got, oh, say fifty bucks, you can buy your share of the grub and another jackass, and I can show you what to look for."

"Naw. I got to get home."

"Yeah, I can see you're a cowboy. Cowboys don't like to walk. Me, I've walked damn near as fur as I've rode. Maybe further. Come out here from Missoura with a ox train, and I walked ever' step of the way."

"Did you ever find any gold?"

"Found me a little color up above Black Hawk. 'Nuff for another stake. Say," he said nodding at a red streak on the left side of Billy's shirt, "what happened to you?"

"Nothin'."

No more questions were asked.

It was dark when the train whistled, puffed and screeched into Colorado Springs. Still ignoring Charles, Billy got off, but only long enough to go to the toilet. He bought two more sandwiches and got back on.

Not until they'd rolled through Pueblo and reached Trinidad at daybreak did he approach Charles. "Whatta you think, Chas?"

"Well," Charles said, stretching his legs one at a time, "it appears you are out of danger now."

"I heard about that telegraph. All the laws have to do is telegraph down the line and they'll have other laws on the lookout."

They stood just outside the depot, watching the city come to life. "I'm still not certain of what happened," Charles said. "All I know is you said a man robbed you and you robbed him and you had to run."

After looking around to be sure no one was within earshot, Billy told the whole story. "All I meant to do was get my money back. Just happened that I found his money first. I shoved it in my pocket without thinkin'."

"It served him right. What did you do with his gun? And where did you spend the night?"

"I dropped it in the dirt at the end of the alley. I spent the night sleepin' on the ground next to a big building. I waited 'til I heard the train whistle before I went to the depot."

"It's ironic," Charles said. "No one came to the hotel looking for you. You could have stayed there. And as far as the police sending telegraph messages down here, I doubt it. What you did was not a major crime, and apparently they aren't searching far and wide for you."

"Is that so? Wal, I wasn't takin' any chances. Whatta you say, wanta get our horses and go on south now?"

"I would certainly like to shave and clean up. I didn't get much sleep on the train. I worried so much about you that I didn't get much sleep the night before either. And you, you must be really tuckered."

Running his hands over his face, Billy said, "I reckon

99

I do look like a porcupine. Maybe you're right. It might be a while before we get another chance to shave with hot water."

At the livery barn they found their horses well fed, and their blanket rolls in the saddle room where they'd left them. Charles suggested checking into the hotel on Commerce Street, but Billy wanted to eat first. "Them railroad sandwiches done hit the bottom of my stomach like a rock," he said. "I need some hotcakes and bacon and coffee."

In a restaurant next to the hotel, they parked their knees under a vacant table. But before they could order breakfast, a hulk of a man in baggy wool pants with a six-gun on his hip loomed before them. Looking at Charles, he said:

"You're one a them, ain't you?"

Surprised, Charles asked, "One of who?"

"Them Maxwell land grabbers that've run honest folks off their land. Stand up, mister, so I can pound your snotty rich man's face in."

A long groan came out of Charles. "Ohhh, no. Not again."

Twelve

It was Billy Johnson who stood up. "I wanta tell you somethin', mister." He positioned himself between the hulk and Charles. "This here is my friend, and he don't know nothin' about any Maxwell land, and if you don't get your ugly mug away from us I'm gonna take that hogleg pistol away from you and cram it down your throat. Get it?"

The hulk took two steps back. He looked Billy up and down. His hand stayed away from the gun. The belligerent look faded from his face. "You sure he ain't one of 'em?"

"I said he ain't and he ain't."

"Wal, if he ain't one of 'em then I done wrong. I don't wanta bother any innocent folks." He spun on his heels and walked out the door.

Everyone in the restaurant was looking their way with a mixture of puzzlement and irritation. When Billy sat again, Charles shook his head sadly. "I don't belong here. I'm definitely out of my element in the West. I should have stood up to that man myself." Still shaking his head, he went on, "I thought, now that Colorado is a state, that there would be law and order."

"Know what I think, Chas? I think that no matter how many laws they've got and law officers and ever'thing, there's still gonna be hard cases and thieves and cheats and killers. And I'll tell you somethin', I ain't ever goin' anywhere again without a gun."

A young waitress who had started toward them was now standing still, wondering if the two customers were dangerous. Looking up at her, Charles forced a smile. "It's all right, miss. It was nothing serious. Really it wasn't."

The red streak on Billy's left side had Charles worried, but not Billy. "Just peeled the hide off," Billy said. "He didn't have time to aim."

He had taken off his shirt to wash himself in the hotel room. Again they had only one bed, but Charles had resigned himself to sleeping double. They did have warm water fetched by an old man with a hump in his back.

"We have to put something on it. I'll go to a store and get some iodine to prevent infection. You can't ignore a wound like that."

"Naw." Billy grinned a sheepish grin. "It's a long ways from my heart."

"I'm going to get something." Charles put his hat and coat on and went out the door.

The Raton Pass was the shortest route over the mountains, so the two partners decided they'd pay the toll and get down to the Clifton House as soon as possible. Before they left Trinidad, Charles bought a pair of saddlebags like Billy's and abandoned his gladstone bag. The saddlebags rode easier. Blanket rolls were tied behind the cantles on top of the saddlebags. They headed south toward Fisher's Peak, but went around it and followed the Santa Fe railroad under construction on the narrow wagon road built by entrepreneur Richens Lacy Wootton. The railroad barely left room for wagons, not enough room for wagons going in opposite directions to pass. A southbound stagecoach pulled by six horses passed them at midmorning. Before noon they'd left the pinyon, scrub cedar and juniper and were in the tall pines. Near the divide, they came to the toll gate. Uncle Dick Wootton was a giant of a man, but good natured. "Light and rest your saddles," he said with a smile.

"Naw," said Billy. "Thanks just the same, but we'd like to get down to the Clifton House before dark." They paid their fifty cents toll and rode on. Once they had to leave the road and ride across the rails and up a steep hill a short distance to let a long wagon train pass.

"How much further to the top?" a mule skinner yelled.

"Only a mile or so," Billy yelled back.

A railroad steam engine with a string of cars attached sat idly near the end of the line. Work crews sweated and swore, setting ties and laying rails on top of the ties. Fresnos pulled by two-horse teams leveled and graded the roadbed ahead of them. "They've progressed four or five miles since I came by here in a stagecoach only a couple of weeks ago," Charles commented. "They're going to be over the mountain in a short time." The two young men rode around the workmen with only a "Howdy." By dark they were down on the yucca flats, but still three miles from the Clifton House. The Santa Fe trail was so well worn they had no trouble following it in the dark.

Billy hallooed the house when they rode into the yard. The short hostler came out, carrying a lantern. It's Billy Johnson and Chas Manderfield," Billy said. "We've been all the way to Denver and back."

After watering and feeding their horses, they went into the house, where the woman fried some meat and warmed a pot of red beans for them. She and the skinny man sat across the table and insisted on hearing everything that happened to them in Denver. The two partners didn't tell everything, but they did say they were convinced that Matthew Wyker had been murdered.

"Say," Billy asked, "did a man about Matt Wyker's size come by here a week or so after the last time you saw 'im?"

Charles added, "He would have been traveling south and he would have had a blond young woman with him."

"Yeah, I rec'lect that pair," the skinny one said. "Yeah, now that I think of it, he wore a hat like Matt Wyker's. Didn't talk much. Ate supper and got back on the stage."

"Come to think of it, I rec'lect them too," the woman said. "Didn't think nothin' of it, though. How come you're askin'?"

Charles explained. The skinny one said, "Well I'll be blowed. There we was a-lookin' at Matt Wyker's killer and didn't know it."

"He didn't look like a killer," the woman said. "We've had men come by here that I wouldn't ever turn my back on."

"They didn't spend the night, then?" Charles asked.

"Nope. They run them stages twixt here and Wagon Mound in the dark."

The two partners rode into Wagon Mound themselves the next day just before dark. They first saw the landmark that the town was named after—a high, oblong, treeless, flattop hill that had the shape of a team and a wagon. At dusk they saw dim lights.

The town was a shipping point for farm products from the nearby Canadian River Valley, and freight wagons were parked near the livery corrals. Billy and Charles paid for feed for their horses, bought some crackers and two tins of sardines at a general store and spent the night in their blankets on the ground near the corrals. By sunup they were on their way again.

Staying on the Santa Fe Trail, they rode past high mesas capped with sandstone and over rolling hills covered with yucca and cholla cactus. A few miles from Las Vegas the southbound stage came up behind them. The passengers waved and so did the teamster, but he kept the horses going at a good trot.

Charles groaned, "We should be traveling by stage. They change to fresh horses and they travel faster."

"Like I said before, we might need horses in Albuquerque."

"Yes, I know. I agreed at the time. But after being on this horse for three days, I hurt all over. Even my feet hurt, if you can believe that."

Chuckling, Billy said, "I b'lieve it. You oughta get you some ridin' boots. They fit a stirrup better. With them shoes you havta put your weight on your toes. That gets tiresome."

Las Vegas, Territory of New Mexico, had a hotel, four saloons, two restaurants and two general stores. A wooden windmill stood right in the middle of the plaza. Here the north-south wagon road divided with one fork following the Santa Fe Trail west and the other running south to Lariat and on to Carrizozo. Charles Manderfield almost collapsed when he crawled out of the saddle at a livery barn. "How can anything filled with hay be so hard?" he said. Chuckling, Billy said, "By the time you get back to New York you're gonna be walkin' bowlegged." Charles did walk spraddle-legged until after they'd fed their horses and were settled into a room at the hotel. Not until they'd had a meal in one of the restaurants and he'd had a bath in a tin tub of tepid water did he begin to walk normally.

"This is a tough sonofabuck town," Billy said. "I'd like to go downstairs and drink some beer, but hell, there's men down there that'll challenge you to a shoot-out if you even look straight at 'em."

"Is there no law here?"

"Yeah, sure. They hang somebody ever' once in a while. But that don't keep men from killin' each other."

Charles was in his underclothes. "I'm not going down, then. I'm staying right here. I wish I had something to read."

Billy was still fully dressed. "What do you want? I'll go down to one of the stores and get somethin'."

"Oh, a newspaper. It doesn't matter which newspaper. I would just like to keep up with what is happening in the world."

"That's somethin' I can fetch. I was afraid you'd want a book, and I wouldn't be able to read the words on it."

"You can read, Billy. All you need is practice."

"I'm gettin' better all the time."

"You can sign your name, can't you?"

"Shore. I learnt to do that a long time ago."

"Well, if you want to practice reading, I'll help you. When you come to a word you can't read, I'll show you how to read it."

"I'd shore appreciate that. I shorely would."

He bought a two-day-old copy of the *Santa Fe Gazette* and took it to their room. While Charles read one page, he tried to read the headlines on another page. "Here's a long word," he said, pointing to a headline. "Let's see, there's a *R* and a *A* and a *I* and a *L* and another *R*. I'll bet it's *railroad*."

Looking over at the page, Charles said, "Correct. All you need is practice."

Billy dropped the page when a gunshot sounded down on the street. He hurried to the window and looked down. "Damn. Somebody shot somebody down there." Two more shots split the night. Men were yelling. Billy said, "Gaw-ud damn, they're shootin' the hell out of things."

"Isn't it dangerous to be standing next to the window?"

"Yeah, but . . . I gotta go down and see what's goin' on."

"Billy, I wish you wouldn't. You can't get involved. We've got better things to do."

"Yeah, but . . . I know you're right, but I just gotta see what's goin' on." Shifting his gun belt and pulling his hat on, Billy went out the door. Charles heard his boots thumping on the stairs, and he put the newspaper down and worried.

In thirty minutes, Billy was back. "There was some shootin'. Feller was killed. Feller that killed 'im was grabbed by some of the men on the street and took to jail. Feller said he was nothin' but trouble ever since he came to town a couple a weeks ago. Said this is his second killin' since he come to town."

"Oh my," Charles said. "Boy, will I be glad to get back to civilization where men don't kill each other on the streets."

Undressing, Billy asked, "Don't they have no shootin' in New York?"

"No. Well, yes, in some sections of the city. There aren't so many guns, however. The favorite weapons are knives and pieces of lead pipe."

"But they kill one another?"

With a sigh, Charles said, "Yes."

It was a long day's ride from Las Vegas to Santa Fe,

107

and the boys had an early breakfast in a cafe crowded with excited men. Billy asked one what the excitement was about and was told: "There's gonna be a hangin'."

"Who, that feller that killed somebody last night?"

"Yeah, him."

"Does he get a trial?"

"Haw," the man said with a snort. "We done tried 'im."

Billy said no more, but Charles had to ask, "And the judge sentenced him to hang immediately?"

"The judge ain't got nothin' to do with it, and the shurff's over to Santa Fe lookin' for somebody."

They had their horses saddled and their saddlebags and blanket rolls tied behind the cantles when they heard a mob of loud voices coming from the plaza. "I'm gonna have a look-see," Billy said.

"Billy, don't. Don't get involved."

"I'll see you back here."

Again Charles waited. Waited and worried. "Gosh damnit," he said to himself. Then he added, "I mean goddamnit." The babble of voices grew louder, then louder still. Finally a cheer went up. Then it was quiet. Ten minutes later, Billy was back.

"They hung 'im," Billy said, face sober. "I heard his neck snap. It sounded like when you step on a stick and break it."

"How awful."

"They said all he did was hang around the saloons and pick fights, and he killed two men, includin' one last night. They just got tired of 'im and hung 'im from that windmill in the plaza."

"That is uncivilized."

"Don't they ever hang nobody in New York?"

"They have fair trials."

"Yeah, then what?"

"Then . . ." All Charles could do was shrug.

Billy got off his gray horse and adjusted the latigo.

Looking up, he said, "Well anyways, I saw a bay horse wearin' a double *M*."

"A double *M*? My uncle's brand?"

"Yup."

"Well, what . . . is there something significant about that?"

"I dunno. We gotta find out."

Thirteen

Charles stayed on the ground and hung onto the bridle reins. He was pensive a moment, then said, "I think you're right. There may be a perfectly logical explanation, but we should try to find out. Does anyone claim the horse?"

"Yup. Said he bought 'im from ol' Cornwell, the gent that owns this barn."

Glancing around, Charles said, "Wonder where he is?"

"He's a comin'."

The livery owner was walking toward them, head down, from the direction of the plaza. His battered gray hat was pulled low, and his baggy denim pants were held up with red suspenders. When he was close, he said, "Well, that's one less troublemaker."

"I seen it," Billy said. "Heard his neck snap."

"Yeah. The sheriff ain't gonna like it when he gets back, and the judge is gonna be madder'n a rattlesnake, but they ain't got no kick comin'."

Charles asked, "Why is that?"

"He kilt a man two weeks ago, and the sheriff arrested 'im, then let 'im out on bail. The judge said he was entitled to bail. Now he's done gone and kilt another man."

With a wry grin, Cornwell added, "He won't do it again."

They were all silent a moment, then Charles cleared his throat and said, "Mr. Cornwell, we have a question. Uh . . . Billy, you ask him."

"It's about a horse," Billy said. "A bay horse wearin' a Double M brand. Two *M*s joined."

"Yeah? What about 'im?"

"Sir," Charles answered, "that brand is registered to my uncle, Joseph J. Manderfield, who owns a ranch near Lariat."

Cornwell's tone became defensive. "I bought that horse two-three weeks ago. Got a signed paper to prove it."

"Would you mind, sir, telling us whom you bought it from?"

"Gent name of Wilkerson. Said he was on his way to Santa Fe. The horse was ganted up and lame in the right fore."

"Do you know a Wilkerson, Billy?"

"Nope."

"I fed 'im up and rested 'im and shod 'im, and he's a good horse."

Billy said, "His name is Sourdough. He was in the Double M remuda."

"You recognize him?" Charles asked. "Out of a whole bunch of horses?"

"Shore. He wasn't in my string, but I know 'im. A waddy name of Ross rode 'im. He was plumb gentle."

"Well, I bought 'im and I had a right to sell 'im."

"We're not accusing you of any wrongdoing, Mr. Cornwell. We're only trying to figure out . . . you see, we're looking for, well . . . what do you think, Billy?"

"Did he sell his saddle? Maybe I can recognize his saddle?"

"No, he kept it."

"Wal." Billy scratched the ground with the toe of his boot. "This Wilkerson could of got ol' Sourdough from Jake Ingalls, or . . . hell, I don't know. Maybe it don't mean nothin'. You say he was on his way to Santa Fe?"

"Yeah. Took the stage."

"We're goin' to Santa Fe," Billy said. "What did this gent look like?"

Cornwell shrugged his shoulders. "Nothin' different about 'im. A little bigger'n you, maybe. Needed a shave, and he looked like a man that shaved ever' few days or so. Wore a hat like yours, but it was almost new. And I b'lieve it was brown. Boots like yours. That's all I remember."

Riding out of town on the Santa Fe Trail, the two young men were silent until Charles asked, "Do you think there is any significance in the horse, Billy?"

"Aw, I don't know. None that I can think of."

"Wouldn't Mr. Ingalls put his own brand on the horses he bought from Matthew Wyker?"

"Maybe not. When a feller gets a horse he likes, he don't wanta mark 'im up any more'n he has to." After another moment of silence, Billy added, "Too bad you didn't get down here in time to buy ol' Sourdough yourself, Chas."

"Why do you say that?"

"He's just what you need—plumb gentle and he's got a runnin' walk that's easy to ride and gets over the country in a hurry."

"Yes. This horse's trot is awfully hard on the, uh . . ."

"The ass."

"Yes, the, uh . . . ass."

Grinning, Billy said, "Purty soon you're gonna quit talkin' like a girl. And like I told you, if you had some ridin' boots, you could put more weight on your stirrups and take some off your ass."

They were getting into the rough, rocky country

112

again. Pinyon and scrub cedars were taking the place of the yucca and cactus. At noon they caught up with four mule-drawn freight wagons with the name *Don Otero* painted on the sides. A wheel was off one of the wagons. Five men were trying to pry the wagon axle off the ground with a section of tree trunk for a fulcrum and a long pole for leverage. The two young men got off their horses and lent their weight to the end of the pole. It took some straining and grunting, but eventually they raised the axle high enough to slip the wheel onto the axle.

"Obliged to you," said the heavyset man who appeared to be the boss "I learnt long ago to carry a extra wheel. Never know when you're gonna bust one. We're fixin' to have some dinner and you're welcome to eat with us."

"I've heard of Don Otero," Billy said. "You haul freight down to Lariat, don't you?"

"Usta haul freight ever'where. Damned railroad's puttin' me outa business. I had to move my headquarters seven times now."

The mule skinners had a fire going and coffee boiling. The two partners shared the coffee, fresh bacon and warmed-over beans. Then Don Otero hollered, "Hitch 'em up, boys. There's miles to go."

Traveling was uphill now. Charles and Billy walked their horses. It was dark when they topped Glorieta Pass, near the site of the only Civil War battle fought in the territory. The night sky was clear, the trail easy to follow. Dismounted, they rested a moment, squatting on the ground. Charles inhaled deeply of the clean high altitude air and the sweet smell of cedar and pinyon.

"I have to admit," he said, "that one could become accustomed to the out-of-doors and grow fond of it."

113

"I like the high country," Billy said. "I like campin' in the Mangases when we're gatherin' cattle. But the prairie is purty too. 'Specially early of a summer mornin', when the air is cool and the birds are singin' their heads off."

"Yes. I can understand that."

After a long moment, Billy stood, stretched. "Wal, let's get horseback. There's things to do and things to see in Santa Fe."

The city was several centuries old, and it showed it. Most of the deteriorating buildings were adobe. The plaza was lighted with lamps, but was full of dark shadows. Freight wagons were parked on one side of the plaza, and the dirt streets around the plaza were dotted with piles of horse and oxen manure. One building near the plaza stood over all else, even the trees. It was the St. Francis Cathedral, built only a few years earlier and one of the most beautiful structures Charles had ever seen.

When they rode by it he had to rein up and stare.

"Ain't that somethin'?" Billy said. "Bet there ain't nothin' like that in New York."

"No sir," Charles said, still staring, "there is not. What architecture. I've never seen anything like it."

"The Mexicans built it. The Spaniards, I mean. They built churches almost ever'where they went."

Shaking his head in admiration, Charles said, "Beautiful."

On the other side of the plaza was the Palace of Governors, a long, low building with a roof that covered the plank sidewalk. And on the other sides were the saloons and dance halls, with lanterns hanging over the doors. Tinny piano music and laughter poured out of them. Near the center of the plaza a handful of Mexicans were playing a guitar and singing in Spanish.

"Damn, Chas, let's get these ol' ponies fed and get us

114

some chuck and then go listen to the music."

By asking, they found a series of pens made of verticle juniper sticks, and by hollering, they pursuaded a Mexican to come outside his two-room adobe house and let them leave their horses there. For fifty cents in silver, he allowed them to water their horses out of a hand-dug ditch, put them in an empty pen and throw hay over the fence to them.

They found a room in a one-story hotel a block from the plaza, and while Charles was admiring the hand-crocheted spread on a big brass bed, Billy was splashing water over his face and wiping dust from his boots. "Now then," Billy said, "let's go c'rouse a little."

"I'll go with you to a restaurant, but then I'm going to bed. I'm very tired."

"Hell, Chas, you'll forget bein' tired when one a them purty señoritas latches onto you. There ain't no women purtier then these señoritas."

"No, I've been on a horse for four days now, and we've been told it's another long day's ride to Albuquerque. I need some rest."

But after a meal of roast pork, corn and tortillas, Charles allowed Billy to pull him into a saloon named Cactus Juice. It was a long room that tried to be elegant, but fell short in spite of etched lamp shades, a brass rail along the bar, and a long mirror behind the bar. The mirror was cracked in two places, and the pine bar was scarred. The place was crowded and noisy. Men wearing everything from jackboots and floppy hats to shoes with pointed toes and slicked-back hair stood at the bar, surrounded a roulette wheel and sat at the card tables. In a far corner a piano player was pounding away while two men with beer mugs in their hands stood beside him, watching and listening.

Billy ordered two beers and studied the room. "Now this," he said, "is what folks come to Santa Fe for. This

115

beats the hell out of Denver. Ever' female in here is purtier than anybody I saw in Denver. Except for Wanda."

Charles said nothing, only took a sip of his beer. At
least the beer was cool.

"Know what you oughta do, Chas?"

"What?" Charles asked, disinterested.

"Get your socks washed."

"What?"

"You know what I mean. Get bred."

"Get . . . are you saying . . . ?" Charles put his beer
mug down on the bar and scowled at his partner.
"Surely you don't mean—"

Billy cut him off. "Now there's a purty one. Damn,
she's purty. Hey, she's comin' over here."

The girl was about twenty. Black hair and brown
eyes, olive skin. Two mounds as smooth as milk struggled to escape from the top of her red flowery dress.
Pretty.

Billy lifted his hat and smoothed his hair down. He
fixed a smile on his face.

But it was Charles the girl stepped up to. "Ahlo. You
are somebody, I theenk." She smiled and her teeth were
white and perfectly formed.

A strangling sound came from Charles.

"*Cómo se llama, señor?* My name ees Margarita. I don
speak English so good."

"What, uh. . . . ?"

"She wants to know your name, Chas."

"Why, uh, Charles. Charles J. Manderfield. And,
uh . . ." An embarrassed smile flashed across Charles's
face. "Your English is much better than my Spanish."

"You nice." Then her eyebrows went up and her
mouth formed an O. "You not live here, I theenk. I
theenk you live far away." She stood close.

Charles felt his face turning red. She was beautiful.
"Why, uh, as a matter of fact, I came from New York."

A puzzled frown settled on her face. "New York? I not hear of New York. Where ees New York?"

"It's a long way east."

"I hear of Sain Louees. I hear of Kansas. But I not hear of New York."

"Well, actually," Charles said, trying to assume a serious tone, "it's as far east as you can go without crossing the Atlantic and . . ."

Billy was laughing. He wasn't trying to say anything, just laughing at Charles's embarrassment.

"Not funny," the girl said, frowning at Billy. "He's nice man." She stood so close her breasts touched Charles's arm. She smiled up at him. "I theenk you ver nice man. I theenk you ver important man."

Still laughing, Billy said, "That's what you get, Chas, for wearin' that little hat and that long coat and them shiny shoes."

"It's really not funny, Billy."

Suddenly Billy's laughter fell from his face. In a half whisper he said, "Uh-oh."

A strong rough hand shoved Charles back against the bar. A burly shoulder crowded between him and the girl. An angry dark face with a thin mustache towered over him. Charles went numb with shock.

Again Billy said, "Uh-oh."

Fourteen

The man was tall for a Mexican, over six feet. Billy guessed he was part Yaqui or Apache. He swore at Charles in Spanish: ". . . *pendejo cabrón*." He grabbed a handful of Charles's shirt front and shook him until his head was rocking. Billy had his hand on the butt of his Remington, but he made no move. As long as the Mexican didn't use a weapon, Charles would have to take care of himself.

Without looking at the girl, the man swore at her too: "*Puta*." He hit Charles in the mouth with a big fist. Charles's head snapped back and his face went white with fear.

Billy knew his partner was no match for the big Mexican, and he wanted to help. But he could do nothing as long as the fight was fair. Again a fist smacked into Charles's face. The New Yorker offered no resistance, didn't try to fight back, didn't know how.

Men had gathered to see what was happening. Billy hoped a lawman of some kind would intervene. Nobody did. Then when Charles took another punch in the face, Billy had to do something. He couldn't just stand there and watch his partner beaten to pieces. Drawing the Remington, he started to push his way between the two. It wasn't necessary.

The girl jumped onto the Mexican's back, swearing at him in Spanish. One arm was around his throat and another was around his face, pulling on him. She got him turned around, then beat at him with small fists and kicked at him with slippered feet. The Mexican covered his face with his arms.

"*Bastardo,*" she screamed. "*Bastardo malo.*"

Grabbing Charles by the coat, Billy said, "Come on, Chas, it's time for us to vamoose. Come on." He pulled Charles to the door. A trickle of blood was coming from the New Yorker's mouth, but at the door he looked back and said, "I have to do something. He'll beat her."

"Naw, Chas, it's the other way around. I'll bet she can handle him and another *chingao* like him."

The crowd had forgotten Charles now. They were watching the man try to protect himself from the girl's furious attack.

"Come on, Chas, let's git."

Outside, Charles wiped his mouth, saw blood on his hand and groaned. Billy said, "It's my fault, partner. I shouldn't of dragged you in there. I should of shot that *chingao* sumbitch. I should of let you go back to the hotel like you wanted to. It's all my fault."

Billy filled a bucket with fresh water from a barrel and carried it to the room. Charles ran his tongue over his teeth for the sixth time and said, "I don't think anything is broken." He washed his face out of a china basin, then said, "I don't belong in the West. I didn't know what to do. I've never had to defend myself."

"I couldn't of whupped that big sumbitch either, Chas. I was about to stick this Remington in his face."

"You would have shot him?"

"Wal, you know, a gun makes all men the same size."

"But you could have killed him."

"Tell you one thing, Chas—if you'd a had a gun he wouldn't of jumped on you like that."

The New Yorker's jaw was so sore he couldn't chew the ham he'd ordered in La Cocina across the street. He did manage to chew and swallow a stack of hotcakes. Again his partner apologized. "I oughta be the one with a sore jaw. It's all my fault. Maybe we oughta stay here today. Them ponies've jogged some distance, and they're gettin' leg-weary. You could use some rest too."

Charles didn't argue over that. He did need rest, he said. But he went with Billy to the Mexican corral to water and feed their horses. Billy picked up a forefoot of his gray gelding, then a hindfoot. "He'll make it to Albuquerque," he commented. "The ground's pretty soft 'tween here and there. We'll go around some mountains, but not over 'em."

"What are you saying?"

"Them shoes're gonna have to be pulled off and new ones tacked on. If I can't borry some tools I'll havta pay somebody to do it. Let's have a look at your horse's feet."

"Speaking of shoes, I wonder where I can buy some boots?"

They found a store that sold everything from Levi Strauss pants to Stetson hats to Mexican saddles and boots. "The important part," Billy advised, "is the shank. Right here." He put his finger on the bottom of the boot, between the widest part of the sole and the heel. "This's where the stirrup fits, and it's gotta be made of hard leather. Doubled leather. Maybe even three layers. That way you can ride your stirrups when you want to without pinchin' your foot."

Billy offered more advice when Charles walked awkwardly in the new boots. "Best way to break 'em in is stand in the creek with em, then walk 'em dry."

Back at the Mexican's corral, Charles stood in the hand-dug ditch until the boots were soaked. "The problem now is I don't want to have to walk that much."

"Won't take long. Let's go over to the plaza and watch the people go by. There's people from ever'where in this town. There's some from St. Louie, and Dodge City and Mexico City. There might even be some from New York."

It was interesting, Charles had to admit. "Do you ever try to guess where they are from or what they do for a living?"

"Them mule skinners and bullwhackers all look alike no matter where they come from, but you can pick their bosses out of a crowd. See that un? He's wearin' the same kind of hat and boots, but he's got on a clean shirt, and he's wearin' wool pants, and he shaved this mornin', and he ain't chawin' tobacco."

While he was thinking of tobacco, Billy pulled the makings out of a shirt pocket. He offered the sack to Charles, though he knew his partner would decline. When Charles shook his head, Billy asked, "Don't they smoke tobacca in New York?"

"Some men do. Most men who smoke smoke pipes and cigars."

"Yeah, there usta be a lot of pipe smokin' around Lariat. My pop smokes a pipe. Me, I never could keep the damned things lit. Cigars, now, that's somethin' you don't see much."

"My Uncle Joseph was here in Santa Fe. He and Matthew Wyker brought an ox train of hardware and other trade goods all the way from Kansas City. They made a lot of money. My uncle might have sat right where we're sitting."

121

"They usta camp in the plaza. I reckon folks around here don't allow that no more."

"My Uncle Joseph is probably dying. I should go back to see him and Aunt Bertha. Their ranch is not too far from Albuquerque."

" 'Bout a day and a half on a fresh horse."

"But not yet. We may be wasting our time, Billy, but I have to try. I can't go back yet."

"Wal, it's only another day's ride to Albuquerque, and we oughta find Matt Wyker's killer down there. I hope we find 'im before he spends all that money."

"If he is still assuming Matthew Wyker's identity, we should be able to find him." Suddenly Charles stood. "There is very little chance that that man came here, but I'll ask."

They walked to every hotel they could find and got nowhere. At their own hotel, the owner, a Dutchman from St. Louis, checked every page in his registration book that had been signed in the past three weeks. Once, he thought he'd found it. *"Ach,"* he said, then, "Oh no. It starts with a *W,* but it's Vilkerson."

"That's the gent that sold ol' Sourdough in Las Vegas."

"When was he here?" Charles asked.

"Let me see. *Ach,* it was June twenty-von." The Dutchman's blond head bent over the book as he turned pages. *"Undt* twenty-two *undt* three. *Ach,* I remember him now."

"What did he look like?"

The brow wrinkled over the ruddy face. "I tank he vas nodding to remember. Chust like ever'body else. Now I remember, he vas askink about the railroad."

"The railroad?"

"Ja. I tolt him I don't tank the railroad iss comink here. I hear talk that iss too much hill to Glorieta Pass."

122

Charles's eyebrows went up. "Is that right?"

"He didn't belieff it either. He said iss comink over the Raton Mountains and it must be comink here. He said it iss the Santa Fe railroad and it iss comink to Santa Fe."

"Well," Charles said thoughtfully, "that's what I thought too. That's what most people think."

Charles still wore a puzzled frown when he sat on the bed in their room. "You know, Billy, perhaps . . . I'm a civil engineer, not a railroad builder, but you know, perhaps he is right. What is the terrain like south of here?"

"As I rec'lect, it's flatter'n a pancake."

"Then perhaps the Santa Fe railroad will bypass Santa Fe. Perhaps it will go around the hills and on to Albuquerque, and build a junction somewhere east of here."

"Wal, like the man said, they're buildin' over the Raton Mountains. Why not build over Glorieta Pass?"

"It's terribly expensive, and there was no way around the Raton Mountains." Charles chuckled. "It's ironic, isn't it. They named their railroad the Atchison, Topeka and the Santa Fe and they're going to bypass Santa Fe."

"That sounds like cheatin'."

"Oh, they will no doubt build a spur into Santa Fe. They can't just ignore an important trade center. But I'll just bet the main line will go straight to Albuquerque."

"Wal, what's all this got to do with us and Matt Wyker's killer?"

"Oh, nothing. It's just that, as a graduate engineer, I can't help thinking about things like that. It's interesting."

At noon Charles was happy to fill up on Mexican beans and goat cheese. His sore jaw tolerated that. Billy tore into a flank steak and said, "I got boots that ain't this tough. A wolf couldn't chew this. Wanta swap, Chas?"

"Thank you, no."

"Wal, would you mind holdin' your foot on it while I try to saw off a piece?"

With a small chuckle, Charles said, "You'll have to stand on your own meat, Billy."

Charles spent the afternoon resting and reading. Billy walked around a while, then sat in the plaza and watched the people. He was facing the Palace of Governors where men in stovepipe hats and swallowtail coats went in and came out. Would he recognize the governor? Naw, he thought. Who cares. He walked over to the corral. Their two horses were standing head to tail, fighting flies. They looked contented. "Rest easy, boys. Tomorrow we travel."

With nothing else to do he returned to the hotel room, sat in the one chair and picked up a page of a newspaper. Charles was propped up on the bed, reading. Aloud, Billy read, "S-A-L-O-O-N. *Saloon*. Now, let's see, S-H-O-O-T. *Shoot*. No, there's an I-N-G. *Shooting*."

Charles said, "Seems a man was shot to death in one of the saloons last night. Terrible."

"Oh. Wal, that makes your little ruckus nothin' to talk about. They forgot all about it a minute after we left."

Rubbing his sore jaw, Charles said, "I won't forget it."

Fifteen

Skirting the Santa Fe River, they rode south onto a broad plain, far east of the Rio Grande. Traveling was easy here — for the horses. Charles was standing in his stirrups and hanging onto the saddle horn to ease the jolts. Billy was as comfortable at a trot as he was in the hotel-room chair.

"How's the boots feel?" he asked.

"B-b-better. My feet feel b-better. Can't say the same about my a-a-ass."

"We can slow down. We ought to get to Albuquerque by dark." Billy lifted the reins slightly, bringing his gray horse down to a jog-trot. Charles followed suit.

While they rode southwest, the Rio Grande flowed straight south until its line of cottonwoods was in their sight. "Did you say," Charles asked, "that there is a store along here somewhere?"

"Yup. Bernalillo. We'll be a little hungry by the time we get there, but we won't starve."

The store in Bernalillo bore a large sign over the front: BERNALILLO MERCANTILE CO. NATHAN BIBO, PROP. Everything from coffins to beads and dolls was sold there.

The travelers found a place to water their horses.

They hobbled them, loosened the *cinchas* and let them graze in a vacant lot. While the horses rested, Charles and Billy bought a loaf of bread and some cheese in the store. Soon they were on their way again. Still keeping the Rio Grande in sight, they came to green farm fields, irrigated by water from a man-made ditch, which carried water from the river. They rode on past the farming community of Corrales and saw the great dome of the Sandia Mountains to the southeast. At dusk they rode into the plaza of Albuquerque.

As in Santa Fe, the plaza here was a busy place, surrounded with stores of all kinds, saloons and restaurants. And as in Santa Fe, a huge church was the biggest building in sight. Most of the buildings were adobe mixed with pebbles and straw. The walls were two to three feet thick. After ogling the San Felipe De Neri church and convent, Charles's eyes roved over the plaza, the people, the stores and the terrain.

"This looks to me like a flood plain," he said. "That river over there has overflowed its banks at times. Have you heard of or seen any flooding here, Billy?"

With a shrug, Billy said, "Naw."

"It's bound to have happened and it will happen again."

"Is that what engineers learn about?"

"Among other things. And where does all the trade come from? I see as many Anglos as Spanish people here."

"I dunno. The U.S. Army, maybe. Last time I was here there was a lot of soldier boys on the streets."

Studying the church again, Charles said, "Weathered, but that only adds to its charm. Do you know how old it is, Billy?"

"Damned old, that's all I know."

They found a livery stable three blocks from the plaza, and a hotel one block from the church. After dropping their saddlebags on the floor in their first-floor room, Charles said, "All I want tonight is some food and at least half this bed. I surely hope we're through traveling."

"We oughta be," Billy said. "We oughta have no trouble findin' this jasper who calls hisself Matthew Wyker. Any idee what to do when we find 'im, Chas?"

"I've been thinking about that. If he's using the name of Matthew Wyker, you can report him to the police as an imposter. It will probably be your word against his, but you knew Matthew Wyker, and your report will start a police investigation."

"Then what?"

"Well . . ." And Charles groaned. "If it goes through the justice system, it will be a long time before we can recover the stolen money."

"Uh-huh," Billy said. "Wal, I've been thinkin' about it too. I don't know how many policemen they've got here, or what they'd do about anything. But I'll tell you somethin', Chas. When we find that *pendejo* sumbitch, I'm takin' my share of the money and I ain't gonna report nothin' to the laws."

"But that's uncivilized."

"Uncivilized or not, I'm gettin' my money."

"Then you would be in trouble with the law."

"Naw. He's a killer and a robber. He ain't gonna go bellyachin' to the laws."

"Well . . . as you said, he's a murderer and a thief. We have to do more than just recover the money—we have to see that justice is done."

"Oh, there'll be justice done." Billy shook his head with a wry grin. "Yessir, they'll be some justice."

* * *

Breakfast was frijoles, fried eggs and tortillas. "Do you New Mexicans have beans for every meal?" Charles asked.

Grinning around a mouthful, Billy said, "It's our favorite fruit. It puts lead in your pencil."

"Yes, umm, it also puts gas in your stomach."

"Ugh. I noticed that last night. Maybe one of us is gonna have to sleep on the floor after all."

"Are you accusing me of . . ." Charles had to change the subject. "I didn't sleep much anyway. The mosquitoes were terrible. I should have known. Where there is a body of water in this climate there are mosquitoes."

"Yeah, they're so big, when I slapped at one it stood up on its hind legs and hit me back."

"Humph."

"I'd of shut the window, but they'd of broke the glass."

"Well, we'll have to make some different arrangements tonight."

"I'll sleep on the floor. That way I can cover up my head without bein' gassed to death."

"Humph."

The plaza was busy. The stores were busy. The irregular streets carried horse-drawn and burro-drawn wagons and carts. "I see a bank over there," Charles said. "I think I'll pull the same trick I pulled in Denver."

"What? Oh, I get it, see if anybody that calls hisself Matt Wyker has money in the bank?"

"Yes, it's a legitimate question."

Halfway across the plaza, Billy stopped and said,

"I'll wait outside. A blind man can tell I'm not a businessman."

While he waited, standing first on one foot and then the other, Charles watched the people. There were almost as many Anglos as Mexicans. He wished he knew what Matt Wyker's killer looked like. Was he still trying to look like a cattleman, or had he shed those boots and the hat and put on the kind of clothes he was used to? No way of knowing. Was he registered with the blond woman in one of the hotels? That they could find out.

Looking at the sign on the window, Billy tried to read. Let's see, he thought, it says *The*—that's an easy word—then C-E-N-T-R-A-L. *Center?* No, *central.* Now, there's a *B* and a *A* and a *N. Bank.* Sure, The Central Bank. Hah. How about that? Now, there's a *O* and a *F. Of.* Then there's a *A* and a *L* and a *B* and a *U* and a . . . let's see now, what's that one? A *Q,* that's what it is. *Albu . . . Albuq . . . Albuquerque.* A happy smile shone like the morning sun on the cowboy's face. How about that?

Then when he saw the puzzled look on his partner's face, the smile faded. "Damn, Chas, you look like Grandpa did when he lost his teeth."

"It's real puzzling, Billy. Let's sit down in the plaza and try to figure this out."

They found a bench. Billy waited patiently for his partner to say more. Finally, Charles spoke. "He was here."

"Yeah?"

"He . . . all right, here's what I learned. A man who identified himself as Matthew Wyker opened an

129

account here. Within the next ten days he wrote drafts on the account. Then he closed it."

"So," Billy said thoughtfully, "he spent some money here by writing bank drafts, then decided not to spend any more money that way."

"Whatever he bought after that he paid cash for."

"Hmm."

"And here's something else: he waited until all the drafts he'd written had been cashed before he withdrew his funds and closed the account."

"Wal, excuse my ignorance, Chas, but he wouldn't have took his money out of the bank until the drafts had been cashed, would he? Wouldn't that of been ag'in' the law?"

"Certainly. But he could have left exactly enough money to cover the drafts, or he could have . . . you know, Billy, it's probable that when he opened the account he didn't know how much money he was going to spend."

"Huh," Billy snorted. "I always know how much I'm gonna spend. All I got. But it is a puzzler, ain't it. Did they tell you how much he spent?"

"No, that would have been unethical."

"Then wherever he is he's still packin' some of that money around."

"Probably."

"Hell, he's a robber hisself. He oughta know how dangerous that is."

Charles was deep in thought. "It's strange. You know Billy, a canceled bank draft is proof. It's proof that the writer paid somebody for something."

"A handshake won't do, huh? Or a signed paper?"

"A signed paper is usually enough, but one can't be too careful. Two kinds of proof are better than one."

"Uh-huh. So whatever he bought he wants to be sure he can prove he bought it."

"That's exactly right."

"Any idee what that could be, Chas?"

"The first thing that comes to my mind is real estate."

"Like land and houses, huh?"

"Yes." Looking around, Charles added, "I don't see any houses worth investing in, unless he bought that church."

"You don't reckon . . . ? No, that wouldn't make sense."

"What were you thinking?"

"Aw, it's dumb. He didn't buy a lot of land so he could go into the cattle business? Naw, his name would be recognized by somebody from Conejos County sooner or later."

"No, the way he did it makes me wonder if he was speculating." Suddenly Charles slapped his knee. "That's it. He's speculating on land. And with the railroad coming south, he has to be speculating on land near the railroad right-of-way."

Billy could only stare at his partner in wide-eyed wonder.

"Yes, by George. The railroad will be here in two or three years. As a matter of fact, the way it's progressing, I'll bet it will be here in two years."

"And," Billy added, "some of these Mexicans that own land around here maybe don't know that and they'd sell their land cheap."

"Well now." Charles was pensive. "It's common knowledge that the Santa Fe is laying rails south, and it will definitely come through here. But . . ."

"But?"

131

"Exactly where?"

"This jasper knows. Or thinks he does. How would he of found out?"

"It could have been easy. The railroad company is planning ahead, and it has the route already picked out. It has the right-of-way already acquired. Whoever it acquired the right of way from would know. Or at least suspect. Or . . . maybe not."

"They could have bought a strip of land without sayin' what they was buyin' it for."

"Exactly. A middleman could have done the buying. If the landowners knew the railroad needed their land, you can bet the price would be high."

"They prob'ly bought land from folks that cain't speak English. But I'll tell you somethin', Chas, these Mexicans ain't dumb. When it comes to tradin' or buyin' or sellin', these Mexicans can dicker with the best of 'em."

"Yes, but suppose . . . suppose the railroad is not coming right through town here. This is a flood plain. This is not a good place to build anything. Suppose the railroad is planning to build near here but not here."

"Only the railroad big shots know where, and they ain't tellin' the folks they have to buy land from."

"Exactly. Enter the middleman, the purchasing agent."

"I heard talk about how Trinidad grew like a Russian thistle when the railroad got there, and Albuquerque'll prob'ly do the same. Now, you say the railroad's already bought the land it needs. And land close to the railroad is gonna be a good place to build a business."

"Exactly. It has happened all over the nation. Where

the railroads have gone, business has prospered.

"So what this hombre is doin' is buyin' land next to where the railroad is gonna build. And when the railroad gets here he'll be able to name his price for it. Is that what you call speculatin'?"

Smiling broadly, Charles patted his partner on the back. "You learn fast, Billy."

But Billy still had a worry frown between his eyes. "That means the *chingadero* knew the right people and found out where."

"He had inside information."

"But, look here, Chas, what worries me the most is he took his money out of the bank. Know what that sounds like?"

"Oh no." When the thought hit Charles he looked sick. "I was so occupied with trying to figure out what he's doing that I didn't think about that."

"He ain't here no more."

A long, painful groan came from Charles. "Damnit. Goddamnit. And we have no idea where he went."

Sixteen

While the two young men were talking, the sun was climbing higher, and with the warmth of the sun came the flies. Big black flies. Charles was continuously fanning his face with his hands. As they sat there a shapely Mexican girl walked by, wearing a lacy shawl over her head. She glanced at the two young men out of pretty dark eyes. Billy smiled and lifted his hat. She immediately shifted her gaze straight ahead.

Billy muttered with a grin, "Too bad I wasn't born good-lookin' steda so goddamn rich."

Charles didn't notice. "I'm at my wit's end, Billy. We've traveled all the way from Denver and we have found that Matthew Wyker's murderer was here, but now we're at the end of the road. We don't know where to turn next."

"We don't even know what he looks like."

"Oh-h-h," Charles groaned. The flies were forgotten. A warm wind whipped up the dust in the plaza. That too was ignored. With a long sigh of resignation, Charles asked, "What do you think we should do, Billy?"

"I ain't givin' up yet. Ask questions, I reckon.

Learn all we can about that jasper. Maybe if we find somebody that knew 'im, we'll get an idee."

Another long sigh, then, "I suppose you're right. Since we are here, we should try a little longer." A pause. "The hotels, I guess. If we can learn where he stayed, we might learn more about him."

Standing, Billy said, "It won't take long. There ain't more'n four or five hotels. I'll help. I've listened to you ask questions enough that I think I can do it."

"Yes. I suppose so. We can divide the chores. I think the first thing I'll do is find the county recorder."

"How come the county recorder?"

"Transactions concerning real estate are public records in the states. I hope the same is true in this territory."

"That way you can find out where the land is he bought, huh?"

"Yes." Charles stood too, wearily. "It probably won't help, but as you said, the more we learn about this imposter, the better our chances are of finding him."

They went their separate ways. Billy learned something interesting in the Amarillo, the first hotel he went to. He asked one simple question: "I'm looking for a gent name of Wyker. He was traveling with a blond woman. Did he stay here around July ten or so?"

The clerk, a dark young man with thick black hair growing low on his forehead, ran a stubby finger down a page of the registration book. "*Sí, señor.* He wass here. But he wass alone."

"When, *por favor?*"

"It wass July ten." Turning pages, he added, "Five dayss. July ten to fifteen. Matthew Wyker from Denver."

"Alone?"

"*Sí.*"

"Do you remember what he looked like?"

The forehead wrinkled, bringing the hairline down to the dark eyebrows. "I theenk he wore a hat like yourss, only brown. And boots like yourss."

"Was he my size?"

"Maybe a leetle bigger."

"Wal, excuse me for askin' so many questions, but I'm tryin' to find Matthew Wyker. Did he say where he was goin' from here?"

"*No, señor.* He no say nothing."

Well hell, Billy said to himself outside. Matt Wyker's killer was here, but alone. What did he do with the woman? Leave her in Las Vegas? Wish we'd asked questions in Las Vegas. Billy started walking across the plaza, head down, thinking. Suddenly he stopped. Wait a minute. A brown hat? Matt Wyker wore a gray hat and his killer had put on the same hat. The jasper that sold ol' Sourdough in Las Vegas wore a brown hat. Gave the name of Wilkerson and said he was goin' to Santa Fe. He wouldn't be here using the name of Matthew Wyker, would he? Aw hell, it doesn't make sense. Naw. Matt Wyker's killer was travelin' with a blond woman. He sure as hell didn't travel horseback to Las Vegas. But . . . he said in Denver he was comin' to Albuquerque. Aw hell.

Billy went back to the plaza, where he again took

136

a seat on a bench. All right, Matt Wyker's killer was here without the woman. He left here on the fifteenth. No, he paid the hotel for the night of the fifteenth, and he would have left the next day. That don't mean nothin'. What we need to know is where he went. The woman. Where did he dump her? If we could find her she might tell us somethin'. Aw hell, she's in Las Vegas, prob'ly, or Santa Fe. Goddamn.

When he looked up his gaze fell upon another hotel sign. He read it a letter at a time: R-I-O V-E-G-A. *Rio Vega*. He had already learned to recognize the word *Hotel*. Just for the hell of it, because he had nothing else to do, he stood and walked across the plaza to the Rio Vega Hotel.

"Wilkerson?" the clerk asked. "No, no Wilkerson."

"Do you remember a man from up north, probably Denver, traveling with a blond woman?"

"Oh yes, I believe I do." The clerk had thinning hair parted in the middle and a thin mustache. He turned pages, studied them. "Yes. This gentleman was here with a blond woman. He signed the register as Mr. and Mrs. Matthew Wyker from Denver, Colorado."

"What?" Billy couldn't believe it. "When?"

"Why, let's see. They were here from July eight to July fifteen."

"Huh?" Billy was still flabbergasted. "Are you . . . yeah, you're sure. No mistake about that. Wal, I'll be . . . do you remember what this gentleman looked like?"

"He was about your size and dressed something

137

like you, only his hat was gray. He had no mustache or beard."

"Wal, don't that beat ever'thing?"

"Do you know this gentleman?"

"Yeah—I mean no—I mean, I think I do. I'm just, uh, surprised that he was here, that's all. You say he left on the fifteenth?"

"He checked out on the sixteenth."

"Was the woman still with him?"

"Yes, and that reminds me—they had a violent quarrel just before they checked out. In fact, they were so loud that I was about to go knock on their door and ask them to be quiet. He came in drunk so much of the time I was glad to see him leave."

"Did they give you any hint about where they was goin'?"

"No, I'm afraid not."

Outside, Billy repeated, "Don't that beat ever'thing." A well-dressed gentleman passing by gave him a quizzical glance. Billy went back to the same bench in the plaza. He wished Charles would show up. He had something to tell him. Like, either the man who called himself Matthew Wyker signed in at two hotels at the same time, or there were two men claiming to be Matthew Wyker in town at the same time. "Don't that beat all?"

A passing *señorita* looked around to see who he was talking to. He lifted his hat and smiled. She too looked away.

Charles found the Bernalillo County clerk and re-corder's office in a crumbling adobe house. The records of land transactions listing Matthew Wyker as buyer were readily available. But the location of the land was a mystery. All he could find were legal descriptions, which meant nothing to him. So he borrowed a sheet of paper from a clerk and copied the descriptions. There were three of them. Then he went in search of a land surveyor.

The surveyor, a short, stocky man named Wilson, was packing his surveying instruments on a burro and was about to leave his clapboard home north of the plaza. "I don't need to look at the markers," he said. "I've been doing a lot of work over there lately."

"Can you direct me to the general location?"

"Go two miles due east and you'll see my stakes. The stakes are numbered." He squinted again at the legal descriptions. "These are lots four, five and six. The other lots along there were already taken."

"Is that along the railroad right-of-way?" He didn't expect an answer and he got none. But the surveyor's eyes narrowed and he answered too quickly, "I don't know anything about that. I'm paid to stake out the parcels. That's all I know."

"Thank you very much."

Charles was pleased to find Billy in the plaza. He dropped onto the bench beside him. "I learned where the parcels are, and I'm almost certain now that they are along the railroad right-of-way. But all this doesn't bring us any closer to the man who is impersonating Matthew Wyker."

"There's two of 'em."

"What? What do you mean?"

"There was a Matthew Wyker in two hotels at the same time. One had a blond woman with him, and the other had a hat like mine, only brown."

For a moment Charles could only stare at his partner in disbelief. "Do you mean there are two men pretending to be Matthew Wyker?"

"Wal, I've been sittin' here thinkin' about that, and you know what?"

Impatiently, Charles barked, "What? What?"

"I think maybe, just maybe, now, one of 'em is the real Matt Wyker."

"But . . . but . . ."

"Look at it this way, Chas. That dead man in Denver could of been somebody else. He was six feet under the ground before we knew about 'im. Then we found out that another man that was prob'ly wearin' Matt Wyker's hat and boots and called hisself Matt Wyker told Wanda he was comin' down here."

Billy paused, then asked, "See what I'm gettin' at, Chas?"

Confused, Charles said, "Yes . . . no . . . go on."

"All right, a man that called hisself Wilkerson went through Las Vegas. He was the same size as Matt Wyker and wore a new hat. Or almost new. A brown hat. One of the Matthew Wykers that was here was the same size and *he* wore a brown hat."

Another pause. Billy pushed his feet out in front and crossed his ankles. "Does this make any sense, Chas?"

"Oh, no, not by any means, but—"

"I know this sounds *estúpido,* but couldn't the hombre that came through Las Vegas be the real Matt Wyker?"

"Why would you think that?"

"I know I'm crazier than a locoed cow, Chas, but it just popped into my *cabeza*. The real Matt Wyker is in cahoots with some ranihan he knew from somewhere. He wants folks to think he's dead so nobody will try to trail him any further. Get it?"

"Oh-h-h." Charles nodded so vigorously that he rocked on the seat of his pants. "Then why did Wilkerson ride a horse to Las Vegas?" Quickly, he answered his own question. "Because if he had traveled by stage from Trinidad he would have been recognized at the Clifton House as Matthew Wyker."

"You're thinkin' the same thing I am."

"So he met his partner here in Albuquerque. His partner was traveling with a woman they'd met in Denver, and he'd told the woman his name was Matthew Wyker. So when he registered in a hotel here he had to use that name."

"Yup. Only thing I cain't figure out is why he used Matt Wyker's name in the first place."

"Because he endorsed and cashed a very large bank draft made out to Matthew Wyker, and to do that he carried papers with Matthew Wyker's name on them."

"Uh-huh," Billy said. Then quickly he added, "But I cain't help wonderin' why. Like I said, if ever'body thinks ol' Matt's dead then nobody'll be lookin' for 'im. But that dead man in Denver wasn't identified, so nobody'll know he's dead."

"What we have to do, Billy, is think back to the beginning and try to unravel all this."

"Yeah."

"So, Matthew Wyker absconded with Uncle Joseph's money. He surmised that sooner or later

141

someone would try to find him and get the money back. If, as you said, the searcher believed him dead, the search would end. So, he placed his easily identifiable orange kerchief on the body of a murdered transient, believing that if anyone followed him to Denver, which a searcher eventually would, well . . ." Charles spread his hands.

"And," Billy continued the line of thought, "he figured that whoever was huntin' 'im would go to the Denver laws, the laws would tell 'im about that dead man and the wildrag, and that would be the end of the trail."

"Yes, and the searcher, if he knew anything at all about Matthew Wyker, would know that he had originally come from Kansas City."

"Then, I reckon, what with telegraphs and all, the laws in Denver would send messages to the laws in Kansas City and find a next of kin."

"Correct. By then the body would have decomposed enough that identification would be impossible. But the next of kin might find a paper with Mr. Wyker's signature on it. The police would compare it with the signature on Jacob Ingalls's bank draft and would then be convinced absolutely that Mr. Wyker had been murdered and the murderer had forged his signature and cashed the draft."

"It's so mixed up it makes a feller's head swim, don't it, Chas?"

"Yes. Mr. Matthew Wyker is devious and crafty. Very crafty indeed."

"He was thinkin', all right. Or maybe he just had an idee and this is the way it worked out."

"That seems logical. It's possible that he and his

cohort accidentally stumbled across the body and saw an opportunity."

"It's hard to believe Matt Wyker's a killer, but maybe they didn't just find a dead man."

"I'm beginning to think anything is possible."

"Wal, it worked. If we'd of gone to the laws steda Wanda we'd of prob'ly gave up. Now we're thinkin' he's alive."

"You're right. He concocted a plan with Mr. Wilkerson, but being a womanizer he didn't want to leave Denver right away. When they found a dead body — or whatever — they stripped it of all identification and placed that kerchief on it."

"Like you said, Chas, ol' Wyker was a crafty sumbitch."

It was well past noon, but the two young men hadn't even thought of dinner. Four Mexicans were sitting under a tree in the plaza, eating tortillas and drinking from a jug of wine. The flies were worse, buzzing around the heads of the humans. A fine dust was swirling through the plaza. Somewhere a burro brayed. A dog barked.

Finally, Charles said, "Of course this is all mere conjecture."

"We got nothin' to do but conject."

"It's totally insane."

"Yeah, a feller'd think we was both croppin' the weed."

"What weed?"

"Loco weed."

"Oh."

"Would you like to take a walk, Billy?"

"Walk where?"

143

"Two miles east. That, I think, is where the railroad has purchased its right-of-way."

"Walk two miles? If the Good Lord wanted me to walk he'd of gave me four legs."

"Yes, you're right. For a moment there I'd forgotten we have horses."

They went to the livery barn, saddled their horses and rode east. The right-of-way wasn't hard to find. Surveyors' markers were everywhere. Billy stayed on his horse and held the reins of his partner's horse while Charles studied the stakes. After finding the stakes he was looking for, Charles stood with his hands on his hips and eyed the terrain—the mountains farther east, the Rio Grande and the line of cottonwoods to the west.

"This is still in the river bottom," he said. "I don't understand why they chose to build here." He took his sheet of paper from a shirt pocket, unfolded it and scribbled some notes on it. Then he mounted his brown horse. His new boots fit the stirrups perfectly, and Billy noticed that he was looking more at home on a horse. "Perhaps they believe this area isn't as likely to be flooded. I don't know. Perhaps they should have hired a civil engineer."

"What was it you wrote down?"

"Some lot numbers. Just out of curiosity, I'd like to go back to the recorder's office."

At the recorder's office Billy again stayed on his horse, holding the reins of his partner's horse. Charles was inside most of an hour. The wind whipped fine dust over the town. The horses were constantly stomping their feet and shaking their heads, fighting flies.

144

When Charles came out he had a wry grin on his face.

"Yessir," he said, looking up at Billy. "There's no doubt about it. The railroad bought a right-of-way through what was private land, and guess who the purchasing agent was."

"No idee."

"A gentleman by the name of John Wilkerson."

Seventeen

They had supper at a table covered with a checkered oilcloth. Charles chewed slowly, carefully, favoring a jaw that was still a little sore. The chili they ate contained so much hot spice that Charles had to take a swallow of water after every mouthful. Billy cleaned his bowl, finished the rolled up tortilla and asked the Mexican woman for more. Charles asked for more water. Then Billy said:

"I've got an idee."

His partner had to take a quick swallow of water before he could reply: "Huh?"

"I'm gonna go c'rousin' again."

"Why?"

"By myself. I don't want no more señoritas wrappin' theirselfs around you and makin' some big Indian mad."

"Well, if you go carousing, you'll go by yourself." Charles took a tentative bite of his tortilla.

"Don't you wanta know why?"

Swallowing with a gulp, Charles said, "I have already asked why."

"To look for a blond woman."

"*The* blond woman?"

"Yup. Her."

"Do you think she's still in Albuquerque?"

"Could be. I reckon I forgot to tell you, but the gent at the Rio Vega Hotel said her and her lover boy had a hell of a quarrel just before they left."

"And perhaps they had a parting of the ways and she is still here?"

"Perhaps. I mean, maybe."

"Or do you just want to go carousing?"

"Wal, both. If you want to bad enough you can go along."

"Thank you, but no thank you."

Grinning, Billy said, "Wal, hell, Chas, with a little practice you could learn to like beer and women. And with your sweet innocent looks you could have the señoritas followin' you around with mattresses on their backs."

"You can have that kind of women."

With Charles safe in the hotel room reading newspapers, Billy walked across the plaza to a cantina named El Toro. Most of the habitués were dark-skinned, but Billy wasn't the only Anglo. He stepped up to the pinewood bar and said, *"Una cerveza, por favor."* Then he looked over the crowd. Not a blond in sight. In a far corner two Mexicans were playing guitars and another a coronet. Billy liked the music. The coronetist lowered his instrument, and they sang about the beautiful Carmelita and the peon who was in love with her but could only dream about her. When a fat man's loud laughter drowned the music, Billy felt like kicking him. Instead, he left.

A half block away on a side street another cantina featured a tinny piano and a hand-painted sign that read CERVEZA FRÍA. Wal, Billy said to himself, we'll see how cold. It was only cool. Must of been kept in a cool cellar, he thought. Again his eyes scanned the room. Not much of a crowd. But, say, there's a blond woman. Not pretty. Too much bosom and too much *estómago y culo.* She was standing near a card table, watching the game, a glass in her hand. The fingers on that hand were covered with rings made of Mexican silver. Billy drank half his beer and sauntered over.

How to do this? What to say? He stood behind her a moment, then decided on a bold approach. "Good evenin', Missuz Wyker."

She half turned. "Me?" One of her front teeth was missing. "Are you talkin' to me, mister?"

"Ain't you Missuz Wyker from Denver?"

"Are you loco? I never heard of no Missuz Wyker and I ain't never been close to Denver."

"Oh. Excuse me all to pieces." Billy left that cantina too, muttering under his breath, "I'll bet she ain't even a real blond."

There were more cantinas. Hell, he thought, I could hit ever' one of 'em and get nowhere. There was no blond in the next one. Down the street was the Golden Ox. He'd try that one.

The girl was pretty, but she wasn't blond. *"Buenas tardes, señor. Un* whiskey?"

"Oh, make that a beer. *Una cerveza.*"

A pretty pout came over her painted face. *"Cerveza?* You look like whiskey man. I like whiskey. We have whiskey together, no?"

He knew he was being used, but he agreed. Two shot glasses of liquid were placed on the bar before them. He paid two quarters. The girl quickly downed hers in one gulp, said, "Ah-h-h." He didn't

148

believe it, and he picked up her empty shot glass and sniffed. Colored water. She looped her arm through his and said, "Drink. Is good." He picked up his own glass, tossed it down and nearly strangled.

"Gaw-ud damn."

"Is good whiskey, no?"

"No. I mean, hell no. *Adiós*."

He didn't have to go far to the next one—just across the street. A dog was barking somewhere. The wind blew. Dust swirled. This one was of a better class, with a mahogany bar, a long mirror, a three-string Mexican combo and coal-oil lamps hanging on chains from the ceiling. It was crowded, but most of the customers here were Anglos. Some were well dressed. The bartender, an Anglo with a waxed handlebar mustache, looked hard at the six-gun on Billy's hip and said, "No guns in here, mister."

"Wal, uh . . ." He started to just leave, but then he spotted her out of the corner of his eye. She was blond, slender and pretty. Sitting at a table with two well-dressed men. Smiling. Billy started toward her.

"Hey, didn't you hear me? I said no guns."

Ignoring the bartender, Billy walked directly to the woman—so directly that she saw him coming. "How do, Missuz Wyker."

Her mouth dropped open in surprise, but she quickly regained her composure. You must be mistaken." The two men at the table were giving him hard looks. The bartender was behind him now, saying, "Either shuck that gun or get out of here."

"I first saw you in Denver," Billy lied. "I know your friend Wanda."

"Wanda?" She stood suddenly. "Listen, I—my name isn't Mrs. Wyker."

"Your name is Effie."

The bartender was threatening, "Get out of here, mister, and I mean right now."

"I have to ask you somethin', Effie."

"Not here. Let's go over to the bar." To the men she said, "There seems to be a mistake here. I'll be right back."

"Do you need some help, Effie?"

"No, I don't need any help."

"Are you gonna git, mister, or do we throw you out?"

Billy followed her to a spot near the bar and near the door. She turned to face him. "Listen, you must have seen me with Matthew Wyker and read the name on the hotel register, but I'm not Mrs. Wyker."

"I know it. It's none of my business what you do, but I'm lookin' for your man friend."

"See here, cowboy." Billy looked into the bore of a short-barreled shotgun in the hands of the bartender. "I told you to git and you'd better git."

"I don't know where he went. The crazy, drunk sonofabitch left town with another man."

"The other man is the real Matt Wyker. I think your friend's name is Wilkerson."

Standing close, talking in a low tone, she said, "You might be right. He let it slip once. Once when he was polluted out of his mind."

"But you don't know where they went?"

"Get away from him, Effie. I'm gonna blow a hole in 'im."

Glancing nervously at the bartender, Effie said, "Just a second, Ed. Don't shoot that thing." To Billy she said, "I think they went south. That's something else he said when he was so loop-legged he couldn't stand up. That's all I know. They got on a stage and I think it was going south."

"No hint at all?"

"They had a scheme of some kind. I don't know what. I suspicioned that they traded wallets in Denver and agreed to meet here. The other one rode a horse from Trinidad to Las Vegas. That's all I know."

The bartender meant business. "All right, cowboy, that's it. I'm gonna count to three and then I'm gonna blast you plumb out of your boots."

"Thanks a lot, ma'am." He turned to leave, then stopped. "Did they leave you broke?"

"Not quite."

"One," the bartender said.

"Wal, I ain't got much, but if you need some eatin' money I can spare a few bucks." Billy reached for the roll of bills in a shirt pocket.

"Two."

"No thank you." She smiled. "That's good of you, cowboy. But I can take care of myself." Another nervous glance at Ed. "You'd better go right now."

"*Adiós*, Effie."

"*Adiós*."

"Three."

By then Billy was on his way out the door.

He didn't want Effie to know it, he didn't want that *chingao* bartender to know it, but he was so scared his stomach was up in his throat. Whew, he said to himself, that shotgun bore looked to be as big as a cannon. That was one of the dumbest things I ever did.

As usual, Charles had the hotel room door latched from the inside, but he quickly got up and unlatched it when Billy identified himself on the other side.

"Did you keep out of trouble, Billy?"

"Yeah, but . . . did you ever look up the barrel of a shotgun, Chas?"

"Of course not."

"Well, I just did, and I'll tell you somethin', it's enough to make a man dirty his drawers."

With an exasperated sigh, Charles dropped onto the bed. "You just can't seem to keep out of trouble. What happened?"

"They went south. Got on a stage and went south, both of 'em. Effie got left behind, but I got the idee she didn't wanta go with 'em anyway. Said the one named Wilkerson was always two sheets in the wind."

Charles asked two questions: "You actually found her? And he was always what?"

"I found 'er, and he was always drunker'n a skunk. The hotel clerk said the same thing."

"Why would Matthew Wyker take an alcoholic as a partner?"

" 'Cause he knows where the railroad is goin'?"

Slapping himself on the side of the head, Charles said, "Of course."

"The railroad's headin' south from Trinidad, and it'll prob'ly go all the way to Mexico."

"I wish we knew for certain."

"What say we get on our horses and head south and see if we can pick up their trail."

"What cities are south of here?"

"There's Socorro, about fifty miles, but there's a

little Spanish town called Las Lunas just a few miles south."

"Socorro. That's not far from Lariat, is it?"

"A half a day's ride."

"All right, let's go south, and if we find no trace of them by the time we get to Socorro, we might as well go on back to Lariat. I'm really worried about my Uncle Joseph. He might have died. My aunt might need me badly."

With a sigh, Billy sat in the one chair. "I know how you feel, partner. If I was in your place I'd feel the same way." He started pulling off his boots. "I don't know what to say. That's somethin' you'll have to figure out for yourself."

"I'm really worried."

"Wal, we can get on our way first thing in the mornin'. No, come to think of it, I got to get my horse shod."

"Las Lunas, you said? What does that mean in Spanish?"

"Wal, *luna* means moon, but I think this is some-body's name."

"You speak Spanish very well, don't you Billy?"

"Naw. All I know how to do is cuss in Mexican."

"Can we open the window, or would it let the mosquitoes in?"

"Best thing to do is cover your head with the bed sheet. I'll sleep on the floor. We should of picked a hotel built out of 'dobe. Them walls are so thick they keep it cool inside."

"Yes. Next time I'll know better."

At breakfast before sunrise, Charles ordered eggs, ham and toasted bread, no beans. Billy ordered everything including beans. Now that his jaw was nearly healed, Charles was beginning to enjoy his food. "These natives do make good bread and marmalade, don't they."

Speaking around a mouthful, Billy said, "Ain't nothin' wrong with Mexican chuck. They know how to cook."

Billy took his horse to a blacksmith, a block from the livery barn, and said, "The hind feet are all right, but the fores need new iron. If I had some tools and a forge I could do it."

The smith was grumpy. "Nobody uses my tools but me. Will that horse stand?"

"Oh, he might jerk his feet a few times, but he ain't bad."

It took nearly an hour. By then the sun was showing itself over the Sandia Mountains, but Charles had their saddlebags packed and their blankets rolled up. They were mounted and on their way when they heard loud voices. It sounded like a hundred people talking excitedly.

"What do you think it is, Billy?"

"No idee. Let's go see."

As they rode through the plaza they saw a mob walking west toward the river, following a wagon. When they caught up they saw a Mexican woman in the wagon. Crying. She was holding onto a side of the buckboard, on her knees, tears running down her face.

"What's happening, Billy?"

"You know what this looks like to me, Chas? I think they're fixin' to hang that woman."

Eighteen

Charles Manderfield's face went white. "Oh no. Why?"

Speaking to a man in a wide straw hat, Billy said, *"Señor, que es?"*

The man answered in English. "She stabbed her husband. Killed him. The judge said she has to hang."

"Oh no," Charles groaned. "That's barbaric."

"He was a no-good pucker-mouthed bottle sucker and he was always beating her, but the judge said she has to hang."

"But this is not justice."

"Maybe we oughta go on about our business, Chas."

"Oh no," Charles said again. "The poor woman. She's so young."

"You don't have to be very big to stab somebody."

"They can't do this."

The wagon stopped under a big cottonwood growing out of the banks of the Rio Grande. The crowd stopped. Someone threw a rope over a limb. The rope had a hangman's noose in the end. The other end was tied to the trunk of the tree. An Anglo with a deputy sheriff's badge pinned to his shirt pulled the woman to her feet. She cried, pleaded.

Charles was almost in tears himself. "That poor woman. They can't do this."

"We oughta go, Chas. This ain't none of our business."

The noose was fitted around the woman's neck. Tears ran down her face. She trembled with fear. She pleaded, "Please, don't. Please, I don't want to die." Sobbing violently, she repeated, "I don't want to die."

Someone whipped the team and the wagon was jerked from under her. She was left dangling by the neck.

Charles cried, "Oh, my God."

But the deputy had made a mistake. He had failed to tie the woman's hands behind her back. Now she had hold of the rope over her head and was trying to pull herself up, trying to relieve the pressure on her neck. Her face was twisted in pain. Her tongue hung out of her mouth. The muscles in her arms strained.

The crowd groaned. Someone swore in Spanish. The deputy swore. He grabbed the woman by the legs and pulled down. While he pulled down, the woman pulled up, desperately. The woman was losing.

Charles hissed through his teeth, "No, by God."

Billy yelled, "Chas, wait. Chas . . ?"

But Charles was on the ground. He ran—ran right at the deputy.

"Chas, don't."

Charles lowered his right shoulder and rammed

the deputy squarely in the middle of the chest. The deputy hit the ground on his back. Slammed down hard.

Charles screamed, "You inhuman bastard. You barbaric son of a bitch."

Billy was on the ground, running. The deputy sat up, reached for the six-gun on his hip. Billy was on him, stomping on his gun hand, stomping hard. He reached down, picked up the gun and threw it into the Rio Grande.

"Come on, Chas. Time to go. Come on, partner." He grabbed Charles around the waist and pulled him back to their horses. "Get on that horse. Let's ride."

"Wait," Charles cried. "Wait a minute." Looking back, he saw that someone had cut the rope. The woman was sitting on the ground, holding her throat in both hands, retching.

"Get on that horse, goddamnit."

Charles tried to mount, but the horse was dancing nervously at the excitement.

"Get on 'im."

Then Charles was in the saddle, and Billy yelled, "Goose that pony. Let's ride."

The excitement had the brown horse eager to run and run it did, carrying Charles across the plaza, down a side street and out of town. Charles hung onto the saddle horn and gritted his teeth. Billy galloped along behind. "South," Billy yelled. "Pull on the right rein."

Charles let go of the saddle horn with one hand and turned the horse south. Billy's gray gelding was running as hard as it could go, but it couldn't catch the brown horse. They were pounding down a

157

wagon road, past a few adobe huts and fenced gardens, and then out onto a sagebrush prairie. The Sandias were on the east and the Rio Grande was on the west. Billy yelled:

"Pull 'im down, Chas. We don't wanta run 'em to death."

Pulling on the reins, Charles got the brown horse slowed to a walk, then stopped. Billy reined alongside. Both young men twisted in their saddles and looked back. They saw no one.

At first they only stared at each other. Then Billy grinned. "Gaw-ud damn, Chas, you just cain't seem to keep out of trouble."

Believing they were safe, they got down and loosened their *cinchas*. Billy reached for the makings and rolled a cigarette. When it was half smoked, he stomped on it with a boot heel, tightened the *cinchas* and mounted. Charles did the same. They followed the wagon road, which paralleled the east side of the Rio Grande. For five miles they didn't speak, then Billy said:

"I don't know how far the stage line goes. It might go no further than Socorro."

"Then they went to Socorro."

"Maybe. I don't know. If they go any further south they'll have to ride in a stage or a wagon."

"A wagon?"

"Yeah, hitch a ride with a string of freight wagons or somethin'."

"Surely they wouldn't go all the way to El Paso."

"They might if the railroad goes that far. That's a long ways from Trinidad, and down there nobody'll know about the railroad comin'. If the railroad builds all the way to Chihuahua it'll prob'ly go straight south from Socorro, down the Jornada del Muerto."

"Down the what?"

"The Journey of Death. I've never been over it, but I've heard about it. It's a damned desert. Men and horses have thirsted to death. But they say it's the shortest way to El Paso, and if you follow the river you travel some extra miles and you go over some rough country."

In a mumbling voice, Charles said, "I hope to God we find them in Socorro."

They rode silently the next few miles to the village called Las Lunas. As in nearly all Spanish villages, the biggest, most impressive building was the church. In a *tienda* they bought some tortillas, tinned beef, a small coffee pot and some coffee. Billy asked first in English then in Spanish where the stage coach stopped. They were directed east, away from the river.

The stage relay hostler was Anglo, and when he was asked whether he remembered two men who looked like ranchers going south, he spat a stream of tobacco, stroked a brown beard and said, "I b'lieve I rec'lect a pair like that. 'Bout ten days ago. Looked kinder alike, only one didn't fit his hat quite right."

"Was that one wearing a gray hat?" Charles asked.

Another stream of tobacco juice discolored the thin soil. "Wal, can't recall the color. They didn't get to get out of the coach very long. Don't take long to change teams."

"How far to the next stage stop?"

"It's, oh, 'bout fifteen miles to Belen. They keep the horses movin' right along."

"Can we get something to eat there?"

"Naw. Ol' Luke, feller that runs the outfit, he'll feed somebody that's starvin', but he don't like to cook, and he'd rather they went on down to Socorro."

The wagon road to Belen had seen plenty of traffic, beginning with the Spanish explorers three hundred years earlier, and it was an easy road to travel. They rode past small Mexican farms where hand-dug ditches carried irrigation water from the Rio Grande. The Manzano Mountains and Bosque Peak were far to the east. By dusk they were riding around another plaza and another big adobe church. Like Las Lunas, Belen was a farm village. Two-wheeled carts passed, pulled by single burros.

Most of the men wore sandals on their feet and wide-brim straw hats on their heads. They were used to seeing travelers, and only nodded in greeting.

Billy remarked, "I don't know what they'd do without those donkeys."

"The beasts of burden owe nothing to the human race," Charles commented.

The stage relay station was easy to find. A long sign on the roof of a rock house read CAMINO REAL STAGE AND FREIGHT. The station was close enough to the river that another hand-dug ditch carried water from the river through two corrals. Three freight wagons and a passenger coach were parked under a cottonwood tree, but all the horses were in the corrals, munching hay.

"Hallo-o-o," Billy yelled. They stayed on their horses untll the door in the house opened and a man in overalls and a bill cap came out. "Is this the end of the stage line?" Billy asked.

"Nope. We're still runnin' on down to Socorro."

Again they asked about two men in cattlemen's clothes.

"Weel, git down and rest a spell. I rec'lect them two."

The young men dismounted and kept hold of the bridle reins. "Did they stay here long?" Charles asked.

"Not long." His smooth-shaven, leathery face split into a grin. "Way I heard it they was askin' all over about buyin' land. They thought they was doin' somethin' smart, but they didn't know."

"Excuse me," Charles said, "but we are trying to locate two men named Wyker and Wilkerson. Would you mind telling us what it is that they didn't know?"

The leathery face smiled widely. "They didn't know we know. Hell, we knowed about that railroad since nearly a year ago. It's the Santa Fe comin' from up north. A feller was here 'bout a year ago dickerin' with the merchants."

"The land owners?"

"Them too."

"I'm sorry, I don't understand."

"What that feller did was, he told the merchants the railroad would come through here if they was to give 'em a strip of land for it. Hell, all he had to do was drop his drawers and bend over and them *mercantes* kissed his ass 'til he barked like a fox."

Billy chuckled at the mental picture, but Charles

kept a straight face. "So the merchants are providing a right-of-way?"

"Yep." The smile disappeared. "But right here is where she stops."

"Would you mind explaining that?"

"Do I look like a fool? You think I'm gonna sell 'em some a my land so they can build a railroad through it and put me outa business?"

"Oh, I see. You're in the freight business too."

"You damned betcha. I was haulin' freight down that Chihuahua Road long before they ever heard of a railroad around here."

"I understand. So, I gather then that Mr. Wyker and Mr. Wilkerson went elsewhere?"

"Took the next stage to Socorro."

"Thank you very much for the information."

"Tell you what, gents, I can't stop the railroad, and I might sell 'em some land, but they're sure as hell gonna pay for it."

"I understand."

"I got 'em by the short hairs. They gotta go through here or way around."

"Thank you very much," Charles said again.

As they rode away, Billy chuckled. "Ol' Wyker met his match in this town. Ever'body here was two jumps ahead of 'im."

Charles said, "Let's see if we can find a hotel. It's getting dark."

They didn't find a hotel, but they did find a grassy spot on the east bank of the Rio Grande where they could hobble their horses and build a driftwood fire.

After drinking boiled coffee and eating tinned beef, they rolled up in their blankets and gazed at

162

the sky. "At least it's not raining," Charles said. "I wonder whether we'll ever find Matthew Wyker and his cohort Wilkerson."

"We're gittin' closer to 'em all the time," Billy answered. "They don't know it, but we're on their tails." He had his saddle turned upside down so the sheepskin skirt lining provided a pillow of sorts. Charles copied him, which prompted Billy to say, "That'll get your saddle skirts bent out of shape, but it makes the ground a little softer."

"I do hope we find them in Socorro," Charles said. After a moment of silence he heard a muffled chuckle come from his partner. He asked, "What's so funny?"

"You. I wouldn't a thunk it of you. You flattened that deputy this mornin' like a fritter."

"I never did anything like that before in my life and I'll never do it again."

Still chuckling, Billy said, "I hope you don't ever get mad at me."

"We're lucky the deputy didn't arrest us."

"He prob'ly ain't figured out yet exactly what happened."

"Good night, Billy."

Socorro was destined to become the biggest city in New Mexico—for a time—but now it was another farming village on the Rio Grande, with another plaza and another adobe church. It was also the last stop before the Jornada del Muerto, something the merchants took advantage of.

Here too—the young men soon learned—it was common knowledge that the Santa Fe would come within two years, and the price of land along the right-of-way was too high for speculation.

They learned too that Wyker and Wilkerson had been here and gone on. The pair had been lucky enough to arrange a ride with a string of freight wagons pulled by four-mule teams. They were lucky because the wagons carried barrels of water and there were enough men with repeating rifles to fight off the Indians.

"Indians?" Charles asked.

" 'Paches," said the stage-stop hostler. "Mescaleros. They've got a likin' for white men's scalps and mule meat."

The two young men had been riding all day, but there was still some daylight left. They dismounted on the banks of the Rio Grande a mile south of Socorro and tried to decide what to do next.

"Whatta you think, Chas? I'm willin' to go on. How about you?"

"All the way to El Paso?"

"Yup. You're only a day and a half's ride from Lariat now. You can go back if you want to."

"What will you do?"

"Go on."

"Well, I have much more to gain by catching that . . . that . . ."

"Son of a bitch."

"That son of a bitch than you have. I . . . yes, I'll go on too."

"I don't know this country, but I've heard about it. I think the next town is a place called Las Cruces, and it must be about a hundred miles, dependin' on which way we go. We can either take the short way and go down the desert, or we can foller the river."

"What about the Indians?"

"Wal, you might wish you had a gun, Chas."

Sitting cross-legged on the ground. Charles put his head in his hands and groaned:

"Oh my, oh my."

Nineteen

The *tendero* had them sized up the second they walked across the veranda and entered the adobe mercantile. Travelers, for sure. The riding boots on the strange-looking one and the spurs on the cowboy's boots told him they were horseback travelers. "Canteens?" He smiled. "Sure. Four dollar."

"Four dollars?" Charles said. "Isn't that a bit much?"

"*No, señor.* They are not too many. Without a canteen you will die on the Jornada del Muerto."

Billy grinned. "Told you, Chas. These people can dicker with the best of 'em. We either pay his price or we die."

They paid the price, and they also paid high prices for tins of beef, a stack of tortillas and four tins of tomatoes. Billy talked the *tendero* into including two empty burlap bags. They priced a lever-action rifle too, but Billy shook his head. "Naw. That's more'n I make in two months. I'd like to have it, but hell, it ain't worth that much. Besides, we have to travel light, Chas. Them ol' ponies are gonna have all they can do to carry us."

"Well, considering the fact that I have never fired a gun, one gun—yours—is all we can use."

Mounted again, they rode south, still keeping the

Rio Grande in sight. "I can't believe I'm doing this," Charles said. "I've been living on this horse for so long I feel as though I'm part of him, and now here I go again on another long journey."

"Aw, this trail got its name a long time ago, before Socorro and Las Cruces was born. You cain't thirst to death in two or three days. It ain't us we have to worry about, it's these horses. You cain't carry enough water to feed a horse."

"How much water does it take to quench the thirst of a horse?"

"A horse'll drink five gallons at a time if he's hot and thirsty. Then he'll come back later and drink some more."

"You're right, we can't carry that much."

"Let's foller this river 'til it turns the wrong direction."

That's what they did. The sun beat them over the head. On their left, heat waves shimmered across a barren plain. The horses tried to slow to a walk, but Billy insisted that they keep to a slow trot. "We'll have water tonight," he said. "Tomorrow is when we'll all get bone tired."

Where the Rio Grande entered the San Mateo Mountains and angled to the southwest, they dismounted in the shade of the only tree in sight. The river was wide and shallow here, and circles of rocks with fire-blackened sticks in the center indicated that others had camped here. Billy loosened the *cinchas* and led his horse to the river. Charles followed suit.

Squinting to the southwest along the river, Billy saw steep banks, treeless rocky hills and deep arroyos. Farther ahead were higher hills spotted with scrub oak and junipers. Canyons split off into two

167

directions. He pointed a forefinger and said, "There's got to be a trail through there, but you can see we'd have to do some climbin'."

"So you think it would be better to travel on the desert?"

"Yeah." Glancing at the sun, Billy added, "Maybe we'd best camp here tonight, drink our fill in the mornin' and start down that Chihuahua Road. Maybe we can make it to Las Cruces in two days."

"Chihuahua Road? I thought it was called the Jornada del Muerto? Or the Camino Real?"

"Aw, they call it ever'thing. Mostly *chingao*."

Billy walked downstream, spurs ringing, looking for a place to hobble the horses. Not until he was out of sight of Charles and the river did he find enough bunch grass for the horses to graze on. When he went back for the horses he found Charles stripped to his undershorts and standing in the river. Brown water swirled around his knees. "Wal," Billy allowed, "I reckon that's one way to cool off."

"It's dirty, but it's cool," Charles said.

By then the sun was sitting on the highest peak to the west, and Billy said, "It'll cool down purty soon. You'd be surprised at how cold it can get at night."

Charles was splashing like a child. He yelled at Billy, "I hope no one else comes along."

"You're safe enough."

Billy untied the blanket rolls and saddlebags and dropped them on the ground, then mounted the gray horse and led the other to the spot he'd picked out. There, he pulled the saddles off and hobbled the horses with the empty burlap sacks he'd brought. The horses immediately put their heads down and started grazing, but Billy had learned from hard experience that horses can go too far with only their forefeet hobbled, so he hunkered down against a low sandstone ledge to watch them. He rolled a smoke, leaned back and let the smoke dribble out of the side of his mouth. The sun had gone down now, and the air was cooling. This was a good spot. It was pleasant. That smoke finished, he rolled another, struck a match and put fire to it.

He heard Charles scream.

As the sun went down, Charles waded out of the water and stood in his shorts until the air dried him off. How fine it was to be able to stand nearly naked out in the open air where no one would see him. He hoped no one would see him. Did something move over there across the river? He watched, eyes fixed on a short bush. Couldn't be. Nothing bigger than a rabbit could hide behind that. Just the same, he dressed hurriedly, now feeling as though he was being watched.

He was sitting on the ground, pulling his boots on when he saw them. Where did they come from? And who were they? There were five. Four men and a woman. An old woman. Were they Mexicans? They just stood there, watching him. The men carried long-barreled rifles, but the guns weren't pointed at him. Yes, they were Mexicans. They had to be. After all, they were dressed in ordinary clothes, shirts and pants and leather belts. But, my God, their greasy black hair hung down their backs like horse tails, and they had moccasins on their feet. And no hats. Mexicans wore hats.

Smiling nervously, Charles said, "How do you do."

169

They only stared at him. He tried again, "Beautiful evening, isn't it?"

One of them spoke in a language Charles didn't understand. The woman stood to one side, watching Charles with eyes as black as sin. She looked to be a hundred years old, with a face as wrinkled as a prune. Coarse, stringy hair with gray streaks in it hung down her back to her waist. Her long dress was calico, dirty, ragged.

Though they had made no threatening moves, fear was building in Charles. He tried again to communicate. "Uh, it's obvious we don't speak each other's language, but I hope we can be friends."

The men began talking among themselves. One of them pointed at Charles and laughed. Charles tried to laugh with him, but all that came out was a scared titter.

He wondered where Billy was. He wondered if he could get away. Perhaps if he just walked away they would leave him alone. Which way did Billy go? South. He'd taken the horses south. All right, move cautiously. No, that wasn't the way to do it. He should move as though he was going somewhere and had no doubt that he would get there. Don't let them see fear.

"It was nice meeting you." He turned and started walking south.

With movements so swift that Charles was taken by surprise, two of the men were in front of him. The other two were behind him.

"What . . . ?" Fear filled Charles's throat and choked off his voice. Then, when one pointed a rifle at him and another drew a long-bladed knife, he tried to bolt.

But strong hands grabbed him by the arms and pinned his arms to his sides. Another hand grabbed his hair, forcing his head back so far he thought his neck would snap. He tried to yell, but all that came out was a gurgle. With one man on each side of him now, holding his arms, he was dragged backwards by the hair. He was dragged to the lone tree. His arms were pulled back, painfully. His hands were tied behind him around the tree. He couldn't move.

Charles tried. He kicked, bent his knees, but could do nothing more. He stopped struggling when the long knife was pointed at his throat. The man holding it barked something at him and put the point of the blade against his adam's apple. Afraid to breathe, Charles stared at the blade until his eyes crossed. A whimper came out of him.

These were Indians. Probably the terrible Apaches he'd read about. They were cruel, and they hated white people.

One of the men picked up the derby hat where it had fallen from Charles's head and put it on his own head. Another pointed at him and laughed. The woman began gathering brush and stacking it at Charles's feet. Then another picked up the two saddlebags and blanket rolls. He went through the saddle bags, pulled out a tin of beef, turned it over in his hands and smelled it. Not knowing what it was, he dropped it and pulled out a stack of tortillas.

But before he could take a bite, another Indian pointed at the hoof tracks, grunted and held up two fingers. The men checked the breeching on their long rifles, then began following the tracks downstream.

That was when Charles yelled as loud as he could—screamed, rather:

"Billy, look out!"

Billy Johnson knew what was wrong the second he heard Charles scream. Instantly, he grabbed bridles and ran to the horses. The Apaches would see the tracks and the sign of two men and they would be looking for him. He didn't know how many there were, but he knew it would be better for him and Charles if they didn't catch him. But he was afraid he wouldn't have time to saddle the horses, so he jumped on the gray bareback and, leading Charles's horse, took off at a gallop down the river.

Hooves clattering on the rocks, the horses picked their way as fast as they could over rough ground, around a shale outcrop and over a small rise. The river had cut through the higher ground here, leaving a steep bank. Billy slid the horses down the bank into the water. Once across the river he reined up and looked back. One Indian was running after him. Only one, but Billy knew that one was the front-runner. There would be more behind him.

Holding both pairs of bridle reins in his left hand, Billy drew the Remington and fired. The pistol bucked in his hand, and the shot echoed among the hills.

The Apache wasn't hit. He stopped and threw the long-barreled rifle to his shoulder. Billy touched spurs to the gray again and took off on a high lope. He heard the rifle fire and a lead slug whistle close to his right ear. Over the broken shards of shale he rode, through the manzanitas and around another small bend in the river. When he looked back again it was too dark to tell whether he was being pursued. Maybe yes, maybe no. The Apache he'd shot at was afoot. He wouldn't chase a man on horseback very far. Were the others horseback by now? He'd soon know.

On foot the Indians could sneak up on him in the dark. On horseback they couldn't. They could creep up on him like a cougar stalks a deer, but only if they knew where he was. The Indian who was chasing him on foot knew about where he was. He had to move. But, then, if he moved, they'd hear him.

Billy slid off the horse. The gray horse would be easy to see in the light of a half-moon. A man on the horse would be an easy target. He hunkered down beside the horse, the Remington in his hand. He listened.

If they were after him they were on foot, their moccasined feet making no sound at all. He listened, strained to see in the dark and waited.

He knew how the Apaches had surprised Charles. A damned Indian could make himself almost invisible. If there was anything at all to hide behind, a damned Indian could make himself look like part of it. Charles wouldn't have been watching. He was easy.

What were they doing to Charles now? An Apache's favorite kind of fun was torturing prisoners of war. They'd get around to it before long. No doubt about that.

Thinking of that gave Billy a strong urge to go back. Immediately. But he couldn't. He'd be no good to Charles if he was killed or captured himself. And if he rode or led the horses back he'd be heard.

He waited. Listened.

The urgency was becoming painful now. They could be eating the chuck that was in the saddlebags and anticipating the fun they were going to have. He could wait no longer.

This time Billy crawled onto the brown horse. The brown wouldn't be so easy to see in the moonlight. Not knowing the country, he had no choice but to follow the same route back to where he'd left the saddles. The Indians could be waiting for him. He rode at a slow walk, leading the gray. The river was clearly visible, a silvery but dirty crooked line among the rocky hills. But the hills themselves were dark, the bushes invisible. The Apaches would be invisible. Breathing shallow breaths, he rode. An Apache could be anywhere — in front of him, behind him or beside him. His throat could be slit before he saw or heard anything.

He winced every time a hoof thudded on a rock, every time a horse blew through its nose. Every muscle, every nerve taut, every sense straining, the Remington in his hand, Billy rode in the night.

Twenty

The four men came back to where Charles was tied to a tree. The woman had piled brush at his feet and was now piling brush on the edge of the river. One of the men took a small box of sulfur matches from a shirt pocket and set fire to the second pile.

Indians aren't supposed to have matches, Charles thought. They're supposed to start fires by striking two rocks together or rubbing sticks or something like that. And where did they get those clothes? The U.S. government was supplying clothes to the Indians on the reservations. Were those garments government issue?

Or—Charles gulped when he thought about it—did they murder some white people and strip the bodies? And who are these Indians? Why aren't they on a reservation somewhere? Again, he gulped when the answer came to him. They had to be renegades who had escaped from a reservation.

Now they were eating the tortillas and drinking from the canteens. They kept glancing at him and grinning evil grins. Charles struggled with his bonds, but it was useless. The more he struggled, the tighter the bonds became. The more it hurt.

The pile of brush at his feet could mean only one thing. Unless a miracle happened, he was going to be burned to death. Burned alive. Sniffing back a tear, he wondered whether he could keep from screaming when it happened. He decided he would do his best to be quiet.

Billy let his breath out with a whoosh when he got back to where he'd left the saddles. It was unbelievable. They could have killed him anywhere along the way back.

Hastily, fumbling in the pale moonlight, he saddled the two horses and tied them to a manzanita bush. Then he tried to imitate an Indian and creep back to where he'd last seen Charles. The spurs. Too noisy. Squatting, he took them off, buckled them together and hung them over the saddle horn on the gray. Then he started off again.

Right now, moccasins would be better than riding boots, but he had no moccasins and he couldn't walk barefoot over the rocks. Slowly, putting each foot down carefully, he made his way upstream. Once, when his ankle turned on a rock, he stopped dead. Listened. He heard voices. Apache voices. They were not excited. Talking in normal tones. All right, another step. Another.

Now he could see the firelight. He wished he were in the higher mountains where there were trees to hide behind. Nothing to hide behind here. Bending low, he moved closer. There were five of them. Four bucks and a squaw. Wearing white people's clothes. Eating the tortillas. Chas was tied to the tree, looking like a man about to be hung. Was there another redskin keeping watch from a dark spot? If not, there ought to be. Apaches weren't that dumb.

Billy dropped to a squatting position and looked nervously around him. Nervously and fearfully. Studied every spot the moonlight didn't reach. There had to be an Indian somewhere near.

The five around the fire sure weren't afraid of anything. They were gulping the tortillas down like dogs, paying attention to nothing else. Soon they would have their bellies full and then they would have their fun.

Squatting in the dark, Billy tried to figure out a plan. Maybe they didn't have a guard out. They knew by the tracks that only two white men had come here, and one had run. Maybe they thought that one was still running and they had nothing to fear. The Apaches were wily, tricky, smart, but they had been known to make mistakes. They weren't perfect.

As he watched, one of the bucks stood and waded across the river. Where was he going? Did they have horses over there somewhere? Apaches could walk a couple hundred miles, but they'd rather ride. Yeah, they had horses over there. That gave Billy an idea.

He'd have to move without making a sound. He'd have to be able to see in the dark. He'd have to out-Indian the Indians.

Slowly, he stood and made his way to the river's edge. In the water, in the moonlight, he'd be easy to see. He had to chance it. Bending low, so low his face was only inches from the water, he waded across the Rio Grande. On the other side, he found a black spot under a cut bank and sat. Under his breath he muttered, "Be still, fool heart. Stop that hammerin'." Then he added, "Not too still, though."

Now to find the horses.

Keeping low, careful, he moved in the direction the one Indian had gone. If he could get close to the horses, their movements would hide the sound of his. He crept, listened, crept again, stopped, listened.

He heard them. First it was the fluttering sound horses make when they clear their nostrils, then it was a hoof thumping the ground. Billy moved closer. He counted five. Hobbled the way white men hobble horses. Where was the Indian who'd come to check on them? Uh-oh.

The Indian was walking back to the river, satisfied that the horses were still there. Billy watched from the black cover of a manzanita's leathery leaves as the Indian splashed across the water.

"Whew," he said under his breath. "Now to get those hobbles off."

They had finished their meal and were looking at Charles. The one who'd left was back. The woman stood and came his way. Charles felt his stomach go hollow with fear. His throat tightened. His knees trembled. She walked up to him, grabbed his hair and forced his head back. She spat in his face. As spittle ran down his face, into his mouth, he was too scared to be angry. He was going to die. His mind said, Oh, please don't. But he kept his mouth shut. Clamped tight. He was determined to keep it that way.

The woman went back to the fire and said something. One of the men handed her a knife. The long blade glinted in the firelight. She turned back to him. Keep quiet, he said to himself. Die with dignity. Keep your mouth shut.

Then the ruckus began.

The Indians jumped up and looked into the darkness across the river. They jabbered, then they ran, ran into the water.

What was it? Horses? Yes, horses running.

The woman stopped in her tracks and watched the men disappear into the dark across the water. She watched for a long moment. Suddenly her eyes widened and she let out a screech. A man appeared. The man ran to the woman and clubbed her over the head. Clubbed her twice. She fell. The man holstered a pistol, grabbed the knife from her hand and was behind the tree, slicing the bonds that bound Charles.

"Come on, partner," Billy said. "Let's vamoose."

Hastily, Billy gathered what he could of their supplies and stuffed them into the saddlebags. He slung the bags over his shoulders and picked up the two blanket rolls. It took only thirty seconds for Billy to pick up everything, but it seemed like thirty minutes to Charles. He wanted to run immediately.

Billy whispered, "Where we're goin' we'd die without this." Charles understood.

They ran in the dark, Billy leading the way and Charles following his footsteps. The gray horse was the first thing they saw. No longer whispering, Billy said, "They're saddled. Get on your horse and let's lope." By feel, Charles untied the reins and climbed into the saddle. Billy handed him a pair of saddlebags and said, "Throw 'em across the fork of your saddle for now. We'll tie 'em on later." Then they were riding, trusting to the horses' good night vision to find a way.

179

It would be dangerous to run the horses in strange rough country where there was no trail, but Billy kept the gray horse trotting where the ground was fairly level. The brown horse followed. Charles asked, "Where are we going?"

"I don't know. Down hill. Out of these hills. The hell away from here."

"Will they chase us?"

"I don't know. I hope they'll spend the rest of the night chasin' their own horses, but I don't know."

"You hit that woman awfully hard."

"Don't feel sorry for her. She was fixin' to cut your pecker off and feed it to you."

"I thought I was going to die."

"You're alive. Let's stay alive."

The horses clattered over the rocks, dipped into shallow arroyos, climbed, slid down low bluffs and were finally on the desert. In the moonlight Billy and Charles could see the country rise into a high dark blob behind them. Nothing but blackness lay ahead. Billy let his horse run a few minutes, then slowed to a walk.

They rode silently. At times the horses' hoofbeats were muffled by soft dirt, and at times they thudded on hard sunbaked earth.

"I want to thank you, Billy."

"Por nada."

"Pardon?"

"It's nothing. It's what partners are for."

"Just the same, you—"

Billy cut him off—*"Nada"*—and Charles got the message: Billy didn't want to be thanked. But Charles had to ask, "You're not mad at me, are you?"

"Naw. It coulda happened to me. Hell, I was half

asleep when I heard you holler. They coulda snuck up on me."

An hour later, Billy stopped and got down. "I don't know exactly where we are and I sure don't wanta get lost on this desert. We'd better stay here 'til daylight."

They unsaddled and hobbled the horses, and Billy said, "I hope they can find somethin' to eat. They've got a hard trail ahead of 'em."

"You rescued our canteens. Thank heavens for that."

"Them damned 'Paches drank some of our water. We're gonna get thirsty, but like I said, it's gonna be harder on the horses."

"Yes." Charles felt like saying he'd be very glad when they reached their destination, but he realized that that was something a child would say. Instead he said, "Well, I'm going to try to get some shut-eye."

"Good idee."

The horses found very little to eat, and by daylight they were standing still with their heads down. The rubbery manzanita leaves and the white manzanita flowers could provide some sustenance to a starving animal, but these two horses weren't starving yet.

With daylight came the realization that the two partners were far from water, firewood or anything else. Dim wagon tracks pointed almost straight south. The hills they had just left and the mountains farther away loomed dark and mysterious in the early-morning light. Nothing but cactus and a few yucca was in sight to the east.

Charles started to mention breakfast, but decided against it. Let Billy mention it first. Billy did. "Let's eat some of that tinned beef and save the tomaters for later. There's juice in those tomater cans, and that's somethin' we're gonna need."

Saddled and mounted, he said, "Let's keep these ol' ponies on a slow trot for a ways while it's cool. The sooner we get off this desert, the better." They rode in silence, the horses settled into a shuffling trot. Charles's throat was so dry it was becoming painful, but he was determined not to complain. When the sun appeared it popped up on the eastern horizon, and within minutes they could feel the heat from it. Heat waves shimmered ahead.

"Looks like a big lake, don't it?" Billy said.

"Yes. I've read about desert mirages."

"That's what it is. And those mountains way over east, they look like they're only a few miles away, don't they."

"Yes."

"I'll bet you could ride all day and not get anywhere near 'em."

For the next two hours only the hoofbeats broke the silence. The ground repeatedly changed from soft dirt to hardpan. Charles counted four varieties of cacti and some sparse bunchgrass.

When he heard the buzzing off to his right he knew immediately what it was. He'd heard a rattlesnake before. This one wasn't as big as the one he'd seen up north, but it was coiled and ready to strike if anything came too close. The riders stayed away from it.

The sun was like a club, beating them over the head. Billy said, "I saw one a them bucks wearin' your hat. You gotta put somethin' on your head." He reined up and got down. "Here, hang one a these gunnysacks on you." He handed Charles one of the sacks he used to hobble the horses. Charles put it on. It helped. "How tight is your cinch? Let's leave 'em as loose as we can. Try to let some air under the saddles." Charles got down and loosened his cinch. "Put your knee against that ol' pony's shoulder when you get on, and pull yourself up with your arms 'stead of puttin' your weight on the stirrup. Maybe your saddle won't turn."

Charles did as advised, and found it an easier, smoother way to mount a horse.

When the sun was in the middle of the sky, they stopped. Charles almost fell when he dismounted. He groaned. "I feel like a piece of old dried leather."

"Yeah, I'd take a pee, but I'm so dry I don't think there's any in me. Time for them tomaters." First they unsaddled to give the horses as much rest as possible. Charles pulled up a handful of brown bunchgrass and tried to get his horse to eat it. The animal put its upper lip on it, then let if fall to the ground. "Poor beast," Charles said. "I'm sorry, my friend."

The tomatoes partially quenched the men's thirst and partially satisfied their hunger. Only partially. Feeling dissatisfied, they saddled up and rode on. As they rode, Charles was sorry for himself. He'd been bitten by a rattlesnake, chased by Indians, beaten in a saloon, made witness to a near hanging, captured and nearly tortured by Indians, and now he was trying to cross a desert. The Jornada del Muerto.

The journey of death.

Twenty-one

Sometime that afternoon the horses hooves clattered on a solid sheet of rock. A lava flow, Charles reckoned. Molten rock had spewed out of a fissure in the earth somewhere near and, instead of piling up, had spread across the desert. Thousands of years ago. On they went, the horses traveling at a walk now. The sun beating on them. Ahead was what looked like a small tree. Shade. Protection from the sun. But as they rode closer it turned out to be a bush with few leaves.

"Creosote," Billy said. "A cattleman's enemy. No grass can grow close to it."

A small cottontail rabbit ran from under the bush and stopped under a cholla cactus. "Coyote bait," Billy said.

Charles was slumped in his saddle, feeling dehydrated, weary to the point of falling off. Then he looked up, straightened up. "What's that?" He pointed to a tall spiral of dust moving swiftly toward them.

"Dust devil."

"It's coming our way."

"We cain't outrun it. Just keep your eyes and mouth shut."

Like a small tornado, the spiral struck. Shrieking.

The sack was blown off Charles's head, and his hair was filled with dirt. His shirt was filled with dirt. His ears were filled with dirt. Then it was gone. He started to say something about it, but changed his mind and instead dismounted and went after the gunnysack.

Billy tried to joke. "After eatin' all that dirt, Chas, you cain't be hungry."

"It's not very good for the digestive system."

Straightening in his saddle, Billy removed his hat, beat the dirt off it against his right knee and said, "Yeah, I reckon it ain't."

The relentless sun seemed to move painfully slow across the sky, but eventually it sat on the mountains far to the west. No sooner had it disappeared than the air turned cooler. It was refreshing. But not enough to relieve the thirst. They found a spot of hardpan ground where a few clumps of grass had survived the desert, and camped for the night. They washed down the last of their tinned beef and tortillas with a few swallows of warm water from their canteens. The horses were too thirsty to eat, and only nibbled at the grass.

Lying on the blankets, covered with another blanket, the two young men looked up at the stars, each with his own thoughts. It was quiet. The wind was still. Nothing moved.

Then the racket started.

At first it was only one, in a high-pitched, weird tone, going, "Whoo-hoo-hoo." Another joined in, then another. Soon they were making as much noise as a class of kids getting out of school.

"What . . . ?"

"Only coyotes."

"They're harmless, aren't they?"

"Yup."

"Will they bother the horses?"

"Naw. A coyote won't jump anything bigger'n he is."

The racket went on, like a dozen people laughing hysterically. The coyotes were close, but invisible in the dark. Dangerous or not, they gave Charles the shivers.

"I like to hear 'em," Billy said. "They're wild, really wild. They're hell on sheep, I reckon, but they don't bother a cattleman much."

"They never bother cattle?"

"Oh, maybe when a calf first hits the ground and the cow is too weak to get up."

"Hits the ground?"

"Borned."

"Oh. Sounds like a hundred of them."

"Three or four pups can sound like a hundred."

"Do they attack in packs?"

"Wal, they don't run in packs, but what draws one might draw some others. Sometimes at night they get together to palaver, like they're doin' now."

"You like to hear them?"

"Yup. They're free. Really free."

Charles listened. The wild, hysterical racket went on, stopped for a moment, then resumed. Now that he was assured that they were harmless, he listened with interest.

Eventually, the coyotes had communicated enough and went their separate ways. Charles lay covered with a blanket, fully dressed except for his boots, his head on his upside-down saddle. In spite of the hunger and thirst, he dozed. He dreamed of a rattle-

186

snake, coiled, ready to strike. He could visualize it slithering along the ground. He awoke with a start.

Something was moving next to his right hand.

Was he merely imagining it? No, there it was again, just a gentle nudge. Charles froze. It moved again, soundless. Now it was crawling onto his hand. Charles tried to whisper for Billy, but fear had his voice choked off. He was afraid to breathe.

It crawled up his arm to his elbow. It wasn't a snake. A spider? Felt like a spider. A huge spider. Poisonous? Everything on the damned desert was poisonous. Still crawling—walking, rather—with what felt like a hundred tiny feet, it continued up to his shoulder. Then his neck.

Charles had to hold his breath to keep from whimpering. Oh, my God. It was on his face. The tiny feet walked onto his right cheek.

Don't move, he told himself. Don't breathe.

It was on his forehead.

Charles couldn't hold his breath any longer. Rigid with fear, he lay there. He felt the thing move again—to the top of his head. In his mind he pleaded, Oh, please, please go away. His heart pounded. If he didn't die of venom he'd die of heart failure.

Was it gone? He couldn't feel it. His breath came out in a whoosh. Did he dare get up? No, it was still there somewhere.

For two hours Charles suffered with fear. It seemed like forever. Billy lay quietly, apparently sleeping. What could Billy do, anyway? Nothing in the dark.

The desert gradually turned lighter. Moving only his eyes, Charles saw the mountains far to the east, across endless miles of nothing. A cholla nearby was only a dark blob at first, but slowly took form. Billy stirred. Charles whispered, "Billy."

"Huh? Whatsa matter?" Billy sat up. "Somethin' the matter?"

Still whispering, Charles said, "I think there's a spider near my head."

"Uh-oh. Be still, Chas. Don't move a muscle." Slowly, Billy stood. "Don't move, now." Barefoot, he walked carefully around Charles, circled him, staying a good distance away. "You say it's near your head?"

"Yes. Can you see it?"

"No. Yeah, there it is. Don't move, Chas."

"W-what is it?"

"A t'rantler. A big sumbitch."

"Oh, my God. Oh God."

"Here's what to do, Chas. Don't move just yet. Stay as still as a rock. Now then, when I holler, you jump up. Jump up as fast as you ever jumped in your life."

"W-what will it do?"

"It cain't reach more'n a couple inches, but it's right next to your shoulder. When I holler, get the hell up from there. *Sabe?*"

"Y-yes."

"All right, now. Get ready. Jump!"

With a shriek, Charles was up. He took two steps and fell onto his hands and knees. He jumped up immediately, turned and looked back. Billy took hold of a corner of the blanket and yanked.

"Gaw-ud damn. That sumbitch is bigger'n my hand."

"It . . . it's a what? A tarantula?"

188

"It sure as hell is. A big, black, hairy sumbitch. How long's that thing been there?"

"A long time."

"How in hell did you stand it? I'd of been so scared I'd of wet my britches."

"I was scared. Why would it crawl on me?"

"Who knows? They like to walk on people. It must of liked the feel of your hide."

"Are they poison?"

"I've heard of people dyin' from a t'rantler bite. We gotta kill that sumbitch."

Looking around, Billy said, "Wouldn't you know it, not a rock or anything. And I ain't about to stomp it with my bare feet."

Billy picked up his cartridge belt and buckled it on. He squinted for a second down the short barrel of the Remington and fired. The boom shattered the desert stillness. It also shattered the spider.

"Do you think there might be another one nearby?"

"Don't know. Shake your boots out before you put 'em on, and watch where you sit."

Charles watched. While they ate a can of tomatoes and drank the juice, he kept his eyes busy, watching. Not until they were horseback did he look at anything other than the ground. My God, what desolate terrain. Nothing but cacti and creosote bushes for miles and miles. Mountains on each side of them, but so far away.

The horses were weak, unable to travel any faster than a slow walk. "The poor beasts," Charles said. "Do you think we'll reach civilization by nightfall, Billy?"

"We ought to."

189

The sun was cruel. Even with the burlap bag over
his head and shoulders, Charles could feel the heat.
The heat and the pressure. When a strange-looking
froglike creature scurried out of their way, he didn't
even ask what it was. Billy told him anyway.
"Horned toad. A snake's favorite dinner."

Revolting.

At noon they dismounted and unsaddled. Billy
used one of the burlap bags to wipe sweat from the
horses' backs. "If there was any kind of breeze," he
allowed, "I'd leave 'em wet. But that sun might blis-
ter a wet back."

"Is there anything left in your canteen?"

"Naw. All we got left is one can of tomaters. You
eat it, Chas. I feel pretty strong."

"Oh no. We'll share it."

"Naw, you eat it."

"Absolutely not. It's share and share alike."

"You sure?"

"Positive."

"Wal, you eat and drink what you want of it and
I'll take the rest."

Charles was careful to eat and drink only half of
what was in the can. Billy made quick work of what
was left. They saddled up and mounted, keeping on
a southerly course. The sun pounded them. Their
throats were painfully dry, their stomachs painfully
empty. The horses plodded along, heads down.

This was what hell had to be like. Hell on humans, horses, anything that wasn't born to the desert. Hell on them too. Always afraid of being killed
and eaten by other creatures.

Billy mumbled around a dry tongue, "Maybe you ain't noticed it, but them hills over west are comin' closer."

"What . . . ?" Talking was painful. "Does that mean — ?"

"We're gettin' closer to water."

"But . . . they're still so far."

By midafternoon they were seeing more green mesquite bushes. And they seemed to be heading toward a junction with the mountains. Another range of mountains was in sight on the east. Billy pointed straight ahead. "Down there somewhere. Won't be long."

"Thank heavens."

Now they were following dim trails through the mesquites. There were a few small strange-looking trees with pods shaped like screws. Charles was curious about them, but it took too much energy to ask. Billy mumbled, "Must be tornillo trees."

The sun was nearing the horizon, spreading a streak of red across the top of the mountains where it reflected off a thin cloud. The horses were still plodding. Charles was slumped in his saddle, feeling only half alive. Then gradually, the brown horse walked a little faster. Billy's gray horse had its head up, ears twitching.

"They smell water," Billy said.

Then they broke out of the mesquites and saw a beautiful irrigated green field ahead. "Yonder she is."

They found a narrow road between two fields, and when they came to an irrigation ditch they stopped to let the horses drink. "Not too much," Billy said. "Don't let 'em founder." After about ten seconds he pulled the gray horse's head up. "We'll let 'em drink

191

again at the river." Charles had to pull hard on the reins to get the brown horse's head up. As they rode on, they saw a Mexican in a big straw hat hoeing in a field. He straightened up, leaned on his hoe and watched them pass. Billy waved. He waved back.

Most of the trees along the river had been cut down for building material, but the few remaining spread welcoming shade for the travelers. On the edge of the Rio Grande, Billy dropped onto his belly, put his face in the muddy water and drank. His horse almost stepped on him, getting its lips in the water. Charles was so hot and thirsty he waded into the shallow stream, dropped to his knees and scooped water into his mouth with his hands, slurping like a hog.

Finally, he stood, let out a long sigh of satisfaction and said, "As dirty as it is, nothing ever tasted better."

Grinning, Billy said, "A little clean dirt never hurt nobody." He pulled his horse out of the water, promising, "I'll let you drink some more in a little while." Charles did likewise.

Feeling as though they had been revived from near death, they sat in the shade of a cottonwood while the horses busied themselves cropping the green grass. After a while, Billy said, "Wal, whatta you think, Chas? Would you do it again?"

"Wal—I mean well—not today, if you don't mind."

"Soon's we rest a while, we're gonna have to go find some chuck."

"There's a village over there. I wonder if that's Las Cruces."

"Don't know." Billy stood. "Much as I hate to walk, Chas, I'll leave the horses here with you and

192

go see what I can see." He unbuckled his spurs. "Might take the saddles off and lead the horses to water again in a little while. I'd do it, but I wanta get over there before dark."

"I will."

After Billy walked away down a pair of wagon ruts, Charles unsaddled both horses and led them to water. He took another long drink himself. He'd seen his partner hobble the horses more times than he could remember, but he didn't know how to do it himself. Silently he cursed. What kind of man am I? I've been traveling on horseback and camping out all this time and I haven't even tried to learn how to do things. I've let Billy do it all. Well, by gosh, I might not do it right, but I'm going to try.

He hobbled the brown horse first. Let's see now, wrap the middle of this bag around the right foreleg, low, close to the ankle, twist it a few times and tie the ends around the left foreleg. There. He stood back and looked at his work. Did he leave too much space between the animal's legs? Yes, probably he did. The horse could still walk. He untied the ends of the sack, gave the middle a few more twists and retied it. Now. Yes, that looks better. The twists between the legs will keep it snug. He hobbled the gray horse. Both animals were so busy cropping the grass they didn't care what he did as long as he let them eat.

Just before it was too dark to see, Billy came back, carrying a load. He dropped a flour sack about a quarter full, then he put down a gallon lard can. "That ain't Las Cruces," he said. "It's called

Doña Ana. There ain't no hotel or cafe, but I met a Mexican who sold me ever'thing we need." He prodded the flour sack with a boot toe. "That's oats for the horses, and in this here can I've got some tortillas and beans that're still warm."

He poured two small piles of grain on the grass for the horses and put the remainder under the tree. "Cain't feed 'em too much at a time. They'll founder. But me, I'm gonna founder myself right now." He opened the lid of the can and pulled out a stack of tortillas The bottom half of the can was filled with red beans in a thick gravy.

"I'll wash our forks."

"Naw. What you do is you spread some beans on one a these fritters, then you roll it up and you start eatin' on one end and chaw your way to the other."

They ate, sitting in the dark under the tree. Charles said, "Delicious."

"Ain't no better cooks than these Mexicans. They can make a meal out of anything."

"Billy, I apologize for asking so many questions, but—"

" 'Sall right. As my ol' Pop usta say, people that ask questions learn things."

"Yes, I was wondering, you mentioned twice that the horses could founder, and I was wondering what you meant. Is it important?"

"You betcha." Swallowing a mouthful, Billy said, "It's a sickness horses get when they drink too much water when they're hot, or when they eat too much rich feed, or, wal . . . lots of things can cause founder. It makes 'em sore-footed. 'Specially the forefeet. If they're foundered bad they never get over it."

194

"Oh. So you can't just give a hungry horse a bucket of grain and expect it to be well fed."

"Good Lord, no. He'd founder for sure on that much grain. Besides, a horse has to have grass or hay or somethin' to munch on. He cain't live on grain."

"Oh."

Stomachs filled, they lay on the ground under the tree. "The hombre I bought this stuff from, he said his brother owns this land, but he don't mind if we spend the night here. He said Las Cruces is only a few miles on down the river, and there's a hotel and a cafe there. What we oughta do, Chas, is go on to Las Cruces in the mornin' and hole up there for a day or two. Let these ol' ponies rest. Then it oughta be an easy day's ride on down to El Paso."

"Uh-huh. You don't think the horses will get enough rest tonight?"

"Don't think so. That's another thing you oughta know about horses. They can go a lot further before they get tired than a man can, but when a horse gets tired it takes 'im a few days on good feed to rest up."

"Oh, I see."

"That's why you need a lot of horses to mount a crew of cowboys. I've had as many as ten I was ridin'."

"I'm learning, Billy. Were it not for you I would have had to give up in Denver."

"When we're in the cities, I have to learn from you."

Silence. The horses grazed contentedly. The night breeze rustled the tree leaves. Then Charles said, "Do you think we'll find him now?"

195

"I'd bet my saddle on it. I can feel it in my bones."

"Yeah—I mean yes—I think so too. I think we're finally going to catch up with that . . . that . . ."

"*Chingao* sumbitch."

"Yeah, that sumbitch."

Twenty-two

Breakfast was cold tortillas washed down with river water. The horses were still weary, but they walked faster than they had the day before. Without stopping, the two young men rode through the village of Doña Ana, following the river past irrigated fields of corn, beans, chiles and pumpkins. The Rio Grande was on one side of the fields and mesquites were on the other. They met burro carts and saw farmers working the fields barefoot, pant legs rolled up. At midmorning they rode into Las Cruces.

"Me, I wanta throw my lip over a mess of bacon and eggs," Billy said. "After that, who knows—I might even take a bath."

"I'll agree to that." Charles said.

The town had the usual plaza and church. Most of the houses were adobe with cottonwood vigas holding up flat adobe roofs. A long one-story building sported a hand-painted sign over the door: HOTEL. Next door was another sign reading CAFE.

Billy's Spanish almost failed him when they hailed a man in sandals, baggy gray clothes and a huge straw hat. The man shrugged. *"No sé, señor."*

"Wal, uh, *caballos,* uh, *heno, donde?"*

A weak smile, but another shrug. Billy tried again. "Uh, *comer, heno, caballos, donde?"*

197

Recognition came over the brown face, and the man smiled broadly. He pointed east. They turned east and soon saw a series of pens made of cut mesquite trunks tied together vertically. The man who watched them approach wore riding boots, denim pants and a wide-brim straw hat. He had the brown face and thick dark hair of a Mexican. Billy said, "*Buenos días.*"

"Mornin'. Where'd you two come from?"

Pleased to hear English spoken, Billy said, "Down the desert from Socorro. Stopped last night on the other side of Doña Ana."

"You're lookin' a little gant, all four of you. Light. I've got some good hay and grain, two bits a day. You can fill your own stomachs at that cafe over there, and the beds in the hotel ain't bad." Grinning, he added, "They wash the linens every few weeks."

Charles and Billy ate, bathed and shaved. There was no laundry in town, so Charles washed his clothes the best he could with a borrowed wash board in a galvanized tub. Billy learned that El Paso was only a day's ride south. Just follow the river.

Thick adobe walls kept the room cool. The mattress was lumpy, but it was comfortable by comparison to the ground. They napped.

As the county seat of Doña Ana County, Las Cruces had a two-room courthouse. When his clothes dried, Charles checked the records for evidence of recent land sales. There were none. The county clerk was Mexican, but she spoke fairly good English. No, she had not heard of the Santa Fe railroad. She had heard of a railroad coming from the east to El Paso.

"From the east?"

"*Sí.* Yes. That is what I hear."

198

"Do you happen to know from where in the east?"

"*No, señor.* I don know."

Later, to Billy, Charles said, "Apparently no one here has heard of the Santa Fe railroad building south, but they have heard of another railroad building from somewhere in Texas to El Paso."

"In a few years there's gonna be railroads ever'where."

"Well, I'm anxious to get to El Paso. Apparently there are two railroad companies headed for the same destination. I wonder which will get there first."

"How come nobody here knows about the Santa Fe?"

"It's possible that they will build on government land east of the farm fields. The government gives land to the railroads."

"Wal, maybe we can start in the mornin'."

"Do you think the horses will be rested enough?"

"I'd like to let 'em rest a couple days, but I reckon one more day's ride won't kill 'em. If their asses get to draggin' out their tracks we can stop almost anywhere."

"Once we get to El Paso they can have a long rest."

At daylight Billy checked the backs of the horses and declared them able to go on. The road down the river was well traveled by freight wagons, burro carts, buckboard wagons and Mexicans on foot. The two young men waved, smiled, but didn't stop to talk. At noon they watered the horses and ate tortillas sprinkled with brown sugar then went on.

It was almost sundown when they rode through a

199

pass between the Juárez and Hueco mountains. Below them lay a wide green valley where the Rio Grande made a quarter turn to the east. The valley along the river was lined with hundreds of houses, mostly adobe. "That," said Billy, reining up, "has got to be El Paso."

"Yup," Charles agreed. "This is as far south as we can go and stay in the U.S. of A."

"I've got a hunch, Chas, that when we get down there amongst 'em we're gonna feel like we're in Mexico."

Billy was right. They rode down a wagon road lined with squat adobe houses. The houses had green gardens behind them and pens for a burro or two. All but a few of the people they saw were dark-skinned and wore cool loose-fitting clothing, with *huaraches* on their feet and big straw hats on their heads. But unlike most Mexicans, they did not smile and wave.

"They appear to be angry about something," Charles commented.

"They ain't too fond of us gringos."

Soon they were in the center of town, where some of the buildings were two-story wood frame with hitch rails in front. A crude sign nailed to a post read SAN ANTONIO STREET.

Other hand-painted signs pointed out the Texas Hotel, Buckshot Saloon, Grubstake Cafe, Acme Saloon, blacksmith, Red Eye Saloon, El Paso Street, Gem Saloon, Rio Grande Hotel, Miller's Mercantile, Jackass Cafe, Mrs. Berryman's Rooms For Rent, Cactus Cafe, Tom's Harness Shop, general store, Cattleman's Hotel and Restaurant, Coyote Saloon.

They saw no sign indicating a livery barn but

looking across the business district to the south, they spotted a series of pens holding horses. When they rode over there they found freight wagons lined up near a small barn. Most of the horses had collar marks on their necks and shoulders. A tall, skinny man in worn-over boots and a black hat stopped raking manure long enough to watch them approach. Twenty minutes later, satisfied that their horses were watered and fed, the two young men carried their saddlebags and blanket rolls to the Cattleman's Hotel.

Owners of the hotel had tried for elegance, with a big lobby, a leaded glass window, etched glass lamps and a few scattered rugs on the floor. But fine furniture had to be freighted too far by wagon, and the clerk's desk and the lobby chairs were of plain pinewood from the nearby mountains. The wooden floor creaked under their feet. The stairs to the second floor also creaked, but seemed strong enough.

"Whew," Charles said, flopping onto the soft bed. Billy looked around the room. It was simply furnished, but comfortable. There was a mirror hanging on a wall with a table and washbasin under it, a chair, a bucket of water, a porcelain chamber pot and a muslin towel. The window overlooking El Paso Street had a lace curtain. A wire was stretched across one corner to hang clothes from. Management provided the wire clothes hangers. "Beats any bunkhouse I've ever been in," Billy said. "I wonder if they know how to cook a steak in that restaurant?"

"I'm ashamed to go down there the way I look," Charles said, "but my stomach says 'Go.' "

"My guts're givin' me a good cussin' too. Hell with the way we look. Let's go put on the *morrals.*"

"Yeah—I mean yes—*morrals*."

The restaurant had also tried to be elegant, with white linen cloths covering a dozen plain tables. The waitresses wore clean white aprons from their throats to the floor. There was no counter. But the two young men didn't need to feel ashamed of their appearances. Most of the customers looked just as bad as they did. Their meal was good: fresh-butchered beef, mashed potatoes and gravy, canned peas, coffee and a pie made of dried apricots.

After taking the last sip from his China coffee cup, Billy asked, "Where do you think we oughta start, Chas?"

"First thing in the morning I'll inquire about recent land transactions, and learn all I can about the railroads. And anything else that sounds like a good investment."

"All I can do is walk around and look at faces. If I see Matt Wyker I'll know 'im. And I can ask in the hotels too."

"Before I do anything else," Charles said, "I am going to buy some clean clothes. And a hat."

Billy chuckled. "You been lookin' like a poor squaw with that gunny sack over your head."

The general store had no derby hats, so Charles bought a cattleman's hat, a Stetson with a high, round crown and a wide, flat brim. "Why isn't the brim curled like yours?" he asked.

" 'Cause you ain't tied it down with a wildrag yet to keep the wind from pullin' it off. What you oughta do, Chas, is take it outside, stomp it flat, then straighten it out again. That way it won't look so new."

Charles also bought a pair of snug-fitting cotton pants and a khaki shirt. Outside, in a vacant lot between the store and the hotel, he dropped the hat on the ground, flattened it with his boots, then straightened it and put it on. "Well?"

"That's better. Now you don't look like an easterner tryin' to look like a cattleman."

"It doesn't feel right."

"Soak it in a stock tank and wear it dry. It'll shape itself to your head."

That's what Charles did, in a galvanized tank at the livery pens. While the hat was drying, he walked to the land office. What he learned there gave his spirits a boost. Sure enough, there were four parcels sold within the past week to Matthew Wyker. The clerk wasn't sure, but he thought they were on the north end of town where that other feller bought a strip of land about a year ago.

"What other feller? I mean, do you happen to recall the other gentleman's name?"

Face screwed up in concentration, the clerk said. "Seems to me it was somethin' like Wilson, or Watson, or—"

"Could it have been Wilkerson?"

"Yeah, yeah, that sounds familiar. Reckon what he wanted that land for?"

"Have you heard of a railroad being built in this direction?"

"Shore. They're comin' from two directions. Ever-'body knows that."

"Two directions? Then you've heard of the Santa Fe coming down from Colorado?"

Again the face screwed up. "No, don't rec'lect hearing about that one."

"Well, excuse my curiosity, but which railroads are you thinking of?"

"We-el, there's the Southern Pacific layin' track

from Tucson, and there's the Texas Pacific buildin'
like crazy from Fort Worth."

"Really?"

"Yep. Ever'body knows about that."

"Thank you very much."

Charles walked. The sun was hot, but walking felt
good to him, even in riding boots, and it dried his
wet hat within minutes. It wasn't far to the edge of
the town, and from there he could see that the only
feasible route for the Santa Fe was through the pass
between the two mountain ranges. He walked in that
direction. Yes, the surveyors stakes were there. Some
were just sticks with small red ribbons on them.
Others were iron stakes with yellow caps driven flush
with the ground. A string of them went straight
north, across two farm fields.

In the near future a railroad would be built across
the fields. Land close to the railroad would be too
valuable for farming. Matthew Wyker knew that and
he intended to make that knowledge pay hand-
somely.

Rested and restless, Billy started his search of the
hotels, the one thing he knew how to do. The Cattleman's was as good a place as any to start. As soon
as he mentioned the name Wyker, the clerk's eyebrows went clear up under his eyeshade. "Wyker?
What a coincidence."

"A coincidence? How come?"

"There is a young lady staying here by the name
of Wyker. She is also looking for Matthew Wyker."

"A young lady?"

"Yes sir. As a matter of fact, there she is now." He
raised his voice an octave. "Oh, Miss Wyker."

Billy looked where the clerk was looking. His gaze fell upon the most attractive young woman he'd ever seen in his life. Prettier even than Wanda, with dark hair curling to her shoulders, an oval face, blue eyes, perfect mouth. Slim, she wore a blue dress that had lace around the throat and on the sleeves. He gulped.

"Yes?" she said.

"Excuse me, Miss Wyker, but you and this gentleman have something in common, and forgive me for being presumptuous, but I thought you'd like to meet."

She came forward, holding her long skirt off the floor with her left hand. "Yes? I am Ellen Wyker." She held out her right hand.

Billy gulped again. He didn't know whether to shake her hand or kiss it. Finally, he removed his hat. A hank of light brown hair fell across his forehead. He took her hand gingerly, afraid of dirtying it. "I'm Billy Johnson, miss. I'm pleased to meet you."

"*Do* we have something in common, Mr. Johnson?"

"Wal, maybe. I'm lookin' for a gentleman named Matthew Wyker."

"Oh? Do you have any idea where to find him?"

"No ma'am, except that I—we—thought he might of come down here."

She stood back and studied his face thoughtfully. He swallowed another lump. "Mr. Johnson, have you had breakfast?"

"Oh yeah—I mean yes—ma'am. We had breakfast."

"Would you care to join me for a cup of coffee?"

"Wal, uh, yeah. Yes."

205

She led the way to the connecting door between the hotel and the restaurant, and to a white-clothed table. Billy remembered his manners and hurried around her so he could pull out a chair for her. He took a chair across the table and dropped his hat on the floor.

"Would you mind telling me, Mr. Johnson, why you are looking for Mr. Wyker?"

"He owes me some money."

"Oh, he does, does he?"

A waitress interrupted long enough to take her order for toast and a poached egg.

"A poached egg?" the waitress asked.

"Oh well," she said, pleasantly enough, "any way will do."

Billy ordered coffee.

She said, "If I don't seem surprised, Mr. Johnson, it's because I've heard this tale before."

Now Billy's eyebrows went up. "Is that so? How come?"

"I've known him all my life. I'm his niece."

Twenty-three

Walking back to the hotel, Charles took off the new Stetson and wiped sweat from his forehead with a shirt sleeve. When he replaced the hat he pulled it low on his forehead the way Billy wore his hat. He wondered if he still looked like a New Yorker.

Before he started up the stairs at the hotel, he glanced through the connecting door into the restaurant — and did a double take. Was that Billy in there seated with a young woman? A very attractive young woman. No, it couldn't be. Yes, it was.

What in the wide world . . . ? For a moment he considered approaching the pair and introducing himself, but then decided that wouldn't be proper. But darn, he would certainly like to know how he'd met her and what they were talking about.

He was still looking back, so full of curiosity he could barely contain it, when he reached the top of the stairs. That's where he collided with someone. Someone soft and feminine.

"Oh, pardon me," he said. "I'm terribly sorry." He bent down to pick up the armload of bed sheets she had been carrying. She bent down too. The brim of his new hat almost touched her face. Hastily, he removed the hat, and now their noses almost touched.

"Please excuse me," he said. Her eyes were pale blue, a little weathered, but pretty. Her blond hair had been cut short, and strands of it hung below her ears.

When she spoke, she was defensive. "It wasn't my fault. You ran into me."

"Yes, yes. I am to blame. I take full responsibility."

"You do?" She seemed surprised. "You admit it wasn't my fault?"

"Of course." They were both kneeling, their faces close together.

"Well, then." She stood, shoulders straight, head up, looking as dignified as her plain gray dress and plain face allowed. "In that case, your apology is accepted."

"May I help you with this?" He had gathered a double armload of the sheets, holding his hat by the brim. "It's the least I can do."

She talked with a drawl, like Billy. "That's kind of you, sir, but I'm afraid Mr. Nussbaum wouldn't like it."

"Oh. Excuse my curiosity, but why wouldn't he?"

"He's payin' me to do this, and he told me not to be sociable with the guests."

"Oh." Now that he was seeing her standing, he understood why. She had a slender but full figure, and a plain but nice face. A little hard around the eyes and mouth, but nice. There were men who would try to take advantage of an attractive hotel maid.

She reached for the load he was holding and smiled weakly. "I do thank you, sir, for your kind offer."

"Quite all right. Permit me to introduce myself. My name is Charles Manderfield."

"I'm pleased to meetcha, Mr. Manderfield." She didn't mention her name.

He watched her walk down the hall, the heavy load in her arms. She didn't walk like an eastern lady, but she wasn't the plodding, dumb servant type either.

Interesting, he said to himself as he unlocked the door to his room. Dropping onto the bed, he ran the morning's events through his mind. Two railroads were building toward El Paso, one from the west and one from the east. That was common knowledge. Another was coming from the north, and apparently that was not common knowledge. Matthew Wyker knew about it and was planning to profit from what he knew. A former railroad purchasing agent was the source of his inside information.

Matthew Wyker was probably still in El Paso. Where?

And who was that young woman Billy was sitting at a table with in the Cattleman's Restaurant?

He couldn't stand it. He had to know. What he'd do, he decided, was go to the restaurant on the pretense of having dinner alone. He'd be surprised to see the two of them. It was the noon hour anyway. They would have to invite him to share their table.

But he didn't have to do that. The door opened and Billy came in, wearing a wide smile.

"Say, Chas, you'd never guess who I just met."

"Never in a million years."

"Her name is Ellen Wyker, and she's the purtiest hunk of woman I've ever seen in my whole put-together."

"Huh? Ellen Wyker?"

"Yup."

"Well, well . . . ?"

"She's Matt Wyker's niece, and she's lookin' for 'im too."

"What?"

"Yup."

Billy sat in the chair, his hat tilted back. "She says he's the only family she has left and she got a letter from 'im posted at Socorro sayin' he was comin' down here. So she come down here to see 'im. Come by train to San Antonio in Texas and took the stage on over here."

"Well, I'll be darned."

"Ain't that somethin'?"

"Well, does she know where he is?"

"No, and she's been lookin' for three days. Sure wants to find 'im."

"Has she searched every place?"

"Checked all the hotels, asked the sheriff, and keeps her eyes out for 'im on the streets."

"He's here. Or he *was* here. He bought some land along the railroad right-of-way." Suddenly, Charles's shoulders slumped, and he groaned. "Do you know what this means, Billy?"

"Yeah." Billy's enthusiasm suddenly turned sour too. "It means if she couldn't find 'im, he ain't gonna be so easy to find."

"And we thought we had finally caught him."

"How long ago did he buy that land?"

"Over a period of several days, and the last transaction was dated only four days ago."

"Then if he ain't here he left on the stage, and somebody oughta remember 'im."

Standing, Charles shook his head sadly, but said, "Let's go ask."

Walking to the stage stop on Texas Street, Billy

said, "Miss Wyker tells me the 'Paches have been raisin' all kinds of hell on the stage road, and they had to have some soldiers ride along with 'em for a day. She said they met a bunch of Texas Rangers lookin' for a gang of killers and robbers led by a hard case name of Whiskey Pete."

"Just wait until the railroads get here. The Indians won't be able to attack them."

Chuckling, Billy allowed, "Naw. Them big engines'll make believers out of 'em."

"But then the white desperadoes will turn to robbing trains."

"There's always gonna be that kind."

The Texas and California Stage Company's office turned out to also be a U.S. Post Office, and the clerk was busy sorting mail. "Folks come in ever' day," he said, "wantin' to know if they got a letter, and they almost never do. You gents expectin' some mail too?"

"No sir," Charles said. "We're looking for a gentleman by the name of Matthew Wyker, and we're wondering whether he bought a ticket here in the past four days."

"Huh. Hmm. No sir, don't remember that name. What does he look like?"

"A cattleman. Average height. Probably smooth shaven. He might have been traveling with a gentleman by the name of Wilkerson."

"No sir. There's always some cattlemen ridin' the stage, but I don't remember nobody named Wyker or Wilkerson."

"Do they always give their names?"

"I always ask. 'Case they get killed by old Victorio and his bunch. So the laws can notify the next of kin."

211

"Victorio?"

"Yeah. He's got a little army of Mescaleros and Chiricahuas on a killin' rampage. Makes travelin' somewhat risky."

"Can't the Army do anything?"

"They chase 'em over to Chihuahua, and that's as fur as they go."

"Darn," said Charles. "Damn," said Billy. "Yeah," Charles said, "damn. Damnit all anyway."

They had dinner in a small cafe on San Antonio Street. "Wal, I don't know what else to do, Chas, so I reckon I'll visit some a these saloons and ask. Way I heard it, that Wilkerson likes his booze, and Matt Wyker don't mind hittin' the bottle now and then."

"We know that Matthew Wyker is a womanizer, if that's any help."

"He almost got shot once for boggin' it to a married woman."

"Be careful, Billy. If you see him, report him to the local sheriff, will you? Then come and tell me."

"Yeah."

The Gem Saloon and Gambling Emporium had gaming tables off to one side of the long bar and rooms in the back for private card games. Two men stood at the bar, each with a foot on the brass rail and a mug of beer in front of them. Two others were shaking dice onto a felt-covered table. "Who?" the bartender asked. "No, don't know anybody by that name."

In the Bullseye, Billy ordered a beer, took a swallow and asked the same question. "Naw," he was told. "Men come and go so fast I don't know more'n a few of 'em. You the law?"

212

"No. I'm no lawman."

"Well, I'd hep you if I could, but I don't know the name of ever' man that comes in here."

In the Acme, when he asked again—wearily—the answer started the same way. "Naw. Well, come to think of it, a gent that Millie is thick with is named Wyker, or Wicker, or somethin' like that. They been thicker'n molasses lately."

"Is she here?"

"Naw. Not now. Don't come in 'til after sundown."

"What's her name?"

"Millie Watson. She owns a half interest in this place."

"What does he look like?"

"Like most of the jaspers that come in here—a beard, a cap like a miner and like that."

"Do you know where he's stayin'?"

"Naw. Millie might know."

"I'll come back later."

Whoever the man is, Billy thought, he doesn't sound like Matt Wyker. This is damned tiresome. And the beer in this damn town is warm. Looks like horse piss and don't taste none too good either. I can stand on the street and look at ever' man that passes, and all I see is mostly Mexicans. None too friendly. Wal, there's another cutthroat joint across the street.

Same question, same answer. Billy had ordered a beer just to have a chance to ask his question. He stood with one foot on the rail and listened to men curse as they rolled dice at a table behind him.

"Looks like piss, don't it?" The voice came from his left elbow. It belonged to a middle-aged man in a bill cap and baggy wool pants pulled tight at the waist with a leather belt. "Yeah," Billy said.

"Mexican beer's better, but they don't like us grin-gos. A man could get his throat cut in one of them Mexican cantinas."

"I kinda got that idee. How come?"

"They was here first and they think this town oughta still be part of Mexico."

"Wal . . ." Billy didn't know what to say to that, so he said nothing.

"Where'd you drift in from? Not that it's any of my business."

"Up north."

"Uh-huh. We-el, in most parts of the country the Mexicans are friendly folks, but not in these parts. Ever hear of the salt war?"

"No."

"We-el, that was some war. Let's have another beer and I'll tell you about it."

Twenty-four

It was too warm in the hotel room, even with the window wide open. Fortunately, there was a screen on the window to keep the flies and mosquitoes out. The two young men should have checked into a Mexican hotel with thick adobe walls. But for some reason the Mexicans here weren't very friendly.

After just sitting for an hour, Charles went back to the street and bought a week-old newspaper from San Antonio, Texas. When he returned he again met the hotel maid. This time she was carrying two chamber pots, holding them at arm's length.

"Good afternoon, Miss uh . . . I don't believe I understood your name."

She smiled weakly. "It's Jennifer Miers. Please excuse me." Then she hurried away as though she didn't want him to see what she was carrying. He understood.

The newspaper read, he folded it and fanned himself with it, wishing he could get some relief from the heat. Billy came in, looking as sour as he felt.

"There's a woman named Millie that might know Matt Wyker, but she ain't come in yet. At the Acme."

"Well, that's something."

"Yeah. Anyhow, I found out why the Mexicans don't like us gringos. It's because of the salt war. Can't say I blame 'em much."

"Someone at the Acme Saloon has heard of Matthew Wyker?"

"He ain't sure. Thinks he might be a gent that's sweet on a woman named Millie Watson. She owns a half interest in the saloon. The way he described 'im he don't sound like Matt Wyker, but I'll go back after dark and see can I find this Millie."

"Oh. I wish I could think of something else to do. I am darned — I mean damned — tired of just waiting."

"Me too."

"What did you say about a salt war?"

"Wal, way I heard it there's some salt flats over east somewhere and the Mexicans've been goin' over there for a hundred years to pick up what salt they need. Then not long ago some rich gringo bought the land it was on and tried to make the Mexicans pay for their salt. He made a mistake. The Mexicans outnumber the gringos around here about ten to one, and they got so mad they took over the town. Killed three white men doin' it."

Charles was listening. He said, "That's capitalism. It's the best economic system devised, but there are some greedy capitalists."

"Yeah, and they got the Army to back 'em up. A bunch of Texas Rangers and some soldiers came over and kicked the shit out of the Mexicans. Killed some and lynched some."

"Hmm. Yes, I can understand why they don't like us."

"Hot in here, ain't it."

"Hotter than . . ."

"The hinges of hell."

"Yeah, yes, hotter than the, uh, the hinges of hell."

"I gotta go outside. Don't know what I'll do. Just stand around and look at faces, I reckon." Billy reached for the doorknob, but before he got his hand on it he heard a creaking from the floorboards in the hall, followed by a timid knock.

Ellen Wyker stood there with a worried frown on her face. She held a small white handkerchief in her hands and was twisting it nervously. "Please forgive me for being so bold," she said. "I . . . I wonder if I could ask a favor of you?"

"Sure, Miss Wyker. You name it."

Charles got up and came to the door. "Is this the Miss Wyker you told me about?"

"Yeah."

"Permit to introduce myself, Miss Wyker. I am Charles J. Manderfield. I understand you are a niece of Matthew Wyker?"

"Yes. He was your uncle Joseph Manderfield's business partner. I, uh . . . Billy, I'm sorry to ask this of you, but . . ."

"But what, Miss Wyker? You just holler frog and I'll jump."

A weak smile turned up the corners of her mouth briefly, then the worried expression returned. "The sheriff was just here. He said a dead body was found this morning. He wants me to look at it. He thinks it might be my uncle."

Charles exclaimed, "Oh my."

Billy put on his hat. "Do you know where to go, Miss Wyker?"

"Yes, I think so. The sheriff said the body is in a shed behind his office."

Charles started to leave without his hat, then remembered and put it on. He walked down the stairs beside the young woman, but at the bottom she hung back and walked beside Billy. On the way to the sheriff's office, boots clomping on a plank sidewalk, Billy said:

"I'll recognize 'im if it's him. You don't have to look, Miss Wyker."

"Thank you."

The sheriff was waiting. He stood immediately when they stepped into his office. He looked like a cadaver himself—over six feet tall, thin, gaunt, with hollow eyes and only a few strands of dark hair combed over the top of his head. "It's back here," he said. They followed him through a back door and across an alley to a clapboard shack. Rusty hinges squeaked as he opened the door. Only Billy went in with him.

The body was stretched out on a wooden bunk, covered from top to riding boots with a linen sheet. "Onliest wound we c'd find was a stab in the heart," the sheriff said. "Didn't bleed much." He pulled the sheet down.

"Huh-uh," Billy said, shaking his head. "That ain't Matt Wyker."

"Any idee who he is? Was?"

"I've got an idee." Billy's eyes took in the boots on the dead man's feet and the gray, wide-brim hat on the floor beside the bunk. "I never seen 'im before, but I'll bet his name is Wilkerson. John Wilkerson. Where'd you find 'im?"

"In a alley behind a Mexican whorehouse. 'Bout daylight this mornin' ."

"Stabbed, you say?"

"We got his shirt off and that's the onliest wound

218

we found. One stab was plenty. Right in the heart."

"That figures."

"What figures?"

Billy wasn't sure himself. It was just a germ of a thought that had popped into his head. He stammered, trying to think of another answer to the sheriff's question. "Wal, uh, we . . . hmmm . . . we think him and Matt Wyker was travelin' together. We think maybe this gent was workin' for the Santa Fe railroad 'til he got to boozin' it up too much. He liked his liquor and his women."

"The Santa Fe railroad?"

"Yeah. Miss Wyker is worried sick. I've got to tell her this ain't her uncle."

"Oh shore." The sheriff pulled the cloth over the dead man's head.

Outside, the hot sun bore down. Relief swept over Ellen Wyker's face when she heard. "Oh, thank heavens."

The sheriff asked, "Want to set down, Miss Wyker?"

"No, I'd like to go back to my hotel. Billy, would you be so kind as to accompany me?"

"Well now, miss, this young fella seems to know somethin' about this dead gent, and I need for him to tell me ever'thing he knows. This here is murder."

"Oh, of course." Looking first at Billy, then at Charles, she said, Perhaps we can have supper together. "Perhaps we can learn from one another."

"You betcha," Billy said.

"We would be honored," Charles said.

"Say about eight o'clock? We can meet in the lobby."

"Fine."

"It will be our pleasure, Miss Wyker."

"Now then, gents," the sheriff said as Ellen Wyker walked away, "let's see can we find some chairs to set on in my office."

They told the sheriff everything—except about the dead man found in a Denver alley. Charles did most of the talking, which was all right with Billy. He concluded with: "Some of the railroad executives should know something of Mr. Wilkerson's background."

"The Santa Fe? Never heard of it."

"We believe it was kept from the public until the right-of-way was purchased."

"Hmm. We got a telegraph here. I'll send some wires. I mean I will if the danged Injuns ain't pulled the wires down. They do that sometimes just out of meanness. Now about this Wyker fella. Any idee where he might be?"

"I'm sorry, we do not," Charles said.

Now Billy had to buy new clothes. He brushed off his hat and boots and put on the new cotton pants and blue chambray shirt, shook out his bandana. "I don't look as good as you do, Chas, but no matter how much money I spend I don't look good nohow."

"You look better than most men around here. At least you've shaved and your hair is combed."

"Good thing that don't cost anything. I'm about busted."

"I can finance us for a few more days, but that's all."

"Soon's supper's over I'm gonna have to go look up this Millie. After that, I don't know what to do."

According to a big clock on a wall in the hotel lobby, it was five minutes after eight when Ellen Wyker came down the stairs. Both young men stared. She wore a light-blue dress with a white belt and bow in the middle, patent leather slippers, and a white ribbon in her hair. "Beautiful," Charles gasped. Billy whispered, "Ain't she somethin'?"

Both young men pulled out a chair for her at a dining room table. She chose the one Billy had pulled out. Charles opened the conversation. "Tell me, Miss Wyker, what brings a lady like you to the Wild West?"

"Restlessness." She sat with her hands folded in her lap. Billy did the same. "May I be frank? I mean, we're just barely acquainted, but I have to talk to someone."

"By all means," Charles said.

"Why sure," Billy said.

"I divorced my husband a year ago, and I have been rather depressed and very restless. Oh yes, let me back up a step. I lived in Kansas City. I received a letter from Uncle Matt, posted from Socorro, Territory of New Mexico, saying he was coming here. I just took it upon myself to come here." The blue eyes turned to Billy. "You've lived on the frontier all your life?"

"Wal." Unconsciously, Billy folded his arms on the table in front of him. "I was raised in Conejos County, and this is the furthest I've ever been from home."

"Interesting. You must tell me all about it." Then, not wanting to ignore Charles, she turned her blue eyes to him. "And you, Mr. Manderfield. Billy tells me you have just recently graduated from a New York university."

"Why, yes, Columbia, actually."

"You must be very well educated." Back to Billy:

"Do you mind my calling you Billy? Please call me Ellen."

"Sure."

"I'm called Charles."

Billy had been taught not to talk with his mouth full, and he was silent during most of the meal. Ellen managed to talk and eat at the same time. "I'm not surprised that Uncle Matt owes you both money. He's always been like that. My parents were both killed when a riverboat sank on the Missouri, and Uncle Matt paid for my board and room and my tuition until I married."

Billy stopped chewing and swallowed in case he needed to say something. He didn't. Charles said, "He has always been like that?"

"An entrepreneur. Always investing in things. Sometimes he won, sometimes he lost. His investment with Joseph Manderfield in carrying trade goods to Santa Fe was one of his wins."

"It had to have been a terribly hard journey over the Santa Fe Trail."

"Oh, Uncle Matt wasn't afraid. He isn't afraid of anything. He likes adventure."

All that was left of the meal was chocolate cake. Billy finished his so soon he was ashamed of himself. "Tell me, Billy, does your family own a ranch?"

"No. We've got four homesteads put together. That's, uh . . ." He tried to add the number of acres.

Let's see now," she said. "I've read somewhere that a homestead is one hundred and sixty acres, is that right?"

"Yeah. I mean yes."

"That's six hundred and forty acres. Most farms in Missouri and Kansas aren't that big."

"It ain't enough to support a family in Conejos County. My brothers and me, we work for the big cow outfits."

"Oh, I see. Then you're a real cowboy."

"Yes."

"Interesting."

Charles didn't understand the lady's interest in a cowboy, but he managed to smile through most of the conversation anyway. He was somewhat relieved when Billy finally said, "Uh, please excuse me, Ellen. I have to go and see somebody." Silently he hoped Charles wouldn't tell her who he had to see. Charles said, "Ellen, perhaps I could interest you in another cup of coffee. Or tea?"

"I'm sorry you have to leave, Billy. Another time? Honestly, Mr. Manderfield, I have had all the coffee I need. I feel like retiring early tonight."

As the young cowboy walked out of the restaurant and down the plank walk, he too was sorry. Sorry that he had to leave the company of a beautiful refined young woman and go and ask questions of a saloon floozie.

Twenty-five

The Acme had changed, now that it was dark. Crowded, almost shoulder to shoulder. The bartender had been right. Men with beards were as plentiful as men without beards. When Billy asked for Millie Watson he was directed to a blond woman seated at one of the tables idly watching a card game. He walked over.

"Miss Watson? My name is Billy Johnson, and I'm lookin' for a man you might know."

She turned speculative gray eyes on him. Her hair was piled on top of her head, and her dress was cut so low he couldn't understand what kept those things from popping out. "Who might that be, cowboy?" Her voice was deep, almost as deep as a man's.

"A gent named Wyker. Matt Wyker."

He'd hit paydirt. He knew it by the way her expression changed from idle curiosity to surprise. She stood. "Come over here, will you." He followed her to an empty corner table and sat across from her. "Who did you say you are?" she asked. He repeated his name.

"Why are you looking for . . . what did you say his name is?" She knew, and he knew she knew. Excitement welled within him. He tried to hold it down.

"He owes me some money."

"He owes you some money? How much money?"

"I don't mean to be smart aleck or anything, Miss Watson, but that's between me and him. Do you know where he is?"

She leaned forward and crossed her arms on the table. Her fingernails were long and painted bright red. "Are you mad at him?"

"Wal"—he leaned forward too—"that depends. If he pays me I'll call it even." That wasn't quite true, but this woman was being devious. She was silent, studying his face. He let her study him, let her think it over.

"Well, I am acquainted with a gentleman named Wyker. We are business partners. Sort of."

"Oh, I was told that you own half of this business. Does he own the other half?"

A short chuckle came from her. "No, not him. I don't think he's the kind to stay in one place long enough."

"Then he prob'ly talked you into investin' in some land next to a railroad right-of-way."

Eyes wide, she asked, "How did you know?"

"I know Matt Wyker." When she only stared at him, he said, "Do you know his travelin' partner, John Wilkerson?"

"Oh, him." She made a sour face. "The sop. Yeah, I've met him."

He considered telling her that John Wilkerson was dead, but he decided not to. What she knew about John Wilkerson was between her and the sheriff. "Wal, I'm askin' you again—do you know where I can find Matt Wyker? I'd be much obliged if you'd tell me."

The speculative look was back. She tilted her head to one side, studying him. "You're a good-looking kid. But you're a cowboy, a hired hand. Surely he doesn't owe you very much money."

"Just some wages."

"Oh." She chuckled. "Is that all? You wouldn't kill a man for wages, would you?"

"Not on purpose."

More speculation. She leaned back in her chair, smiling. "All right. You don't look like a killer. You don't look dangerous at all. He's staying at my house."

Excitement was so high he had to fight to hold it down. "Ahem. Would you please tell me where that is?"

After Ellen Wyker excused herself and retired to her room, Charles felt restless. He wandered out onto the plank walk, stood for a moment in the dim lamplight from the hotel window, then went back inside. He was feeling a little down and rejected. He couldn't understand it: Ellen Wyker had no interest in him at all but she couldn't learn enough about his cowboy partner. After all, he was her kind and she was his kind—educated, refined. Women were strange creatures.

Inside the lobby, though, was another young woman, and it occurred to him that, yes, she was just as attractive as Ellen Wyker. In spite of her plain working-woman's clothes and lack of makeup, in spite of the menial work she was doing, Jennifer Miers was neat and clean, and she carried herself with dignity.

"Good evening, Miss Miers," he said, tipping his hat.

She was sweeping the floor with a straw broom. "Oh, good evening, Mr. Manderfield."

"Is your work never done?"

"Why, yes sir, I'm almost finished for the day."

He didn't understand why, but for some reason he

226

wanted to visit with her. He wanted to visit with someone. "Would you care to join me for a cup of tea in the restaurant when you finish?"

"Oh, well, sir, I . . ."

He could see she was flustered. "Just a cup of tea. Nothing more."

Glancing back at the desk clerk, she stammered, "Why, sir, I . . ." And then she reached a decision. "Yes sir, I will be happy to join you."

When she returned to the lobby, she had changed to a dark blue dress, snug at the middle, showing a truly fine hourglass figure. Her short blond hair had been brushed until it shone. The desk clerk scowled at her. She ignored him and took Charles's offered arm.

The house that Millie Watson directed Billy to was four blocks from the Acme saloon in a part of town where the only light came from windows in flat-roofed adobe huts. Dogs barked at him. It was so dark he could barely see the street. But the house he was looking for was easy to find. It was bigger than most, made of pine lumber, and it had a pitched roof. Thin, transparent lacy curtains covered the windows.

What did town folks do when they wanted to hail someone in a house at night? Did they knock on the door? Or did they stand outside and holler like country folks did?

Walking up to the house, Billy couldn't help but see through a window into the front room. He stepped close, feeling like a thief in the night. A man sat in a wooden rocking chair, reading a newspaper. A bearded man with thin hair on his head, wearing riding boots. A dog at the next house barked furiously.

The man lowered his newspaper and listed his head as if wondering what the dog was barking at. The man was Matthew Wyker. He listened for a moment, then folded the paper, stood and moved toward the front door. Billy had to make a quick decision.

Should he confront Matt Wyker right here and now or wait until daylight? Or should he slink away, fade into the night? Come back early in the morning. Here and now it was dark. He would have to step inside to be recognized. Also, maybe Charles would like to be present when the confrontation finally happened.

He backed away, got into the dark of the night. The neighbor's dog was still making a fuss. The front door of Millie Watson's house opened and Matt Wyker stood in the light, trying to see into the darkness. Billy stood still making himself invisible, until Matt Wyker went back inside and shut the door. Then he tried to walk away.

But the dog was furious. It knew a prowler was in the neighborhood, and it wanted to warn everyone. A door at the next house opened, and a man's voice said, *"Qué pasa?"*

Billy made a mistake. Instead of standing stock still, he kept walking, and too late he discovered he had lost the street and was walking across a vacant lot. He stumbled into a shallow ditch, scrambled back to his feet and walked.

"Alto! Ladrón!" A shot was fired. Running footsteps came his way. *"Ladrón! Ladrón!"* Another shot. Looking back, Billy could see flame spurt from a gun barrel.

His feet told him to run. But goddamnit, he was no thief and he would not run. Besides, if he ran he would look like a thief trying to escape in the dark.

But goddamnit, he couldn't just stand there and be shot either. Another shot was fired, and this time the muzzle blast was closer. Running footsteps were coming closer.

Not knowing what else to do, Billy drew the Remington and fired a shot in the air. The footsteps stopped. Then Billy realized he'd done something else *estúpido*. The muzzle blast from his gun gave away his location. Now he had to run. Run or kill somebody. He holstered the Remington and ran.

Two more shots followed him, but he was in the dark, staying off the street, running across yards, running across a garden. More dogs joined in the racket, but none chased him. Billy ran until he was in back of the Cattleman's Hotel. There he leaned against the building and got his breath. This walking around in the dark was dangerous in a town like El Paso. Folks in this town shot first and then struck a match to see who they'd hit. Now he was sure that he and Charles would have to wait until daylight to go back to Millie Watson's house.

She had not lived an easy life. At first she was reluctant to talk about herself, but Charles managed to gently coax it out of her. Raised in a large family on a dry dirt farm in East Texas, she'd hired out to a ranch family as housekeeper and cook. She liked the job, was good at it, and worked at it for five years — until the family sold their holdings to a conglomerate. She followed another ranch couple to El Paso, where they intended to establish a second ranch. Indian problems caused them to change their minds. Jennifer was unemployed again until she found a job at the hotel. But she preferred ranch life. Cleaning rooms and emptying chamber pots was not to her liking at all.

It wasn't the ranchers and cowboys that made the work disgusting, it was the drummers, the gamblers and the eastern businessmen. They seemed to think that because she worked at a lowly job she should be happy to accept a few dollars for special favors. Cowboys were not known for tidy housekeeping, but they were respectful, surprised and grateful when they discovered that someone had cleaned up after them. They always thanked her kindly.

But instead of talking about herself, she wanted to know what it was like living in a big city, going to a university. After hearing Charles describe it—the noise, the overcrowding, the crime, the smoke-filled air—she wrinkled her nose prettily and said she believed she'd stay in the West. Charles understood why.

She was pretty. When she smiled she showed beautiful white teeth—not the result of expensive dental care, Charles deduced, but of good genes. No university graduate, of course, but Jennifer liked to read. Her favorite reading was *Harper's Magazine* because it gave her a small insight into other sections of the nation.

"Do you own a ranch, Mr. Manderfield?"

"Well, no, but I may find myself manager of a ranch in New Mexico Territory."

"If you happen to need a housekeeper. I can do the job. I'm a good cook, and I can chop wood, and I can harness and handle a team. I can ride a horse too."

"Ahem. Well, I can't promise anything, but I will keep that in mind."

Yes, he definitely would keep Jennifer Mier in mind.

How damned long was Charles going to sit in

there and talk to that girl, anyway? Billy had something to tell him. But Charles had a smile on his face and was enjoying himself. It wouldn't do to interrupt. Billy wanted to grab him by the shirt collar and drag him outside.

The girl was nice. In fact, the more Billy looked at her, the better she looked. But not like Ellen Wyker. There was nobody like Ellen Wyker.

Come on, Chas, he said under his breath. Haul your New York ass out of there.

Finally, they came out into the lobby. The desk clerk scowled at the girl, and she shot him a worried glance. Then she smiled and ignored him. At the door to a back room, she said, "Goodnight, and thank you," to Chas, then went through the door. Charles was smiling until he saw Billy's urgency. Then the smile faded.

"C'mere," Billy said, motioning Charles outside. When they were on the boardwalk, he said, "I found 'im. He's got a beard, but I'd know 'im anywhere. He's right here in town."

"W-what? Are you sure?"

"Sure I'm sure."

"Well, let's go. My God, is it really he? We've found him at last?"

"Yup."

"Well, let's go—"

"Not right now," Billy said. "I just got shot at for walkin' around in the dark."

"We'll have to wait for daylight?"

"Yeah. I don't think I'll sleep much, but we havta wait."

"My God."

Neither young man slept. They tried, but were too excited. "Do you know," Charles said, "how far we have followed Matthew Wyker? Of course you

231

do. I had no idea, when I started out to look for him, that I would have to travel this far. I can't believe I did this. I can't believe we have actually caught him."

"What I cain't do is I cain't hardly wait for *mañana*. I cain't wait for another look at 'im. Ain't he gonna be surprised? He'll dirty his drawers. He'll choke on his own spit."

But they waited, each watching the one window for a sign of daylight. Finally, it came.

Billy led the way, half running. "Him and his woman'll prob'ly be in bed, but we'll hammer on the door 'til he gets up. They'll be mad, but not as mad as we got a right to be."

Huffing, Charles said, "You know, Billy, I'm glad you've got a gun. I didn't think I'd see the time when I'd say that, but I'm glad."

They hammered on the door. Hammered again and again. It took ten minutes to get a reaction from inside. Then the door opened, and Millie Watson stood there in a wraparound robe, her blond hair sticking up in all directions, her lip rouge smeared, her eyes puffy. She barked, "What in holy hell do you want?"

The answer was short: "Matt Wyker."

"Well, he ain't here. He was gone when I got home a couple hours ago. Took his stuff and hauled ass."

Shock. Silence. They looked at each other. They looked at the woman. They spoke in unison: "He's gone?"

"That's what I said, didn't I. He's gone."

Twenty-six

It took a while for the news to soak in, but finally Billy said, "We apologize for wakin' you up so early, but we havta find Matt Wyker. Any idee where he went?"

"You're that cowboy that was looking for him last night, aren't you?"

"Yes, ma'am."

"Well, all I can tell you is he took his stuff and left before I got home last night. I mean this morning."

Charles said, "I too apologize, madam, but it is imperative that we locate him. I understand you were in business with him."

Millie Watson gathered her robe tighter around her and ran a hand over her hair. "Not exactly. He talked me into investing in some land, that's all. Now I suppose it was a con job of some kind."

"Is the land along a railroad right-of-way?"

"Yeah, that's where it's supposed to be."

"Then," Charles said, "it's probably a good investment."

"How do you know so much?"

"Miss Watson, we have been following Mr. Wyker all the way from Denver, Colorado. We know what he has been doing."

"Oh, is that right?" Her voice softened. "Well, all I

can tell you is he talked about goin' to Kansas City to wait while the railroads build here. He said once he had nothing to keep him here."

"Did he say how he would travel?"

"No, but I can guess. He'll take the stage to San Antonio or Fort Worth, and the railroads from there."

"Where is the first stage stop east of here?"

"Why, I believe it's Ysleta."

"Did he take everything he had with him? Everything he brought with him, I mean?"

"No, he left some of his clothes, but I don't think he's coming back in the near future."

"Did he take more than he could carry on a horse?"

"I don't know. He had two pairs of saddlebags. I guess he could get it all on a horse."

"Thank you, madam, and again we apologize."

"Yeah, all right. Is that true, what you said about our investment?"

"It is speculation, of course, but I would guess that your investment is safe."

"Well, I can't tell you any more about him. Somebody must've heard you were looking for him and warned him. He sure left in a hurry." She shut the door.

The stage office wasn't open yet. They had to wait outside in the early-morning light. They had concluded that Matthew Wyker had either bought a ticket here or had gone to a stage stop somewhere east where he could board a coach without attracting attention. It was after sunup when the ticket agent appeared

"You fellers again?"

"Yup," said Billy, "and we're askin' the same question."

"Let's see now, it was a feller named Wyker you was askin' about, wasn't it?"

234

"Yup."

"Same answer."

Charles asked, "Is there some place east of here where he could buy a ticket and get aboard?"

"Shore. There's Ysleta, Hawkins station, Fort Quitman. There's lots of places."

"When does the next stage go east?"

"Day after tomorra. 'Bout sunup. Providin' the soldiers or the rangers escort 'em through Dead Man's Pass."

"Thank you very much."

"Wal, Chas, should we ride out of here before breakfast or after? It might be a few hours to Ysleta."

"After breakfast, then."

They intended to grab a quick breakfast and be on their way, but when they walked into the hotel restaurant they had to change their plan. Two young women were seated at a table for four and insisted that they join them.

"We got acquainted the first day I was here," Ellen Wyker explained, "and now we're roommates."

"Ellen is kind enough to let me share her room," Jennifer Miers said. "I . . . was fired this morning."

Ellen said, "All she did was—how did he put it?—'Fraternize with a paying guest.' You, Charles."

"I knew better, Charles. It's not your fault. I was warned not to be too friendly with the guests."

"But," Charles stammered, "all you did was . . . and you were fired?"

Jennifer's eyes were downcast. "Yes. I didn't think that would ever happen to me."

"Why, that's an outrage. Who is responsible for this?"

"Mr. Nussbaum. But he did warn me. It's my own fault."

235

"Anyway," Ellen said, "I invited her to share my room until she finds another job or until I leave. Old Nussbaum didn't like it, but I told him to like it or lump it. I half expected him to order us both out, but apparently he doesn't want to make a fuss of it. And I did pay in advance."

Billy had been quiet, listening, his eyes going from one young woman to the other. Now he said, "That's the neighborly thing to do, Ellen." Then he remembered the job that lay ahead of him and Charles. "We got to throw down some chuck and get goin' ."

"Oh?" Ellen's eyes locked onto his. "Where? I mean, it's probably none of our business—unless it has something to do with my uncle. Does it?"

"Wal . . ." Billy looked to Charles for help.

"We have to be honest, with you, Ellen. Yes, we're still trying to find Matthew Wyker."

"And where are you going?"

"He was here in El Paso. He left late last night. We think he is planning to board the eastbound stage somewhere east of here—where he would attract no attention."

"Can we go with you?"

"Oh no," Billy said. "We don't know for sure where to find 'im, and it might be dangerous."

"My uncle is not a dangerous man. Evasive at times, but not dangerous."

"Oh, my goodness, no," Charles said. "Billy is right. We're not certain about anything. And there are Indians on the warpath and desperadoes, and a character called Whiskey Pete, and Mexicans who hate us gringos."

"We both can ride, and we can rent horses at the livery. What do you say, Jennie, shall we tag along?"

"Well, no, not if Charles doesn't want us to."

"Billy, can't we go?"

"Wal . . ." Again he looked to Charles.

"We'd, uh, rather you didn't."

Ellen smiled a broad smile and said, "Jennie, let's go to our room."

"Whew," Billy sighed when they had gone. "For a minute there I thought we was gonna have company whether we liked it or not."

"Let's get some breakfast and be on our way."

Later, riding east at a steady trot, following the Rio Grande, Billy said, "It's not that I don't like their company. That Ellen, she can go with me anywhere anytime, except today."

"Yes, if we were going on a picnic, there's no one I'd rather have for company."

Suddenly, Billy reined up. "Uh-oh." Tall weeds along the river had obscured their view to the east, but now that they had rounded a small bend the view ahead lengthened. "Tell me, Chas, that I ain't seein' what I think I'm seein'."

"Oh God, it's . . ."

"It's them, ain't it?"

"It's them."

The young women sat astraddle their saddles, wearing long dresses that covered them down to the calves of their legs. Polka-dot bandanas covered their hair. They smiled widely as the partners rode up, although Jennifer's smile was tentative. Ellen spoke first. "Well, you didn't say anything like absolutely, positively, no way in the world."

Jennifer's smile faded, but she forced it back. "You did leave the question only partly answered."

"Besides," Ellen added, "I'm sure that if Uncle Matt knew I was looking for him he'd come forward. And beside that, Billy has a gun."

237

"Yeah," Billy grumbled. "One gun. One short-barreled *pistola*."

"I hope," Charles said, "that it's not far to Ysleta."

Ysleta wasn't far. But Matthew Wyker wasn't there.

"That sounds like the feller that stopped here 'bout daylight," said the stage company's employee. "Seemed some disappointed when I tol' 'im the eastbound is waitin' for some hep from the U.S. Army. Too many 'Paches and robbers."

"Any idee where he went from here?"

"I tole 'im about a place three-four miles that-a-way." The hostler pointed northeast. "There's a spring and a cabin there, and a corral for his horse. Don't think anybody's stayin' in it now."

The two young men looked at each other. Charles asked, "What do you think, Billy? Would he go there by himself?"

"Wal, like Ellen said, he's not afraid of anything." To the station keeper he said, "Was he packin' a gun?"

"Yeah. Had a repeatin' rifle." You . . ." He glanced from the young men to the women. "You ain't takin' them women up there, are you?"

Billy said, "Maybe you ladies ought to wait for us here."

"Oh no," Ellen said. "We've come this far and it's only three or four miles farther. Besides, if he thinks you are a threat to him he might use that rifle. With me along he won't."

"Whatta you think, Chas?"

"What do you think, Billy?"

"I don't wanta get in a shootin' match with Ellen's uncle. Or anybody else if I can help it."

"Jennie," Charles asked, "what do you think?"

238

"I'll tag along."

"Let's go."

They picked up a dim trail that wound through hundreds of acres of mesquites so tall they couldn't see over them. Thorns grabbed at the women's dresses and soon had them in tatters. They rode silently, single file, Billy on his gray horse in the lead. Looking back, he grinned. "How do you like playin' cowboy?"

Ellen said, "Now I know why cowboys wear those leather things on their legs."

Breaking out of the brush, they looked up at a long high ridge to the north. Straight ahead were more mesquites. "We either climb that hill or fight the brush," Billy said. "I've got a hunch that cabin is under the hill."

They crossed a small grassy park and rode into the brush again. "Whoever would build a cabin around here?" Ellen asked.

"Dunno," Billy said. "Maybe a cow camp, maybe a hunter's camp. I dunno."

When they broke out of the mesquites again, they saw the cabin. It squatted under the ridge, a rock and adobe structure with a tar-paper roof. Water seeped out of the bottom of the ridge, but flowed only fifty feet before it seeped back into the earth. A bucket-sized hole had been dug and lined with rocks where it would be filled with water. A corral built of mesquite sticks was between the cabin and another hundred-or-so acres of brush. One horse was in the corral.

"Wal," Billy said, "he's here. Somebody is. You-all wait here 'til I find out." He urged his mount forward cautiously. When he was close he hollered, "Hallo-o-o."

The door opened and a bearded man came out, pointing a rifle at Billy. But before he said anything,

Ellen Wyker yelled, "Uncle Matt!" She kicked her horse's sides and rode up.

The bearded man spoke, "Well for . . . Ellen, what in the world are you doing here?"

"Looking for you, Uncle Matt." She slid off the horse, tried to rearrange her dress and went to her uncle. He put the rifle down and wrapped his arms around her.

Charles and Jennifer rode up.

Holding his niece at arm's length, Matthew Wyker said, "I wish you hadn't come, Ellen. I'm on my way back to Kansas City."

Everyone else remained silent. Then the bearded man's eyes went from one to the other. "Hello, Billy," he said. "Don't tell me you tracked me all the way here to collect your wages."

All Billy said was, "Yup."

Dismounting, Charles helped Jennifer off her horse, then turned to the older man. "Permit me to introduce myself, Mr. Wyker. I am Charles J. Manderfield."

Matthew Wyker's shoulders slumped, and he shook his head. "Joe told me about you. I guessed it was you looking for me last night."

"You know why."

"Yeah. Can we go inside?" He turned and led the way. The cabin was sparsely furnished—a barrel-shaped sheet metal stove, a wooden bunk covered with a dirty quilt, a table and a chair. A few sticks of firewood were piled near the stove.

Charles was blunt. "Where's my uncle's money?"

"Out in the bushes. I hid it in case the wrong people came along."

"You don't deny that you owe my Uncle Joseph about twenty-five thousand dollars."

Ellen had her arm looped inside her uncle's arm.

240

"It's a mistake, isn't it, Uncle Matt?"

"No, I'm afraid not. But my intentions were good. I was planning to pay him back with interest once my investments paid off." He paused, then added, "That is, I was planning to pay Bertha if Joe passed on."

Charles was tempted to say something sarcastic, but for Ellen's sake he didn't. "We know about your investments," he said.

"You do? Then you know I stand to make a profit of at least five hundred percent."

"How much of the money is left?"

"Enough. I didn't have to spend as much as I thought I would. Most of the land was already taken."

Again Charles was blunt. "Get it."

"I'll be right back." The bearded man went out the door. Charles watched from the open doorway as he disappeared in the mesquites. Billy went to the one window.

Suddenly Billy said, "Uh-oh." He yelled through the window, "Get back in here, Matt! Run, Matt!"

"What's wrong?" Charles said.

Matthew Wyker was running. Running awkwardly, carrying two pairs of saddlebags. He got to the door. No farther. A rifle cracked from back in the brush. Matthew Wyker fell across the door sill, half outside and half inside. As he fell he pitched the saddlebags inside.

His niece screamed.

241

Twenty-seven

Billy left the window and grabbed the older man by one arm. "Help me, Chas. Let's get 'im in here." Charles grabbed the other arm. They pulled the man through the door.

Ellen was crying, "Uncle Matt. Oh no, please no." She knelt beside him. "Uncle Matt." With tear-filled eyes, she looked up at Billy. "What happened?"

Billy slammed the door and slid the bolt latch into place. "Get away from the door. Get back." He hurried to the window, stood to one side and peered out.

There was no curtain on the window, no glass. A wooden shutter hung wide open on leather hinges. Billy stayed to one side, but kept careful watch. Charles got his hands under the wounded man's armpits and dragged him away from the door. Ellen followed, and sat beside her uncle. Charles opened one of the saddlebags.

It was stuffed with packages of U.S. greenbacks.

Matthew Wyker shuddered, gasped, and was still. Ellen wailed, "Uncle Matt! Oh, my God, Uncle Matt." Jennifer knelt beside her and tried to comfort her.

Billy's eyes searched the brush outside.

Charles asked, "What do you think, Billy?"

"I think somebody else is plannin' to use this shack. He saw Matt Wyker and shot 'im. Whoever he is he's feelin' us out, tryin' to decide whether to try and shoot us out of here."

"Could there be more than one out there?"

"Could be an army."

"The money's here. I haven't counted it yet."

"Won't make no difference if we cain't get out of here." Billy added, "Damn—I mean durn—I wish we'd brought that rifle in with us."

"Where is it?"

"Just outside the door, but I wouldn't open the door right now."

"Well then, what do you think we should do?"

"Wait and see what happens. Chas, would you look through one a those cracks in the other wall and see what you can see?"

"I'll do it," Jennifer said. She stood, hurried to the far wall and dropped to her knees, putting an eye to a crack between the rocks. "I don't see anybody."

"Keep lookin'." To Charles he said, "Chas, will you take over here a minute? Keep your eyes peeled, but don't stay in one spot, don't give 'im time to draw a bead on you."

Voice shaky, Charles said. "Y-yes, of course."

Billy went to Ellen and put an arm around her shoulders. She turned to him and buried her face against his chest. He wanted to say something, but didn't know what to say. He stroked her hair and let her cry.

Then Charles gasped, "Oh God." He ducked aside as a gun spoke outside and a lead slug zinged through the window and thudded into the far wall.

"Ever'body get down," Billy yelled. "Hit the floor." He ran to the window, glanced out, drew the Remington. "Durn, there's more' n one."

Charles glanced out too. "Oh God, there are too many."

More shots poured through the window. Gunfire from outside came so fast and furious that it sounded like one continuous earsplitting roll. Splintery holes appeared in the door. Billy yelled, "Get down. Flat."

A heavy shoulder hit the door from outside. Again and again. The door crashed open. A bearded face appeared.

The Remington in Billy's hand roared. The face disappeared. Another face took its place. Again the Remington roared. Gun smoke filled the room, stinging eyes and noses.

"Stay down," Billy yelled. Jennifer was lying flat next to the bunk. Ellen was kneeling, covering her ears with her hands. "Ellen, get over there with Jennie. Chas, see if you can shut the door. Keep low. Don't get in the doorway."

Turning back to the window, Billy sighted down the short barrel of the Remington and fired at a figure in the brush. "Damnit, there's too many of 'em."

For a moment, all was quiet. Charles pushed the door closed, but it hung on broken hinges, leaving a gap between it and the doorsill. The two women were wide-eyed but still. The acrid odor of gun smoke brought tears to Jennifer's eyes.

Charles said, "Do you think they're . . . ?"

Gunfire drowned out the rest of his question. It poured through the window like a swarm of angry hornets, slamming into the wall over the women's heads, forcing Billy back, drilling more splintery holes in the door.

Billy swore, "Damnit." He didn't dare show himself in the window. But he had to show himself, had to return the fire, couldn't let them just step up to the window and blaze away.

Quickly, he glanced through the window, picked a target and fired. Immediately, he ducked back. More angry hornets swarmed through.

It was hopeless and Billy knew it. He hadn't had a chance to count the men outside, but there were at least a half dozen. They knew there was only one gun inside. It was only a matter of time until they poured so much gunfire through the window and door that they could just walk in and take over. He had no idea who they were, but they weren't Indians nor Mexicans. Outlaws. Robbers and killers. They intended to use this cabin for a hideout. Maybe had already used it. Two men, two women and one gun were all that stood in their way.

Well, by God, he was going to get as many of them as he could.

Jennifer yelled, "Can I do anything?"

"No. Keep down." Moving fast, Billy again glanced out the window, again picked a target and fired.

"Maybe I can get to that rifle out there," Jennifer yelled.

"No. Stay put."

Again Billy squeezed the trigger. The Remington's hammer clicked on an empty shell.

"Damnit."

Charles asked, "What's wrong, Billy?"

"Gotta reload."

"Oh God."

His fingers felt like sausages as he plucked cartridges from his belt loops and stuffed them into the gun cylinder. He couldn't move fast enough. Jaws clamped shut, he muttered, "Move, fingers. Dammnit."

"Oh God."

And then Charles jumped to his feet. He yelled, "I'll get that rifle." He yanked the door open. Billy yelled, "Chas, don't. Don't, Chas."

His voice was drowned in gunfire. Lead slugs whined through the open door and smacked against the wall. Charles had to step over a dead man to reach the rifle. A bullet knocked his new Stetson off his head. Another plucked at his shirt. He got his hands on the rifle, jumped back inside.

"Hit the floor!" Billy yelled.

Charles dropped to one knee, facing the open door. A bullet plowed a furrow in the dirt floor beside him. He yanked the lever down on the Winchester and jerked it back up. The action threw out a .44 casing but shoved another bullet into the firing chamber. Charles squinted down the barrel and pulled the trigger. The recoil slammed the butt of the gun against his right shoulder. The boom of an exploding cartridge stung his ears. He jacked the lever down again.

"Take that!" he yelled as he yanked the trigger. He kept firing and yelling, "Take that! And that! And that!"

Gun smoke was so thick that neither young man could see across the room. Billy shoved the sixth bullet into the cylinder and cocked the hammer back. Just in time to shoot at a face in the window.

Charles was still firing and yelling, "Take that!"

Then it stopped.

The only sound was the women coughing in the gun smoke. Through stinging eyes, Billy tried to see outside. Charles was still kneeling on the floor in front of the open door, squinting down the rifle barrel, but not firing.

The smoke was rising, clearing the air. The women stopped coughing. It was so quiet that Billy could hear his ears ringing. Charles heard himself breathing. All were afraid to move, to speak.

Then a man's voice yelled from outside; "Hey-y-y in there. Hallo-o-o the house."

Charles looked at Billy. Billy looked at Charles.

"Hey-y-y. Is anybody alive in there?"

"Huh," Billy snorted.

"Hey-y-y. It's Captain Jacobs, Company D Texas Rangers."

"What?" Charles said. "Huh?" snorted Billy. "Hallo-o-o the house. Don't shoot."

"Wal, I'll be durned."

"I'll be durned too."

"Hallo-o-o. I'm comin' over there. Don't shoot."

"My God," said Charles. "I hope we haven't been shooting at Texas Rangers."

"Not likely," Billy said.

The man who stepped out of the mesquites wore a six-gun in a low-hanging holster, and a silver star on his left shirt pocket. He held his hands shoulder high.

"How can we be sure?" Charles asked.

Billy yelled out the window, "Shuck that gun."

The man was close enough now that he didn't have to yell. He had long gray sideburns showing

under a broad-brim gray hat. "One thing a law officer never does," he said with a drawl, "is give up his
weapon."

"Who's with you?"

"An even dozen rangers."

"Wal, we ain't givin' up our weapons either."

"I'm not askin' you to. I'm goin' to call my men
out. You have nothing to fear now." He half turned
and waved his left arm. Twelve men walked out of
the brush, wearing six-guns and carrying repeating
rifles. Captain Jacobs turned back to the cabin. "Is
anyone hurt?"

"Dunno." Billy turned to the women, "Are you
hurt?"

"No," Jennifer said. "I'm not," Ellen said. They
stood, their dresses torn and dirty.

"Chas?"

"Don't think so."

The Texas Ranger stepped over two bodies and
came inside. "What are you-all doin' here?"

Billy answered, "We don't feel like tellin' you just
now. What're you doin' here?"

Instead of answering, the ranger said, "Do you
know what you just did?"

"Don't tell me we was shootin' at lawmen."

"Nope. What you just did is you just wiped out
Whiskey Pete and his gang."

Two dead men were sprawled near the door, and
three others lay between the cabin and the brush.

"Huh?"

"What?"

"We weren't far behind 'em. Picked up their trail
right away after they robbed the westbound yesterday at El Muerto." The cabin was soon filled with

248

heavily armed, hard-eyed men. All wore silver badges.

"Well, I'll be durned," said Billy, holstering his Remington.

"Me too," said Charles.

Twenty-eight

Ellen Wyker made sure the rangers understood that the dead man on the floor wasn't one of the gang. "This is my Uncle Matt Wyker. They murdered him."

"Yeah," Billy said. "Shot 'im in the back." He picked up the two pairs of saddlebags and handed them to Ellen. "This is hers." She took the bags without opening them.

It was a solemn procession that rode through the mesquites back to Ysleta. From there the bodies were transported in a wagon to El Paso. A curious crowd gathered outside the sheriff's office, full of questions. Was it true that most of the Whiskey Pete gang had been killed?

As soon as Billy and Charles could find a moment of privacy, they reached an agreement:

"We don't have to tell about the dead man in Denver, do we?" Billy said. "No," said Charles. "We're both thinking the same thing, but we aren't sure, are we?"

"No. That one in Denver and John Wilkerson was killed the same way. Wilkerson was a boozer that talked too much. That's all we know."

"The whole thing was a very elaborate deception

for a man who intended to return the money, but all we have is a suspicion. No use mentioning it. Ellen is feeling badly enough."

"No use kickin' a dead man."

"We agree on that, then?"

"Right," said Billy.

Their whispering was interrupted by the ranger captain. "Look here," he said, handing Billy a sheet of paper. Billy slowly read a few words, then handed it to Charles. Charles read it. "REWARD: $5,000 for Capture DEAD OR ALIVE of WHISKEY PETE, Notorious Robber of Stage Coaches and Relay Stations."

"Which one was he?" Charles asked.

"The one closest to the door," the ranger said.

"Billy shot him. The reward does to Billy."

"They'll have to mail it to me," Billy said. "I'm not sticking around here any longer than I have to."

Finally, they were allowed to go to their hotel, the four of them. Not until they were in Ellen's room with the door closed did they open the saddlebags. Ellen pulled out bundles of U.S. paper currency. There were other papers, deeds to land in Albuquerque and El Paso. "The correct thing to do," said Charles, "is to go through probate. But that would take forever, and a good portion of the money would go for legal fees. What do you suggest, Ellen?"

"We can settle it here and now. It's really no one else's business."

Charles agreed to twenty-five thousand dollars. Billy asked for forty dollars.

Ellen couldn't believe it. "Forty dollars? That's all? After all you went through?"

"That's what he owed me."

"But Billy, you can't settle for such a small amount."

"That's all I got comin'."

Charles said, "He'll get a five-thousand-dollar reward. Maybe more."

Ellen counted twenty-five thousand dollars, which Charles stuffed into his own saddlebags. Billy put forty dollars in his shirt pocket. Besides the deeds, there was three thousand dollars left of the late Matthew Wyker's estate.

"Those deeds will be worth a lot of money in a few years," Charles said.

They had supper together and talked of the immediate future, ignoring stares and whispers of other restaurant patrons. After supper they sat in a corner of the hotel lobby and talked until midnight. The next day they buried Matthew Wyker in a small cemetery reserved for Anglos. A church pastor was paid to pray over the body before it was buried in a plain wooden casket.

Back in the hotel, Charles and Jennifer left Billy and Ellen to visit alone in her room. Later, the four of them talked again. When Charles had a chance to draw Ellen aside, he had to ask an embarrassing question: "Are you sure? Forgive me for saying this, but you know that infatuation can—"

She cut him off. "I know what you're thinking. Let me explain it this way. I was married to the wrong kind of man. I've known too many of the wrong kind. I've thought it over very carefully and thor-

252

oughly. Billy is the most honest and loyal man I've ever known." She smiled a happy smile. "I'm just crazy about that guy." Then she turned serious again. "The answer is no. No, the novelty of being married to a cowboy will not wear off."

Charles said simply, "I believe you."

It was near the middle of August. Charles Manderfield and Jennifer Miers climbed wearily from the stagecoach at Lariat, Territory of New Mexico. Their next stop was Isaac Enderlee's general store. After Enderlee stopped expressing his surprise and pleasure at seeing him, Charles had a question of his own: "Do you know the Johnson family?"

"Shore. Everybody knows the Johnsons."

"When you see them, or one of them, will you give them a message? Tell them I have news of Billy Johnson and to come to the Double M Ranch." Quickly he added, "It's good news. They'll be surprised. I don't mean to be mysterious, but I'd like to tell them myself."

An hour and a half later, a rented horse pulled a rented buggy into the yard at the Double M. Two weary but happy travelers got out. Charles had to holler, "Aunt Bertha? Hello-o-o, Aunt Bertha."

Soon he was almost smothered with hugs and kisses. His first question was, "How is Uncle Joseph?"

"He's still with us, but failing. The doctor is certain now that he has bone cancer. He has been refusing his morphia and enduring the pain so he would be conscious when you came back."

Charles introduced Jennifer. "She's going to help with the work, but she's not just a hired girl. She means more than that to me."

Aunt Bertha looked knowingly from one to the other and smiled. "I think I understand." She hugged Jennifer too.

Inside, Joseph Manderfield opened pain-filled eyes. "I would've bet the ranch you'd be back, Charles. Your old dad would have."

Charles stood beside the bed. "I've got your money, Uncle Joseph. I've also got a permanent partner. Do you know Billy Johnson?"

"Yes, I know Billy. A good boy. The whole Johnson family is good people."

"Billy was married in San Antonio, Texas. I was a witness. Billy and his bride are still in Texas, looking for cattle to buy. We're going to restock the ranch."

The pale eyes brightened. "You're going to stay here, then, and manage the ranch?"

"Yes. I and Billy. And of course we'll see that Aunt Bertha has everything she wants. I brought a friend with me. Well, she's more than a friend. I'd like you to meet her."

Joseph Manderfield finally gave in and drank his glass of warm water with tiny crystals of morphia dissolved in it. He went to sleep with a smile on his face.

And while the women worked in the kitchen and chatted happily, Charles went outside to see that the rented horse was watered and well fed. He looked around him. He looked at the Mangas Mountains, now purple and wild in the evening light, at the plains of St. Augustine, broad and seemingly endless, at the juniper thickets and at the tall timber high on the mountains, and he said aloud:

"We're gonna get acquainted, you and I. You're my home."

THE SEVENTH CARRIER SERIES
by Peter Albano

THE SEVENTH CARRIER   (2056, $3.95)
The original novel of this exciting, best-selling series. Imprisoned in an ice cave since 1941, the great carrier *Yonaga* finally breaks free in 1983, her maddened crew of samurai determined to carry out their orders to destroy Pearl Harbor.

THE SECOND VOYAGE OF THE SEVENTH CARRIER

                                       (1774, $3.95)
The Red Chinese have launched a particle beam satellite system into space, knocking out every modern weapons system on earth. Not a jet or rocket can fly. Now the old carrier *Yonaga* is desperately needed because the Third World nations — with their armed forces made of old World War II ships and planes — have suddenly become superpowers. Terrorism runs rampant. Only the *Yonaga* can save America and the free world.

RETURN OF THE SEVENTH CARRIER   (2093, $3.95)
With the war technology of the former superpowers still crippled by Red China's orbital defense system, a terrorist beast runs rampant across the planet. Out-armed and outnumbered, the target of crack saboteurs and fanatical assassins, only the *Yonaga* and its brave samurai crew stand between a Libyan madman and his fiendish goal of global domination.

QUEST OF THE SEVENTH CARRIER   (2599, $3.95)
Power bases have shifted dramatically. Now a Libyan madman has the upper hand, planning to crush his western enemies with an army of millions of Arab fanatics. Only *Yonaga* and her indomitable samurai crew can save the besieged free world from the devastating iron fist of the terrorist maniac. Bravely the behemoth leads a ragtag armada of rusty World War II warships against impossible odds on a fiery sea of blood and death!

ATTACK OF THE SEVENTH CARRIER   (2842, $3.95)
The Libyan madman has seized bases in the Marianas and Western Caroline Islands. The free world seems doomed. Desperately, *Yonaga*'s air groups fight bloody air battles over Saipan and Tinian. An old World War II submarine, USS *Blackfin*, is added to *Yonaga*'s ancient fleet, and the enemy's impregnable bases are attacked with suicidal fury.

Available wherever paperbacks are sold, or order direct from the publisher. Send cover price plus 50¢ per copy for mailing and handling to Zebra Books, Dept. 3850, 475 Park Avenue South, New York, N.Y. 10016. Residents of New York and Tennessee must include sales tax. DO NOT SEND CASH. For a free Zebra/Pinnacle catalog please write to the above address.